Bestselling author Alan Gold began his career as a journalist, working in the UK, Europe and Israel. In 1970 he emigrated to Australia with his Czech-born wife, Eva, and now lives in Sydney, where he divides his time between writing and running his award-winning marketing consultancy.

MINYAN

Alan David Gold

flamingo

An imprint of HarperCollins*Publishers*

Flamingo
An imprint of HarperCollins*Publishers*, Australia

First published in 1999
by HarperCollins*Publishers* Pty Limited
ACN 009 913 517
A member of the HarperCollins*Publishers* (Australia) Pty Limited Group
http://www.harpercollins.com.au

HarperCollins*Publishers*
25 Ryde Road, Pymble, Sydney, NSW 2073, Australia
31 View Road, Glenfield, Auckland 10, New Zealand
77–85 Fulham Palace Road, London, W6 8JB, United Kingdom
Hazelton Lanes, 55 Avenue Road, Suite 2900, Toronto, Ontario M5R 3L2
and 1995 Markham Road, Scarborough, Ontario M1B 5M8, Canada
10 East 53rd Street, New York NY 10032, USA

National Library of Australia Cataloguing-in-Publication data:

Gold, Alan, 1945-.
  Minyan.
  ISBN 0 7322 6400 6
  I. Title.
A823.3

Cover photograph by Brett Odgers
Printed in Australia by Griffin Press Pty Ltd, Adelaide on 79 gsm Bulky Paperback

5 4 3 2 1
03 02 01 00 99

*This book is dedicated to
the memory of
Julian Alexander Gold
1972–1982
who loved being told stories*

ACKNOWLEDGEMENTS

This book started to take shape in my mind half a century ago when my mother and father first began telling me the stories of my heritage. As I grew older and the tales grew increasingly complex and metaphorical, they enabled me to put my people's history into context. But only when I became a father and began to tell my own children stories of our heritage did I begin to comprehend the vast store of wisdom and human experience which is embodied within the legends.

Storytelling is perhaps the oldest of all the arts of humankind. There's not one nation, not one people, not one religion which doesn't have its fund of stories and legends. Because Jews have suffered dispersion and separation from their ancestral lands for most of the last 2000 years, we have perhaps acquired more stories and legends than most other peoples. Indeed, for a nation of so few, it would be hard to conceive of a greater fund of stories having been created by any people.

The events and the stories in this book are, of course, purely fictional, but no work of literature develops in isolation and for many of these stories I have to thank the Jewish communities of both Leicester in England and of Cremorne in Sydney, Australia. With their help and with the help of such great minds as Isaac

Bashevis Singer, Hayyim Nahman Bialik, Martin Buber, Shalom Aleichem and Ahad Ha'am who were at the forefront of the modern Jewish and Yiddish storytelling tradition, I have been able to compile these fables.

But there are also many people of the modern world who have helped me enormously. My wife Eva was a fund of knowledge where my own inadequacies showed through. I test-drove most of the stories on my three wonderful children, Georgina, Jonathan and Raffe and they were perceptive in picking up and helping me to correct weaknesses.

Michael Benstock, friend and an encyclopedia of matters Jewish, read, advised, and helped me correct the text. Dr David Brooks and Dr Philip Levine were also generous in their insights. The story of the Hasidim on the farm as told by Mr Glick comes from a delightful time which my family and I spent when we were guests of Frank and Audrey Marks at their stunning property in Wollombi, north of Sydney. The story of the Buddhist's Tree comes from Rick Le Plastrier. My thanks also to Rabbi David Rogut of Lindfield Synagogue for kindly providing the beautiful menorah which forms the cover of this book.

Jill Hickson and the team from Hickson Associates, my literary agents, as always were unstinting in their support.

And this book would never have been written without the assistance of the extraordinary Jenny Roberts, friend and associate, who lived and breathed every word.

The amazing people at my publishers, HarperCollins, have enabled me to see horizons much further distant then I ever realised; Barrie Hitchon, Angelo Loukakis, Laura Harris, Jim Demetriou, Christine Farmer, Kate Thomas, Darian Causby and Karen-Maree Griffiths, as well as the best sales and marketing team in all of literature ... each and every one of them a fable. And finally, but by no means last, my editor Deonie Fiford whose wonderful support, keen insight and sharp intelligence have made working with her on this project an enormous joy.

A NOTE ON PRONUNCIATION AND SPELLING:

Transliterating words from one language to another is fraught with difficulties. In this book, I have attempted to use modern Israeli Hebrew pronunciation except where the characters would obviously not do so. Hence, Israelis and people who hale from Sephardic origins say 'Shabbat' instead of the Ashkenazaic 'Shabbos'.

In terms of spelling, the most vexed group of letters is 'Ch'. Modern spelling would see the famous Jewish bread spelt 'Hallah', rather than the more traditional 'Challah'. The name of the Biblical matriarch 'Rachel' should by rights be spelt 'Rahel', but this would cause confusion. Hence, where I have used a commonly known word like Challah (bread) or Cheder (room), I have stayed with the traditional.

To those who find this discomforting, I apologise.

THE MINYAN

How should I begin? Where do I start? They sound like universal questions ... like the meaning of life, or why are we here? But it's much more prosaic than that. I'm looking for a way of capturing your attention. You see, there's now a theory that readers actually help to write the books they read by bringing their life experience to what they're reading. So on this journey, you're going to help write this book!

But that doesn't answer the question. How to begin? Well, for this, I'm going to need your help. You see, this isn't a book which should just be read. Like any good story, it improves if you can hear it in your mind, or see the characters in your imagination. So it should be listened to with your imagination open.

I'm going to tell you some stories ... ten stories in all. Ten? Does the number have any significance? Oh yes! Great significance. But that will become obvious as I start to tell you my stories.

But before I do, let me begin by reassuring you that you don't really need to remember the names of the people who are taking part in the minyan. In England or America, a character who you meet in these pages named Smith, would be called Smuelonovitch in Russia, Schmidt in Germany, or something musical and romantic in Italy, like Smilini. No, all you have to do

1

is to remember their faces, listen to their tales, journey with them where their storytelling takes you and see if it awakens any memories from your own childhood.

For no matter what their names are, they will always be Smith or Brown or Cartwright to the people in their Chevra.

But therein lies yet another problem. I thought that the main difficulty I would have would be with names. Because I'm sure that some Jewish names will sound uncomfortable and foreign to your ears. You see, the Jews are the most diverse and disparate of peoples and they've picked up all sorts of names from many different countries. All the Jews have ever wanted to do is to live like all the other people in the country where fate happened to put them. Just be normal, and be allowed to practise their religion in freedom and with dignity. Alas, over the past 2000 years, this was so rarely the case. Only occasionally in the long, black night of the Jewish expulsion, were the Jews ever allowed to go to the synagogue and pray without fear that some madman would want to destroy them just for being Jewish. It was all the fault of the Romans, of course. The bleak and unforgiving nightmare of the Jewish people began with the creation of the Jewish nation by Abraham. Since then, we've been enslaved by the Egyptians, conquered by the Babylonians, and the Greeks; but the real problem started with the Diaspora, when the Romans destroyed the Temple, and sent all of the Jews into exile in 70AD. It all happened when the Emperor Vespasian decided that enough was enough, and kicked all the Jews out of Judea for causing problems for his ... but I'm racing on. I haven't told you what the other problem is yet.

The other problem that you're going to have reading this book happens when I use words like minyan and Chevra and Aron Hakkodesh. These are words which are known to most

Jews, but there's no guarantee that you are a Jew. In fact, it's a fair-to-even chance that you're not Jewish, but you simply happened on this book as you were browsing in the bookshop, stopped to read the title, and thought 'Minyan! Now that's a serious spelling mistake for the author to make. Surely he means "minion".' We all know that this means an obsequious follower or dependent, or a subordinate official.

But no. I really do mean minyan. A minyan is the minimum number of men in a Jewish community that must come together in order to say prayers. Fewer than a minyan — and that's any number under the magical ten — and there are certain crucial prayers which cannot be said. (Remember? I mentioned the number ten at the beginning.) Without ten men, there can be no proper Jewish service ... and that means all the men must go home saddened and ruing the decline of their religion.

Oh, and another thing. I keep on saying the word 'men'. I'm not being politically incorrect. Judaism is one of the oldest of all the religions on earth, and when the rabbis were codifying its rules together, the feminist movement wasn't exactly front-page news. You see, even to this day in an Orthodox Jewish service, only men count towards a minyan. Don't get angry with me. I didn't come up with the idea.

But to get back to the other problem. It's simply this: I'm going to have to use Hebrew or Yiddish names and words all the way through this book, while the characters are telling their tales. It's completely unavoidable. I've put a glossary at the back to help you in the early stages, but by the time Mr Dub has told his story (I'm sorry, but I can't quite remember when that happens) you should be fairly familiar with the words so that you don't have to keep on flipping to the back to understand everything that goes on.

So, there are the two major problems covered. One of the problems was about the storytellers' names. Don't worry about them. And the other was the way that on occasion they use Hebrew or Yiddish words. Again, don't concern yourself. You'll get used to it. From now on, it's all plain sailing.

So, where to begin? Did you see that? I just said 'so' twice at the beginning of a sentence. That's a typically Jewish trait. Like saying 'Nu?' all the time. Or answering a question with another question. Why do Jews always answer a question with a question? Why not?

Where does this minyan take place? It usually takes place in a shul or a synagogue. Sometimes a minyan meets in a person's home if there is no shul nearby or if they're saying prayers for the dead. Sometimes, like at the Wailing Wall in Jerusalem, a minyan may just happen. Ten men come together and shout excitedly, 'Minyan! Minyan!' and they start to pray.

But in the case of this particular minyan, the minyan that I'm talking about, this minyan took place in a little shul in a town … somewhere. Don't let it upset you that you don't know where or in which country. Why is it that today we have to know all the details before our minds are at ease? It's television, isn't it? All these hourly news reports giving the age, the address, the birthplace, the history, the biography of people in the news. So, we've grown up in our fact-based global community with a pressing need to know. But what is there that you simply must know about our congregation in our little shul? The size of Mr Yarblonsky's hat? What Mr Cohen had last night for dinner? See what I mean? In our little community, not all that much happens which you simply must know. All you need to know is that in this small shul in this town in this country, ten men got together regular as clockwork on a Friday night to say prayers for the introduction of the Sabbath.

Now, the Jewish Sabbath begins when the sun goes down on Friday night and ends when the sun goes down on a Saturday night. We have an injunction from God that we are not allowed to do any work and that it is good to go to the synagogue and to pray. Then we go home and have a beautiful meal and play with the children, talk to our wives and husbands, sit in the most comfortable chair in our warm and welcoming home and read our favourite books. Of course for Jews, turning on the light or the television or the airconditioning or the stove is a form of work, so we don't do that. But there are ways around it, and I'm sure that when you read the story told by Dr Josephs, you'll see what I mean.

So what do these men do in this shul? Well, they walk in before the sun goes down and there they greet each other. These days, it's usually the same familiar old faces, like comfortable furniture. Already sitting at his wooden bench, studying the words of a psalm, nodding his head, his lips kissing each other as he intones the words to himself, is Mr Dub. Mr Dub is a cabinet-maker. He has been making cabinets, furniture, sofas and cupboards for over sixty years now. There aren't many people around like Mr Dub with his love of craftsmanship. Those who were have gone out of business, because people won't pay for craftsmanship any more. What they want is a good product at a reasonable price. And Mr Dub was brought up to believe in the best products and never mind about the price. So Mr Dub makes the occasional piece of furniture and he spends his week waiting for Friday night when he washes his hands, his face, the back of his neck, combs his hair, takes off his apron and hangs it up behind the joinery door, takes off his shirt stained with linseed oil and puts on a crisp white tunic specially ironed for him by his wife. It smells of starch. It smells of the beginning of the Sabbath.

He kisses his wife and depending on the weather puts on an overcoat. No, that's not quite right. He always wears an overcoat, even in the height of summer. As he gets older, he feels the draughts a lot more in the shul. He carries with him his tallis in the tallis beitel. And he walks up the hill to the little shul where the light is already on, even in the daylight, and where he can smell the musty comfort and age-old familiarity of his seat in his place and of the books that surround him. And as he sits down, he fingers the beautifully carved wood and the intricate filigree, like frosting on an expensive (and now forbidden) cake. What the members of the shul don't know, and what he will take with him to his grave, is that beneath the seat where the rabbi sits is a particularly delicate piece of carving, something which Mr Dub spent hours over when he was very much younger and a great deal more impetuous. When his hormones still raced around his body, and the sight of a young woman would prevent him working properly for hours at a stretch. Because beneath the rabbi's seat is a picture of a bunch of grapes. And the pendulous fruit is in precisely the same shape as the early bosom of Mrs Markovitch ... but that's another story, and one which it's very unlikely Mr Dub will tell. After all, Mrs Markovitch and Mrs Dub are on the Ladies Auxiliary Committee together and if it ever came out, the roof of the shul would be blown sky-high ... even if it was forty years ago.

Standing near the steps leading up to where the rabbi prays is Mr Dayan. Mr Dayan is a butcher, a kosher butcher. He has a big curling grey beard, and spends much of his time stroking it. Even when he is praying he strokes it. When he is angry, he strokes his beard. When he is thinking, he strokes his beard. And when Mr Dayan is happy, when Mr Dayan roars with laughter at a joke from a customer or somehow hits a bone wrongly and his cleaver bounces back up and shocks the customers, even when Mr Dayan laughs hysterically, he strokes his beard. When doesn't Mr Dayan stroke his beard? For that, you'll have to ask Mrs Dayan.

And slowly the other members of the shul walk in to say their prayers as we approach the Sabbath. I won't introduce them all to you. You'll meet them soon enough. But the one whom you must meet is the man who walks in last. Our very own Rabbi Teichmann. But does he come in last because he is so important? No, not at all. Rabbi Teichmann comes in last because he has only just returned to the shul. He was visiting Abe Flaxman, the beggar. Yes, some Jews are beggars. Poor Abe is an embarrassment to the community. He sits on the street corner, cross-legged, with his cap in front of him as people walk by. Looking at them imploringly and making little noises with his throat, not really words, more like bird calls. Little imprecations to let people know that he's sitting down there on the pavement, near the gutter, as low as a man can go (unless he's dead, of course).

Poor Abe. He's really down and out. Too much wine, too much whisky, lost his wife and his job, the usual story. I won't go on because he doesn't come to the shul any more, and so he isn't in the minyan. But he's the reason that Rabbi Teichmann is so late tonight. You see, in the cold weather a couple of months back, Abe developed tuberculosis and he started to cough up little bits of blood. Even he was frightened, so the place where he sleeps, a kind of dosshouse, took him to the hospital and the doctors listened to his chest, and they decided that he should remain there. But Abe doesn't like it because he thinks he's going to die in there and so they phoned the rabbi. The rabbi immediately went down to comfort him and to give him some money and to promise him that he would look after Abe, so that when he comes out he can spend some time at the rabbi's house and get himself back on his feet. And when Rabbi Teichmann left Abe's bedside, Abe was feeling a lot better.

But I'm wandering again. I was telling you about how Rabbi Teichmann was the last to walk into the Friday night service to celebrate the coming of Sabbath. It starts with the usual prayers, psalms and lots of loud chanting and lots of mumbling and people bowing to the Aron Hakkodesh, which is where the holy scrolls are kept, the five books of Moses. And they pray and they bow and they shout out prayers and the rabbi shouts louder to make his voice heard. And then there comes the time to say the most beautiful prayer of all. It's what we call the shema'. It's one of the verses from Deuteronomy and it's when the writer of that beautiful book tells the chosen people of Israel, 'Hear O Israel, the Lord our God, the Lord is One'. When we say the word 'One', we have to emphasise it, so that anybody listening knows that there's only one God in our book. No sons, no mothers, no brothers or aunts or uncles. Just God.

And the service continues. We welcome the bride of the Sabbath and everybody feels a profound sense of fulfilment. Everybody that is, except Rabbi Teichmann. You see, he's a bit like a scorer in a sports match. And the score he's keeping is the number of men who come to the shul on a Friday night. Remember what I told you at the beginning? That there have to be ten men. Well, in this particular shul, in this particular community, there were always eleven men. Ten members of the congregation and the rabbi. But one of the members of the congregation, a regular, has moved with his family to another country and, try as he might, Rabbi Teichmann has been unable to attract any other man in the community to take his place on a regular basis. Now, this is very serious because while he was playing the game with one spare, Rabbi Teichmann felt a degree of confidence. But when you have no reserves sitting on the bench, then every player counts and the more Rabbi Teichmann looked at his tiny Friday-night congregation, the more insecure he felt when he counted all of the players.

They were old. They were tired. They were prone to illnesses. And one good cough or cold meant no Friday-night prayers, and that meant that Rabbi Teichmann wouldn't be able to welcome the Sabbath as his bride.

Now Rabbi Teichmann is a lovely and learned man, a gentle soul, someone who never causes anger within the community, someone who is as familiar with the holy books as he is with his face when he wakes up and looks in the mirror. And that was both his problem and his blessing.

Because these days a rabbi has to be political to succeed. Being saintly isn't enough. You actually have to get out there and make your presence known. Write imposing articles in newspapers, stir up the imagination of the public by declaiming on this and that, scribe learned dissertations for important magazines that don't have pictures on their glossy covers, make lots of speeches in long cold halls. Why? So that the great rabbinic court, the Beth Din, gets to hear about you and the next time the rabbi of a big shul curls up his toes and lies down for his eternal rest, it's your name that springs to mind.

But Rabbi Teichmann? No. He was happy just being in his small community, visiting the sick, teaching the little children in cheder, helping bar mitzvah boys with the delicacy of their task, comforting grieving widows and patiently explaining to the doubting why they're wrong to doubt. But most of all Rabbi Teichmann loved the joy of standing up on the bimah in the shul and acting as a conduit for God.

A rabbi is a very different kettle of fish from a Catholic priest. In fact, rabbis are more like a mullah of the Islamic faith — a teacher, a wise man, a righteous and good man. In Catholicism, priests are ordained by bishops who were ordained by other bishops who in their turn were ordained by other bishops and other bishops were ordained by yet more bishops, all the way back to the time of Christ who ordained Peter who ordained Linus who ordained Anacletus who ordained Clement ... you get the point.

So a priest in a Catholic community is somebody who acts by ordination as an intermediary between the congregation and God, and who can trace his ordination all the way back to Christ. Not so in a synagogue. Anybody in a synagogue can stand up and lead the congregation. Even little boys as young as bar mitzvah, that is thirteen years and a day, can lead the congregation. It's all one big community. You don't even need a rabbi. Just ten men. So when Rabbi Teichmann stood to lead the congregation he knew that he was nobody special and he knew in his heart that he was privileged to have been entrusted with the care of the people who came to him as their leader.

Rabbi Teichmann lived close to the synagogue. Four doors away in fact. It was an old house, bought by the community and given to him as part of his salary package. He was lucky to get free board and accommodation because there wasn't much else in the job for him financially. His wife, counting the change in her purse a couple of days before he was due to be paid his salary, used to joke that for the wages a rabbi was paid, the most suitable man for the job was a Catholic priest. At least they took a vow of poverty.

In fact, without the free board and accommodation, Rabbi Teichmann would probably be sitting in the gutter next to Abe the beggar, making birdlike noises to passers-by in order to supplement his wages. But somehow, every week, he and his wife Sarah and their eight children got by. It was a clean house, a not particularly tidy house but a loving house.

Most people think that rabbis work only on a Friday night and Saturday morning. Not Rabbi Teichmann. He was always busy with the thousand and one things which were needed to be done in the community. This meant that he didn't have as much time as he wanted to devote to the study of the holy writings. Some people take novels to bed with them, others the newspaper or a magazine. Still others watch television until they fall asleep. But Rabbi Teichmann's relaxation was to follow the intricacies of the Talmudic scholars as they wrestled with momentous questions in Babylonia or Jerusalem. It was these knotty questions of life and death that gave him the subject for his Friday-night lessons or his Saturday-morning sermons.

And it was the wisdom of the Talmudic scholars which gave Rabbi Teichmann a clever way of guaranteeing the return of each of the nine men left in his Friday-night minyan, whether they were sick or well, exhausted or lively. In fact, if Rabbi Teichmann was halfway right, they would crawl to shul on crutches rather than miss out in the coming weeks.

Because what Rabbi Teichmann was going to do was to tell them a story. Not a lesson. Not a sermon. Not words of wisdom. Nor even quote the great books of Moses or Isaiah or Samuel. He was going to tell them a story.

And on this particular Friday night, at precisely the time that his traditional lesson was about to start, the nine men, scattered like fallen leaves on a lawn, closed their books and sat back deep into their seats in anticipation of the next twenty minutes. For no matter how learned Rabbi Teichmann was, for his declining

11

congregation, it was the end of a hard week for each of them and this was the bit of the service which they hoped wouldn't take too long so they could bid each other 'Good Shabbos', and return to their homes and the warmth of a Friday-night meal.

As Rabbi Teichmann faced them, there was a glint in his eye and you should have seen the expression on their faces when Rabbi Teichmann said ...

RABBI TEICHMANN'S TALE OF THE SHIPWRECK, THE PROSTITUTE AND THE POT OF HONEY

'My grandfather, alav ha shalom, came from the great Czech city of Prague. Has anybody here been to Prague, I wonder?' asked the rabbi.

A couple of people slowly and reluctantly put up their hands. It was like being back at school.

Mr Dub looked at Mr Dayan, who raised his eyebrows, and shrugged his shoulders. There was nothing private about the gesture. But nothing Mr Dayan did was ever private. He was too big and muscular to be subtle. No, it was a body movement designed for all the rest of the congregation to see. As well as the rabbi. It said 'Come on rabbi. Stop messing around. We've got a meal to go to, and wives and sons and daughters to get back to ...'

The rabbi counted the hands ... well, it was pretty easy — two out of nine ... and said, 'As you know, I returned to Prague a few years back in order to trace my family history. Most people think that the Jews only recently arrived in Bohemia, maybe a couple of hundred years ago. But when I delved into the history of the Jewish population, I found out that Jews first settled there in the ninth century. Nobody knows where they came from. Maybe they were merchants from the east, trading between the Franks and the Germans and the inhabitants of Byzantium, or Kiev or some other busy and bustling metropolis where the women were keen for the latest in fashion, and the men eager to do business and to trade. But one thing I do know; when these early Jews followed the banks of the Vltava as I did, and set eyes on that unbelievable castle in the air, they would have thought they had landed in paradise on earth.

'And there, they built their synagogues and their schools and set up what is needed for people to live a good Jewish life. And it lasted, on and off, for a couple of hundred years. They probably lived alongside gypsies and Hungarians and Slavs and Croats ... and there were possibly some Welsh, Spanish and other exotic people thrown into the melting pot in ancient Prague. It all came to an end in the year 1096 when the Jews of Prague were forcibly baptised during a series of pogroms which were set off by that great and courageous march of history, the Crusades.'

By now, quite a few people in the congregation were looking at each other in disquiet.

When a rabbi speaks from the pulpit you have to look straight at him in case, God forbid, he should look at you, and your eyes and attention are elsewhere. When the Pope spoke from his window in St Peter's Square, did any of the tens of thousands of people below the balcony look around, wondering where the ice-cream sellers were? No, they stared upwards so that they didn't miss a word.

And so the congregation of even the smallest shul in the world would sit, apparently transfixed, listening with rapt attention as they learnt about the proper way to glean a field after a harvest in biblical times, or the right way to pronounce the word Amen, or the dangers of assimilation.

But tonight, Friday night in our little shul, there was no such vigilance paid. On this night, Mr Dub looked at Mr Dayan who looked at Dr Josephs and everybody looked at everybody else. Tonight should have been a shiur, a lesson. Twenty minutes of Rabbi Teichmann droning on about the obscure past, and struggling to find a moral, an irony, some nexus to link the ancient past to the uncertain present. Usually our beloved rabbi would talk about how, in the days of the Talmud, Rabbi Someone of blessed memory said ... or Rabbi Someone Else, may God rest his eternal soul, agreed, but also added ... And the congregation had learnt to sleep with their eyes open.

But today, the congregation was being treated to a history lesson ... no, worse ... a travelogue. Why, they were not too sure. If they wanted to know about the glories of ancient Prague, they could go to Mollie Caplan who'd just opened up a travel agency. Maybe the rabbi had shares? A rabbi's job was to be a rabbi, not to sell travel. But he was still the rabbi and they would have to listen.

Within seconds Rabbi Teichmann could tell that his congregation wasn't exactly following where he was going with the story. So he got back on track with the tale about his grandfather.

'What I'm going to do tonight, is to tell you a story about my grandfather, how he left Prague, and what happened to him.'

Any good storyteller can judge his audience, so he threw in some bait.

'This story concerns my grandfather's shipwreck, a prostitute, and a pot of honey.'

The words were hardly out of his mouth, when all movement in the shul stopped. Squirming bodies no longer writhed, mouths half-open in stifled yawns suddenly gaped, heavy eyelids closing in the welcome relief afforded by a surreptitious doze popped open in amazement.

What did he say? Something about a prostitute and some honey? No, he must have said 'Prosecute' or 'Constitute' or maybe even 'Institute'.

Rabbi Teichmann looked at his congregation, and drove home the message. 'A prostitute and a pot of honey,' he repeated for good measure. 'And a shipwreck. Sounds like a dirty joke, doesn't it? But it's not. It really happened to my grandfather, and I'll tell it to you the way that he told it to me.

'My grandfather was born in 1880 in the ancient Prague area known as Malá Strana. His father, my great-grandfather, was a rabbi of one of the shuls in the old Jewish quarter. Not the chief rabbi. Nothing exalted like that. Just an assistant rabbi, whose job it was to open the shul and take Shaharit on cold mornings, and teach cheder every Sunday. Now my grandfather, Reb Isaac, grew up amongst great books, and the shul was his second home. He would use its quiet and comforting walls to protect himself from the shouts and clamours of the city, and often you could find him at night sitting there in the glow of the candlelight, just reading one of the holy books. Everyone said that my grandfather was destined to become a rabbi. His father was proud of him. His mother was worried about his eyesight. His brothers and sisters thought that he was peculiar, because unlike other kids their age, he wasn't interested in tag or fighting or chasing horses through the cobbled streets, or ringing the doorbells of unpleasant people. All he ever wanted to do was to curl up with the great holy books, and learn about what Moses did, or what Samuel said, or how Ezekiel and Hosea ranted and raved about immorality.

'Am I making him sound like a dull and studious sort of chap?' asked Rabbi Teichmann of his audience. No, they all intimated, shaking their heads, wondering when he'd get to the good bit and tell them about the prostitute and the pot of honey.

The rabbi nodded in satisfaction. He'd caught their attention. 'So, my grandfather, alav ha shalom wasn't all study. He made friends with boys who weren't studious at all. Nice boys, good Jewish boys, but not boys who would go on to become rabbis. These friends, these people with whom my grandfather spent much of his time, were boys who would follow their fathers into the family business; or so their fathers hoped. But they were wrong. Because these boys, these friends of my zeida, had no intention of following their fathers. No! These lads had seen their fathers work day and night in order to put food on the table. Why should they do the same thing, the boys reasoned. These weren't the old days. These were modern times. Nobody should work like that.

'But before I go on to tell you about the shipwreck, the prostitute, and the jar of honey ...' You see, the rabbi was getting into the swing of being a storyteller. Playing with his audience, dangling the bait ... 'Let me tell you something about the conditions in which Jews in Europe found themselves at the end of last century.

'Since the great revolutions in the middle of the nineteenth century, the walls of the ghetto had fallen. Jews, who were living in the darkness of the walls, were suddenly blinded by the brilliant light of emancipation. Rabbis, fathers and mothers warned their children against rushing out into unfamiliar territory, which even they could see was seductive.'

The rabbi shrugged his shoulders and continued, 'Even in those days, they didn't know what to do with their kids! And just like ours, their kids didn't listen. Certainly not the kids in Malá Strana. Well, that's not quite accurate. You see, there were some voices which they listened to. One in particular. One day, into their town, came a young revolutionary, a Zionist, an emancipist, a socialist. A young man burning with fervour and anger, a man who presented himself as a modernist, telling the rabbis and the leaders of the community how their ways were wrong and how the old teachings had done nothing for the Jews for thousands of years.

'I can't begin to describe to you the way in which this young man split the community. The older people thought he was a disciple of the devil. But the young thought that his was the voice of pure reason, the most musical and poetical voice they'd ever heard. Wherever he spoke, this young man, in halls or in homes, young people would gather around like hungry fish at feeding time. He would stand there in his cloth cap and his three-piece suit, thumbs tucked into his waistcoat and declaim how Jews must take their lives into their own hands, how they should no longer cower under the shadow of the great castles of European aristocracy but should go out onto the streets and proudly proclaim to the Catholics and the Protestants, "I'm no different from you".

'Well! You should have seen the reaction amongst his young and impressionable audience. It was like lighting tinder in the forest. The young saplings were ready to explode in angry flames. The more he spoke, the greater his passion, the more the young men in his audiences nodded, clapped, cheered and whistled. And that includes my grandfather. Wherever he spoke in Malá Strana my grandfather and his friends sat at the young man's feet listening to the revolutionary words. But unlike his friends, who believed they were listening to a messiah, my grandfather knew he was listening to trouble. For everything the young revolutionary said contradicted what my grandfather had been brought up to believe.

'Conflict was everywhere in the once-peaceful Jewish community of Prague. It was a conflict started by this young man, and the others who followed him. Disputes grew, separating sons from fathers, and rabbis from their communities.

'But did the young man care about the trouble he'd begun? No! He just upped and departed, to go and spread his revolution to the other great cities of Europe, and in his wake, he left the flotsam and jetsam of emancipation floating in the troubled sea that he had stirred up. For months after the young man's visit, the youth of Malá Strana talked about nothing but the excitement of their modern times and tried to come to terms with the conflict between the importance of their ancient religion and the need to leave the security of the ghetto.

'Every evening they would sit in a corner of one of the kosher coffee shops which used to abound in Malá Strana, drinking glasses of sweet tea and eating deliciously moist yeast and poppyseed cakes, and discuss things. Oh no, they weren't going to make the mistakes their parents had made. This was 1897. The age of the entrepreneur, of resourceful men who made fortunes out of paper. There was electric light in America and huge ships plied the seas regardless of wind and currents, driven by coal and steam. People could speak, and their voices could be played back to them on a phonograph. There was almost nowhere that modern man had not explored and mapped on the surface of the earth. Nature was being tamed. It was the culmination of everything that man had been put on the earth to accomplish.

'My zeida listened to their confidence with delicate scepticism. He didn't rant and rave like Hosea. And while Hosea might have railed against the weakness of ancient Israel, my grandfather didn't shave his head and wear sackcloth and cover his face with the cold ashes of the fire, and go out into the marketplace and denounce the modern ideas. But when his friends talked about the new movement of socialism, and especially when they talked about the new Jewish philosophy of Zionism, there was a zeal, a passion in their eyes which my grandfather found worrying.

'The Zionism which was preached by Theodor Herzl was unstoppable and it impelled my grandfather's friends to unbelievable heights of excitement. Why, they reasoned, should they follow their fathers into trades as tailors or silversmiths when the whole world was changing? Modern science was rapidly replacing craftsmen. The skill of the artisan's hands no longer counted as worthy in an age which was beginning to see the advent of mass-produced products. The tensions between my grandfather's friends and their families was palpable. These boys were eighteen, nineteen, twenty and yet they had no trade or profession. Nor were they even students because universities were closed to boys who came from the old Jewish quarter. The only education open to them was the Hebrew books, but they didn't want a traditional Jewish education, they weren't interested in the ancient books and they reasoned that the joy of learning for its own sake was a part of the Old World. Part of the world that was rapidly disappearing in the maelstrom of modern ways.

'You may be wondering how this affected my grandfather. On the one hand, he was listening with great interest and curiosity. On the other, he would search the great books for explanations of why these things were happening. He read Jeremiah in order to see if there were parallels between the Babylonian exile and the condition of the Jews in the Diaspora, and he read about King

David and the problems he had encountered. But nowhere in the great books did my grandfather find the answers to the problems that were troubling him. He was pulled this way and that. He knew there was something missing but he didn't know what.

'One day my grandfather met his friends as usual. But this time, something was different about them. There was more than fervour in their eyes. There was a kind of insatiable curiosity. It had been building over several weeks now and had reached a point where they could control themselves no longer. "Why don't we cross the bridge?" they said.

'"Bridge?" my grandfather asked.

'"Sure," they insisted, "go over the bridge. Walk over the Vltava. Go into the New City. Find out what's there."

'My grandfather frowned and shook his head. "Are you mad? We're Jews. We can't go wandering."

'"Why not?" they demanded. "We've been told we must go out and confront the Christians. Meet them head to head."

'"But..." began my grandfather.

'But his friends would accept no buts and so, despite his misgivings, the three of them crossed the bridge from Malá Strana to the part of Prague where all the Christians lived in the shadow of the castle. As they stepped onto the bridge and began to walk, they looked down at the fast-flowing waters of the Vltava. You may know it better as the Moldau which captivated the composer Dvořák. He painted it in sound as a gently flowing bucolic river, but on this day following the recent heavy winter rains it was flowing rapidly and angrily over weirs and around the rocks in its path. The three young men climbed to the apex of the bridge, where my grandfather suddenly stopped, full of doubt and hesitation. But his friends pulled him forward telling him to look towards the future.

'They walked to the other side of the river and entered the Christian part of Prague. Here were buildings of great stature and unbelievable grandeur, houses which stood eternally as symbols of the power and importance of their owners. Many of them had crosses proudly proclaiming the religion of those who resided within, as though the sign was a protection from the evil which dwelt outside. Three- and four-storey structures, houses with decorated eaves whose roofs were made of terracotta tiles. But not all of the buildings were grand. Some were old and tumbledown from which washing hung stretched across the street. And in between the buildings were shops of every kind: butchers, bakers, locksmiths, jewellers, bookshops and shops selling tins and others selling cakes. More shops than my grandfather and his friends had ever seen in their lives.

'Now the people of the Christian part of Prague walked around the three young men, staring curiously at their caps and sidelocks and the fringes of the tsitsith which hung below their jackets. In Malá Strana everyone wore sidecurls and showed their fringes but here they were an exception. They stuck out like sore thumbs. A policeman with a creased brow passed them on horseback and looked at them but he passed on, his horse's hooves clopping over the cobblestones. And the frightened young men quickly left the main road and walked in the backstreets where there were a dozen different inns with lots of laughter and noise and blue cigarette smoke pouring out of the windows. And in one of the streets, women sat on chairs in the November sun, their legs spread open, their skirts dangling seductively, their bodices suggestively uncovered. My grandfather's two friends laughed and nudged each other, one feeling in his pockets to see if he had enough money. But my grandfather, remembering the injunctions of the Prophets said,

"I'm going back. All of this is wrong. Terribly wrong," and as he walked away from them, they laughed at him. He didn't see them until later that night. And he never talked to them about what they had done before their return to Malá Strana and the old ways. Better not to know, he thought.

'A year went by and then one day something happened which changed the course of my grandfather's life forever. A group of townspeople who lived at the foot of the castle across the Vltava decided one day to cross the bridge and to vent their anger at the Jews. Why were they angry? Why does any pogrom begin? Do you need an excuse to start one? No, all you need is somebody to accuse the Jews of something and then you have a riot on your hands. As to what started this particular pogrom, well, that's lost in history. Maybe two people were talking in an inn and one had too much to drink. Maybe he lost his job. Maybe his landlord was a Jew. I don't know. But whatever it was, two angry men attracted the anger of two others and soon the four were a group of hornets buzzing around, their barbs ready, their minds angry, their faces flushed with the desire to hit and kick, to punch and kill. And they attracted more and more until there were hundreds that swarmed around the central handful. The people on the periphery of the group probably didn't even know why they were angry. All they knew was that they were angry. Angry with the Jews for doing something. Drinking the blood of a Christian child; charging too much money in interest; controlling the economy; spreading disease; infecting the town with the pox. We've all heard these hideous blood libels before. With the comfort of distance we can smile at the stupidity of the men and women who believed these things but in those days, there was nothing to smile about. Once there was an excuse for a pogrom, then Jews would get killed.

'And on this particular occasion the group of men grabbed whatever weapons were at hand — knives, hammers, spades, battering rams, anything — and they crossed the bridge at night from under the protective gaze of the castle into the Old City of Malá Strana.

'And there they spread fear and terror and anger and hatred. The Jews who first heard them coming thought it was just a group of gypsies happily crossing the bridge, singing their gypsy songs and playing their gypsy instruments. But the closer these men got, the closer the torches came to illuminate the hatred on their faces, the quicker the Jews of Malá Strana realised that this was no chorus from a comic opera. This was a mob and mobs meant death. Quickly they shuttered their windows, grabbed children from the street and ran through the town shouting out their warnings to their fellow religionists to get indoors. When the mob of men arrived at the south bank of the Vltava, the ancient city of Malá Strana was already empty and boarded up.

'But that didn't stop them. The pathetic shutters were no match for the mallets and sledgehammers. Windows were broken; men, women and children dragged from their houses and beaten; torches thrown into houses which flared incandescently into the night sky. Flames could be seen for miles and miles, and all that could be heard was the roar of fire and the screams of terrified women and children. Fortunately, the fire never reached a conflagration, because the police responded immediately, separating the mob from their victims and helping to put out the fire.

'The following day, a black mood descended on the ancient town. It was as black and grim as the smouldering ruins of the half-dozen houses which were burnt to the ground. You could almost touch the dull grey haze which hung in the air, a haze of confusion, of hurt, of fear. One of the houses which burnt down was the house in which my grandfather lived. It wasn't the target. It was instead, next-door to the shul which the madmen had tried to burn but had been unable to. My grandfather was not alone. The mob had also set fire to the house of the handbag maker and the silversmith, after stripping the shop window of every item of silver and craftsmanship inside. The next day, leaning against a street corner, talking about the events of the previous night, my grandfather and his friends realised they were ruined. My grandfather's two friends had no homes and no family income, and although my great-grandfather was still an assistant rabbi in the shul next-door, they would have to throw themselves on the charity of the community in order to survive.

'Now you can imagine what these young men talked about, can't you? My grandfather recounted it to me as one of his most vivid memories. There was such a feeling of disgust at their fellow citizens, the people who lived underneath the walls of the castle. The very self-same castle that Franz Kafka looked at every day as he was writing his great novels. They spoke of revenge. They spoke of getting a mob of Jews together, storming back across the bridge and setting fire to the homes of the Christians. They talked of poisoning the wells from which the Christians drew their water, or of kidnapping rich Christians and holding them for ransom. They discussed travelling far and wide to seek help from other Jewish communities in great cities who would come in their thousands and hundreds of thousands to support the pathetic and beaten community of Prague.

'And their conversations, whispered and urgent, were overheard by some of the elders of the community who smacked them on the back of the head, clipped their ears and told them not to be so stupid, to keep quiet. They were told, my grandfather and his friends, that these revolutionary fighting words were inappropriate, that responding would make matters worse, only reason and calm would quell the situation.

'But the following day, and the day after that, they all met on the same street corner and talked their talk. And they began to be noticed, the three of them. Standing in a tight huddle at all hours of the day, whispering revolutionary thoughts, until their parents were called in by the Chief Rabbi of Prague who told them to control the boys and prohibit them from uttering these dangerous and revolutionary ideas. And when the parents told the boys, the boys objected. My grandfather, most of all. Does that surprise you?' asked the rabbi of his congregation.

Some nodded. Some shook their heads. 'It shouldn't surprise you. You see Jews throughout history have been considered by those around them to be subservient and docile — the very antithesis of troublemakers. Our history seems to justify this attitude. We were locked in ghettos and never fought. We were exiled from one country to another. We were the subject of pogroms. But think about it for a minute, my friends. History only records the successes of the victors, never the vanquished. Who knows how hard we Jews fought against overwhelming odds? And this was the reason why my grandfather objected most vehemently, for he had in mind the stories of the great kings and the great prophets of ancient Israel, men who grabbed their swords and brandished them at the enemy, impelled by the glorious name of God. "Why should we be terrified to retaliate?" my grandfather asked his father when his father told him what the chief rabbi had said. "Why shouldn't we cross the bridge and strike fear into the hearts of the Christians?" His father shook his head sadly and stroked his beard.'

At this point, Rabbi Teichmann looked at old Mr Dayan, the butcher who was sitting there hanging on his every word and slowly stroking his beard. A glint appeared in Mr Dayan's eyes, an association with what the rabbi was saying.

'My great-grandfather said, "Haven't you learnt anything from the Great Books that you have been studying all your life? Haven't you learnt that reason overcomes fears? That peace is stronger than war? Do I have to remind you of the words of the great prophet, Isaiah who told us: 'They shall beat their swords into plowshares, and their spears into pruning hooks: nation shall not lift up sword against nation, neither shall they learn war any more'."

'It was then that my grandfather knew it was time to leave. That he and his father had diverged too far on opposite paths; that he should get on a boat and sail to the new land, the promised land. Not Palestine, which would soon become the new Israel, but America. America was where the Jews were going. Jews who were fleeing the hideous pogroms, the swords of the Black Hundreds, and the rampant anti-Semitism which made everyday life a living death for the millions of Jews who had lived in the Pale of Settlement for centuries. America beckoned. America, the land of equality, of openness, of decency.

'That was what he told his friends the next time they met on the street corner; his two friends, who were such ardent Zionists yet who immediately agreed to travel with him to America. "What?" he asked. "You would come with me to America? But I don't understand. I thought that you of all people would want to go and fight to make Palestine a Jewish country. That you would follow Herzl." But they smiled and shook their heads and said, "Sure, America. Life is so hard in Palestine. It's all right for some, but life is tough here. We want to grow rich, to prosper. You're right, America is the land of opportunity. We'll go there and make our fortunes and then we'll go to Palestine and help change it into Israel.'"

It was at this point that Rabbi Teichmann realised his audience was beginning to wander. What he was telling them wasn't an uncommon story. In fact, almost every Jew who lived in this country had a parent or grandparent or even a great-grandparent who had left their home under extreme duress and who had trudged the thousands of weary miles along winding country roads or dangerous highways in order to reach a ship which would magically transport them to a different land, full of new and exciting opportunities. And the land they always came to was America. The goldeneh medinah. The golden state. The land of the free. So Rabbi Teichmann knew he had to recapture the congregation's attention.

'Let me ask you a question,' he said. 'Is there anybody who has guessed yet how the prostitute, the jar of honey and the shipwreck come into the story?' Dr Josephs started to put up his hand but withdrew it. Nobody had a clue. 'Bear with me a few more minutes,' said Rabbi Teichmann, looking at his watch. 'Then we'll get on with the service.

'I won't tell you of the unbelievable difficulties which my grandfather and his two friends suffered as they trudged from Prague to Hamburg. Five hundred kilometres as the crow flies but, believe me, the crow was the only thing flying in those days. By the time they had climbed up hills and down into valleys, and avoided huge cities like Dresden and Berlin which they knew would be dangerous for wanderers, they had walked over a thousand kilometres. At the beginning they walked forty kilometres a day — buying food, doing odd jobs, sometimes stealing in order to get through the night. They slept in ditches, in roadsides, in barns, wherever they could.

'The journey didn't take them a month as they had estimated. It took them three whole months. And by the time they came within sight of Hamburg, they were like skeletons. If it hadn't been for the generosity of the Jewish community in Hamburg, my grandfather told me he would have died. The blisters on his feet had turned septic. He didn't walk, he hobbled. One of his friends had such bad dysentery from drinking ditch water, that he nearly threw up his own stomach. But the Jews of Hamburg gave them medical help and food and they rested for a week until they were able to feel like human beings again.

'Now you might think that they had a ship in mind that would take them to America. But no! All they had was an idea of getting a boat. You see, when they were in Prague, they had to escape both the city as well as their families if they were going to leave, and so they didn't have time to make reservations. Time? What am I talking about? They didn't have the money. All they had was a burning desire to go and live in a new land.

'Luckily there was a certain rich Jew in Germany called Rothschild. Of course, you've heard of Rothschild. And Rothschild had a fund to help Jews who wanted to flee Europe, so the boys were able to get an assisted passage to America.

'The captain of a steamship was paid the three fares and the boys were hustled on board at eight o'clock that night to begin the long journey. They kissed the men and women who had helped them and they offered their eternal gratitude. They said that one day they would return as rich men and repay every single pfennig they had cost the local community. How many times had the local rabbi heard that story?' Rabbi Teichmann shrugged his shoulders.

'The first night at sea, the boys celebrated with a bottle of wine and some cheese. The smell of the open sea, the feeling of euphoria as the ship sailed away from Europe, from the dark continent, from the place which had oppressed them all their lives, was something which not even I as a storyteller can explain to you. They felt as if they had never been born and that this was the moment of their delivery on earth. They wanted to strip off all their clothes and dance naked under the cold November sky like pagans at a solstice. But reason prevailed when the following day the captain told them that people who had an assisted passage had to work on the boat and they would be expected to scrub floors, help in the galley, mend broken items, and maintain the ship's chandlery. And so for two days until they put into the port of London in England, the boys happily worked and laughed, and ate and breathed the clean fresh sea air.

'Now the captain was an old seadog. He was a man with something of a reputation. A reputation of theft and aggression, but my grandfather and his friends didn't know this. The day after they arrived in London, the captain said to the three young men, "Why don't you go and look at London? It's a nice town. Go and have a look around before we sail at six o'clock tonight. But be sure you're back by five. I don't want to have to wait."

'So they shook hands and said goodbye to the captain and walked from Black Friars into the heart of London. There they saw Buckingham Palace and Covent Garden and the bustling markets. All around them were thousands of people wearing fashionable clothes, carrying parasols, sitting in cafes, smoking cigarettes and laughing. It was such a difficult place to find their way around in that for the first couple of hours the three boys felt intimidated. The language was hard, the road network so terribly different from Malá Strana, and the city continued endlessly without any horizons. Its tall buildings, imposing squares and monuments seemingly placed in a hodgepodge designed to confound the newcomer. But after several hours of walking and buying horse chestnuts in squares of newspaper, sold to them by red-faced men wearing hats and scarves and standing over hot braziers, they decided that they should return to the ship in order to continue their journey to New York and freedom.

'Trudging all the way back to the Embankment and then along the Embankment to where they had left their ship reminded them of the misery, only two weeks earlier, when they had finally arrived in Hamburg after crossing half of Europe. Their corns and blisters now healed, began to throb like phantom memories.

'They walked past the dock where the ship had been and on for another two miles before they turned back wondering if in their inexperience they had missed the ship. But when they stood on the dock where the ship had stood that morning and saw only a sluggish swell in the water, with filthy papers and bits of flotsam and jetsam, they knew their lives were at an end. They couldn't believe it. The ship had sailed without them. They blamed themselves of course. They had arrived back late. But no! A passing man showed them his fob watch and it was only four thirty. There was another hour and a half before the ship was due to sail. The captain had sailed earlier! And they realised that he'd probably sold their berths to other fare-paying passengers.

'They sat by the wharf, protected from the cold November winds that blew down the Thames, talking nervously about what to do. All their possessions, their clothes, even what little money they had was on the ship. All that remained was what they wore. "We've been shipwrecked," said my grandfather. "It's just like we've been cast off on a foreign shore because our ship has sunk. We're shipwrecked." He shook his head in sorrow. "What are we going to do now?" he asked the other two.

'But they were useless to him for they had no answers, only questions. They sat by the wharf for an hour until a policeman told them to move along. They wandered back along the road they had taken earlier that day, only this time their hearts weren't joyous, their hearts were heavy. In their journey through London they had seen many poor people begging in the streets. Was this all that was left to them? they wondered. But suddenly grandfather had a good idea. "We must go and see the local Jewish community. They're bound to help us."

'And so later that night, they found themselves at the bottom of Edgware Road where a huge edifice to English Judaism, the wonderful Marble Arch Synagogue, still stands to this day. And they went to see the rabbi.

'Now this rabbi wasn't like any rabbi they'd ever seen before. The rabbis of central Europe were hunched from years of study, and wore long coats and fur streimels on their heads. Most of them were Hasidim and in their minds still lived in the eighteenth century. But this rabbi was more like an English aristocrat. He wore tails and a silk top hat, his shirt sleeves had ruffles and he sat behind his huge oak desk looking at the three beggars asking them questions in English which they simply didn't understand. He tried Yiddish but they didn't speak his Yiddish, so he tried Hebrew and my grandfather's eyes lit up. And my grandfather responded in perfect Hebrew. They sat there, old man and young man, both from different countries, communicating as Jews have communicated with each other through the millennia, in Hebrew.

'My grandfather quickly explained what had happened to them and the rabbi shook his head and told them how awful it was but that there was nothing he could do. There were no funds which would help. No charitable institutions for cases like this.

Only for ill-health, not for destitution. But he took money out of his drawer — large pound notes — and gave a one pound note to each of the boys and he said to them, "This will help you get on your feet". And then he said to my grandfather, "And you, young man, please come back and see me in a few days. It's possible you may be able to help me in my work."

'The three boys found cheap lodgings in Soho and the following morning, still with some money in their pockets, they set out to get work. They each went in a separate direction, hoping to support each other. The two boys who were my grandfather's friends came back that night with nothing. They were despondent. They couldn't communicate and they had no skills. They couldn't be silversmiths like the father of one or a manufacturer of ladies' handbags like the father of the other. So what did they do? They walked around asking for work, using their hands to explain what their vocabulary denied. But on each occasion, when the person they were asking asked them what they could do, their answer was nothing. And so they each trudged home wearily and unhappily and sat in their threadbare room on the single hard bed in which the three had slept the previous night and fought back tears of fear and frustration.

'But my grandfather, now he was different. He had left the house in Soho that morning and as he was walking around looking for likely work opportunities, a buxom lady with swelling breasts, bright lips and rouged cheeks, wearing a cloche hat and flowing petticoats, had smiled at him as he walked along. My grandfather had smiled back and the woman had beckoned him over. Being polite, he went and the woman had said something to him which he didn't understand, so he replied in Czech. She tried a smattering of German but again, my grandfather shook his head as he did to her French and Italian, the only languages this very cosmopolitan lady knew. She rubbed her thumb and forefinger together, indicating payment. And it was then that my somewhat naïve grandfather realised that this lady was a prostitute, so he politely bowed and backed away, but she stopped him and beckoned him inside. He shook his head — until he saw a mezuzah on her door.'

The men in the congregation reeled back in horror. A prostitute! A Jewish prostitute! No. They had gone along with Rabbi Teichmann — all the way from Prague and across Europe to Hamburg and then to London — but this they wouldn't go along with. This they refused to believe. A Jewish prostitute! Impossible.

Rabbi Teichmann sensed a rebellion in his congregation and raised his voice sternly. 'You think that there are no Jewish prostitutes? You think that every Jewish woman is virtuous? Let me tell you about Rosie Klein. Rosie Klein was born in England and was beaten by her drunken father. Now it just so happens that her father seduced her mother who was Jewish. I won't go into the details except to say that her father worked as a dock labourer in Liverpool and during his stay in London met Rosie's mother who was a bit wild and attracted to this rough man. They met in Golders Green, made love that night on Hampstead Heath and nine months later, Rosie said hello to the world.'

Rabbi Teichmann held up his hands, almost in apology for having soiled the shul with such an earthy kind of story. But it was necessary in order to explain how Rosie's mother had tried to care for her but was ostracised from the community in Golders Green and so in the way of these things, Rosie became a prostitute at the age of thirteen in order to survive. When she was nineteen Rosie gave birth to a beautiful little boy.

Rabbi Teichmann appealed for calm among the restive souls in his congregation. This was getting beyond a joke. This was not suitable for a Friday-night shiur.

'When the little boy was eight,' Rabbi Teichmann continued, 'Rosie decided that he needed a Jewish upbringing. Now it wasn't easy, as she could attract nobody to help her. No melamed was willing to go near her, especially as she lived with all the other whores in Soho. And so the first Jewish teacher who happened by was my grandfather, of blessed memory, who, as he walked past Rosie, put his hand up and touched the mezuzah. He then kissed his fingers and walked on.

'So astounded, so touched was Rosie that she ran after him, and virtually forced him off the street back into her house. Despite his protestations, he went with her. The inside of Rosie's house was small and dense. The downstairs part was dark and dank, thick drapes which hung as draft protectors over the doors still carried the smoke of cigars from her former customers. My grandfather was repelled by the smells of cigar smoke and cheap perfume and pulled away from Rosie to try to escape, but she forced him upstairs and showed him into her private inner sanctum where a little boy sat at a desk, dressed in a sailor suit. His tongue was lolling to one side of his mouth, carefully writing out letters from a book. He looked up in surprise. The little boy didn't know what Rosie did but there were always men in the house and he was never allowed to go outside his room, except when he held Rosie's hand. For a man to come into their private rooms was unheard of.

'My grandfather was just as shocked. He had no idea what this woman wanted, but her face was different up here to the way it was downstairs. Here her face shone with an innocence that was not apparent in the muted light of the November afternoon street. She beckoned him to sit down, which he did at the same desk at which her son was writing. She spoke to her son, who nodded. My grandfather, of course, could understand nothing. But she fossicked in a bookshelf and withdrew a book of Hebrew, an alef-bet. She handed it almost reverently over to my grandfather, who opened it. It was the same type of book that he had used when he himself was learning the rudiments of Hebrew. In his cheder, whenever he learnt a new letter, an aleph, a bet, a gimel or so on, his melamed would give him a honey biscuit.

'Rosie indicated that she wanted her son to learn the alef-bet but that she didn't know anything about it. My grandfather nodded in understanding. This was a sacred task. This transcended her profession, his poverty, or the theft of his worldly goods by the sea captain. In the next two hours, the little boy learnt how to say *abba* or father, *imma* or mother, *tov* which we all know means good and a few other words. Rosie looked at her watch and realised that she was missing out on customers. This was the busiest time of the day when men from the markets were going home. She used sign language to explain and my grandfather nodded in understanding. He stood up and kissed the little boy on his forehead and, as he walked to the door, Rosie took out a one shilling piece from her purse and gave it to him. He refused to take it, handing it back, shaking his head vehemently. It was his privilege to teach a Jewish soul. Being orthodox, my grandfather couldn't accept money from a prostitute. By sign of language, however, Rosie explained that she was paying him with savings she'd made when she worked in a tailoring factory the previous year. My grandfather wasn't happy, but according to Jewish law, this money wasn't tainted. Rosie was forceful and my grandfather left her home with money in his pocket.

'You should have seen the reaction from the other two boys who were his travelling companions! And when he explained that Rosie wanted him back the following day to teach her son more and that it would mean another shilling, they were ecstatic. That night they went to a pub and the other two drank the warm beer that the English sold and ate bread and a huge nob of Leicestershire cheese, red and exploding with a piquant flavour. My grandfather, of course, refused to eat non-kosher food. The following morning, my grandfather bade his companions goodbye and went to teach the little boy his shiur. But this time my grandfather didn't arrive empty-handed. This time he approached Rosie's house with a pot of honey which he'd purchased in order to sweeten every letter which the little boy learnt.

'After a couple of weeks, my grandfather had earnt enough to move out of the awful lodgings in which the three boys were living and into a nice room with a poor Jewish family in Whitechapel. The other boys he was travelling with knew it was coming, for no matter how much they tried, they could earn no money and not even my blessed grandfather was willing to keep them for the rest of their lives. Without a trade, without a Hebrew education and without a knowledge of English, there was very little that these other boys could do. What happened to them? I don't know. They're just two turn-of-the-century Jewish men who probably found their feet in life if they were lucky. But my grandfather carried in his head everything he needed to establish himself in a new country amongst new people. Through his Jewish education, because he had spent his youth learning as well as praying, my grandfather knew a universal language and eternal customs. He was a part of the international body which is our religion. You see, the only thing of any lasting value, my friends, is what learning we carry in our heads, not the wealth of our possessions.

'And so my friends, my grandfather went on to become a true melamed, a true teacher and eventually he was offered a place in the Marble Arch Synagogue as an assistant rabbi like his father who had been an assistant rabbi in Prague.'

Rabbi Teichmann took out a handkerchief and wiped his lips. He looked at the men of the congregation. If only they paid as much attention when he was telling them about the Talmud as they did when he discussed his grandfather, the prostitute and the pot of honey.

Rabbi Teichmann thanked the congregation for their patience and as he turned around, he heard them say as one, 'Shekoyach' and then he continued with the service.

At the end of the service, the rabbi bade goodnight to his congregants and went to bed happy. During the following week, two things happened. One was that the rabbi racked his brain trying to think of another story to tell the following Friday night. It's not so easy to suddenly find a story. Most of the stories which the rabbi knew came from the Talmud, that vast and unfathomable body of explanations written before and after the life of Christ, concerning debates about the five books of Moses and other matters, and written over a 700-year period in Babylon and Jerusalem. And over the seven centuries in which the hundreds of rabbis that contributed to the Talmud were sitting and debating, the work expanded to include apocryphal tales, legends and words of wisdom on every subject from astronomy to agriculture, science to arts.

The one thing the rabbi didn't want to do was to make his stories sound too much like a sermon. For no matter how beautiful they were, stories from the Talmud tended to end up sounding like sermons. So the only other stories Rabbi Teichmann knew were jokes which he had heard, many of which were unsuitable, as well as stories, which were more like gossip, and tales about his own family. The best tale, unfortunately, he had already told so everything from now on was going to be downhill.

But that was only one of the things that happened. The second thing was the reaction in the community to the rabbi's story. Mr Dub told Mrs Dub who told a friend sitting in a hairdresser's shop who told her husband who told some of his friends one night when they were playing poker. Now you multiply that by the nine people in the shul and you have a lot of people suddenly finding out that a rabbi was standing up on the bimah telling stories about a prostitute and a pot of honey (somehow the shipwreck didn't seem to come into the retelling of the tale).

And eventually the word spread to Mr Nathan, an older man who was a three-day-a-year Jew. All he ever did was go to shul on the two days of Rosh Hashanah and on Yom Kippur. The three holiest days of the year. That's it. Of course he sometimes went when there was a wedding or a bar mitzvah but Friday night and Saturday morning . . . almost never.

But something had happened to Mr Nathan over the past year that had made him rethink his whole existence. One of his closest friends, a man he had befriended when they first came to this country from Russia, suddenly dropped down dead from a heart attack. Now, these two had been boys together, had travelled to this country on a boat and had made good in the same town. They were like alter egos, like blood brothers. They holidayed together, each was the best man at the other's wedding, they were Godfather to each other's children, confidants, they even shared a mistress once. So when Mr Nathan's friend suddenly dropped down dead of a heart attack, a harsh reality dawned on Mr Nathan and he thought to himself, 'Oh God, I'm next'.

From that moment onward, Mr Nathan didn't think about today but only about tomorrow. He got his financial affairs in order, paid back money he'd forgotten to pay to the Inland Revenue Service, and told his occasional mistress that enough was enough. But as he looked back on his life, he kept wondering how society would judge him. Of course, there were the usual outside trappings by which we are all judged superficially. Wealth, house, lovely family, donations to charities. But how would society really judge him? What sort of ethical and moral contribution had he made? How would he be remembered as a man and as a Jew? Certainly in the latter category, he didn't think he would hold up too well and so Mr Nathan made a decision. And the decision was that rather than stay at work till night-time on Friday and then wend his way home to his wife lighting the candles and him struggling to say a b'rachah (he never could get his tongue around Hebrew after a lifetime of avoiding it) he would go to the synagogue just this once and listen to this crazy rabbi and the stories that he told. Maybe then God would judge him a little bit more kindly in his later years ... if there were any later years.

And so the week rolled by and Friday night arrived again. Just before the sun went down, along came Dr Josephs, Mr Dub and the few other regulars who made up the minyan and as they were sitting waiting for the electric clock on the wall to signify it was time to begin the service, the door opened and a cold blast of air blew in and there standing like the redeemer, enclosed in a halo of light, was Mr Nathan. Mr Nathan looked at the congregation and smiled shyly. The congregation looked at Mr Nathan in utter astonishment. A newcomer. A stranger? No! It was Mr Nathan who came to shul three times a year. They smiled at him and he smiled back and the rabbi, about to mount the steps to the bimah to start prayers, walked over and shook his hand warmly, escorting him like an honoured guest to a central seat.

And so the rabbi began the service and the men stood and davened and mumbled and said their prayers out loud. All except Mr Nathan who stood with a prayer book in his hand wondering where the place was. Mr Krohn, an electrician, sidled over to him surreptitiously and offered him his prayer book which was open at the right place. Mr Nathan shook his head saying 'Don't bother,' but Mr Krohn insisted and pushed the book into his hands, taking Mr Nathan's prayer book and instantly opening it to the correct place. The two men stood side by side, one praying to God and the other trying to follow the service. As Mr Krohn turned a page, so too did Mr Nathan and the incomprehensible Hebrew began to take shape. The occasional word that he recognised — blessed, God, Our Lord — he was able to say ... and then the memories started to come back to him of when he lived in Russia as a little boy and went to Hebrew school and was given a honey cake every time he learned a new Hebrew word.

And so the service came to the halfway point when the men sat down at the appointed time for the sermon and all eyes waited impatiently for the rabbi to tell them another story. But Rabbi Teichmann was going to let his flock down. He didn't have another story. Instead, all he had was a parable. 'Let me tell you,' he said, 'a very short story about a very wise rabbi. I won't go into the details but, trust me, this rabbi was very clever. And he had a driver and a coach given him by his congregation so he could travel around the Ukraine from shtetl to shtetl, village to village, to preach his words of wisdom and his sermons. People would pay him so he was able to support himself and his driver and give food to the horse. It wasn't a bad life, but it wasn't all that great.

'Anyway, the rabbi was happy and he was one of the most learned men of his generation. And for twenty years his driver drove the rabbi from village to village where the rabbi was greeted with love and reverence and respect. At each village, as the rabbi was fêted to a meal and drinks after the long journey, his driver would be in the stable feeding the horse and brushing him down and laying a blanket over him. And then when he was finished, he would go into the kitchen, have something to eat himself and then, with the rest of the community, would wander over to the shul hall where the visiting scholar would be applauded for his great wisdom. And the rabbi would stand and deliver a wonderful, extraordinary sermon, relating ancient biblical matters to the traumas of modern-day life and the people would cheer when he came to the end of his sermon. Then the following day the two men would start the journey to another town.

'One day the driver turned to the rabbi as they were halfway between towns and said to him, "Rabbi, for twenty years I've been listening to your sermons three, four times a week. I know them all by heart yet I'm only a simple driver and nobody pays attention to me."

'"Go on," said the rabbi stroking his beard.

'"I was wondering, Rabbi, just once if you would let me have a little bit of the honour and stand up pretending to be you and deliver your sermon. After all, I'm a good Jew like you. I'm as observant. It's just that nobody knows who I am."

'Now this rabbi was a very modest man and he feared that all of the attention he was getting was going to his head and making him arrogant and so he thought, yes it would be good for him to sit in the audience and listen to his own words recited back to him, because then he would learn a lesson instead of teaching it. So before they entered the next town, they changed places and clothes, so the rabbi became the driver and the driver became the rabbi.

'As they entered the town the villagers came out and greeted the rabbi with great love and warmth and he was escorted into the house of the richest man in town and there he was given a sumptuous meal. While this was being done the real rabbi, who was pretending to be a driver, took the horse into the stables, fed him, groomed him, lay a blanket over him and had a meal of milk and bread and butter and a slice of cheese in the kitchens. Then with everybody else in the village he wandered over to the shul to hear the great rabbi give his d'rashah. And the driver didn't disappoint the rabbi. He stood there with the confidence of ages and he thundered from the pulpit. He invoked the words of the learned ancients. He quoted the Mishna, the Gemara, the Book of Job and the other things which he had heard the real rabbi quote from so many times in the past. And at the end of his speech, the audience stood and cheered, women cried and men could hardly speak, and they sat down, each saying to the other that they were in the presence of one speaking with the voice of God. And the local rabbi from the village, impressed beyond measure by the genius of this visiting rabbi said, "Are there any questions?"

'And a young Bible student in the second row, awed beyond belief by the presence of this greatest of all rabbis, tentatively put up his hand and humbly began to ask a question which, at its beginning seemed simple but when he got into the swing of it, showed an amazing, almost breathtaking grasp of the Jewish law. Hardly anyone in the audience was able to understand the incredible complexity or the nuances of the question that he asked. And when the young Bible student had finished asking his question, the driver stood there looking at the young man. He nodded a few times. Everybody in the audience believed that he was formulating the answer. But in reality, he hadn't understood a single thing that he had just been asked. It was all so complex. So he said to the young man "You know, young man, for a student of the Bible, that was a very shallow and superficial question. So shallow in fact, so easy to answer, that I'm going to ask my simple and uneducated driver at the back of the hall to come forward and answer it for you.'"

Rabbi Teichmann licked his lips. He'd come to the end of his story. The men in the minyan had laughed at the appropriate place, but they wanted more. This was only a few minutes. An hors d'oeuvre. It was now time for the main course. So he asked, 'What is this parable all about? Is it about a wise man who was humbled by a fool, and a fool who was humbled when he tried to be wise. Or is it about knowing your place in life? I don't know. But what I do know is that last week, I amused you by telling a story. Now, I can't be the only one with tales to tell. Is there anyone here who would like to enlighten us with his own story? Don't be shy. I really would like one of you to stand up here and tell me a story. I'd like you to come up onto the lectern and just as I did to you last week, you do it to me this week.'

Well, you should have seen the reaction on their faces. One looked at the other, and eventually they all looked around hoping that somebody would have something to say.

And wouldn't you know it? It was Mr Dub who nodded and stood and said, 'You know, Rabbi. I do have a story to tell. Something which I've never told anyone else before. Something about my wife and I.'

'Welcome Mr Dub,' said Rabbi Teichmann, opening his arms. 'Come up here and stand in my place, and I shall take your seat.'

And so Mr Dub walked up onto the lectern, and faced the congregation ... Not as a participant, but as a leader of the service, something which he'd never done before in all his years of going to synagogue. And Mr Dub told a story about ... but that's another story.

MR DUB'S STORY
ABOUT MRS DUB AND
HER HIDDEN LIFE

Mr Dub stood in front of the small congregation and suddenly was lost for words. Down there, sitting amongst his friends, listening to the rabbi every week, it had all looked so easy. For the whole week he had imagined himself taking the place of the rabbi, and telling the congregation the story to do with his wife. The story about his Sophie had grown in his mind ever since Rabbi Teichmann had told his tale of his grandfather and the prostitute. After all, if the rabbi could divulge details of his family, so could Mr Dub.

Of course, he never thought that for one minute, it would be him telling the story. What he planned to do was to relate the tale to Rabbi Teichmann, who would then stand up and retell it, but here he was standing at the lectern, two feet above everybody else, looking down at their expectant faces, wondering how to begin.

Now, as a cabinet-maker, Mr Dub was never much of a conversationalist. Most of the things he used to say were instructions to his staff about how to plane a piece of wood, or how much glue to use. But these days he doesn't have any staff, and what he says when he's alone in his workshop are mainly instructions to himself — things like, 'I must put another carving there to match the carving on the other side', or at times when things are going wrong, he has been heard to say, 'Dub, you're a shmuck. This thing is too high. Now, you've got to re-cut the wood.'

Of course Mr Dub speaks regularly to his wife Sophie, who is a good listener, but after fifty-three years of marriage there aren't all that many things left to talk about. There are the synagogue card parties where Mr Dub speaks a lot and in shul on Saturday morning, Mr Dub talks to the people sitting next to him.

But when it comes to standing up in front of an audience, this is something Mr Dub has never done before. Not once. Never in his life. Which makes you think that the storyteller's art isn't nearly as easy as it looks. But that's another story . . .

The first thing Mr Dub did was to apologise. 'Let me start off by apologising,' he said, 'I'm not like you, Rabbi. Words don't come as easy to me as they come to you. All my life, I've spoken through my wood. The beginning of my sentence has been the raw planks of wood that come to me, seasoned, straight and solid but with a lot of roughness. And the verbs and the nouns are the plane, the saw, the files and the sandpaper. And the full stop is when I deliver the furniture to the customer who says, "Thank you so much. It's beautiful." That's my full stop. The end of the matter. So as you can see, I'm not a learned man. What I'll try to do is to tell a story that nobody here knows. It concerns my wife Sophie. Sophie, you all know. Every Saturday she's in shul. She does many things for the community. She's a real active member of our congregation. Right?' he asked. It came out a bit more aggressively than he thought it would but the response was good. Everybody nodded.

'But did you know that my Sophie wasn't Jewish?'

Well, the reaction was like pouring ice-cold water over their heads. Remember the reaction when Rabbi Teichmann began to talk about the prostitute and the pot of honey? (See, even I've forgotten the shipwreck.) That time everybody stopped moving and not a breath could be heard in the shul. And it was exactly the same when Mr Dub said that his wife Sophie wasn't Jewish.

The Dubs had lived in the community for more years than anyone could remember. They'd always been there. Stalwarts of the community — they were amongst the more religious, certainly the more regular, in attending shul every week. In fact, give or take the rabbi and the rebbetzin and a few other members of the community, you would have to put Mr and Mrs Dub down as being amongst the most Jewish and certainly the most Orthodox in the shul.

But what was this? Sophie Dub wasn't Jewish? Nonsense. It was like saying the Pope was a Buddhist or the Dalai Lama was an American TV evangelist. Nonsense. The congregation was shocked.

But Mr Dub was ecstatic. He stood there looking at the faces and he felt a surge of power, the like of which he had never known before. Control, that's what he had. He had real control over his audience. If only he could get other people to respond like that. Like his children. The moments ticked by and he continued, 'That's right. My wife is a Polish Christian. Well, she is according to the papers which saved her life when the Nazis overran Poland in 1939.'

The rabbi smiled and sat back in his chair. He was the first to understand what was going on and slowly reason dawned on the others who looked up at Mr Dub in eager anticipation of his tale.

'Let me tell you how it all started. My wife Sophie was born in the town of Tomaszów which is southwest of Warsaw by about one hundred kilometres. Now, this was a town like many others before the war. The main town was full of the usual things which towns in those days were full of — town halls, inns, houses, churches, shops and schools. But where the Jews lived in a shtetl just outside the town, were only houses and the occasional shop. If they wanted to drink, they had to walk up the hill to where the Christian part of the town began, and find a corner in the inn, and stay there. But usually, the Jews didn't mix with the Poles and certainly the Poles didn't like mixing with the Jews but this, I'm sure you know, so I won't go into. What I'll tell you, however, is that my wife Sophie was a very adventurous girl when she was young.

'Don't misunderstand me. There were no real barriers like gates or a wall between the two halves of the town. But the Jews kept to themselves, and so did the Christians. Sophie's mother didn't like her going into the Christian part of the town, and so it always seemed to tempt her. She would look up the road from where her house was and she would see a lot of bustle and hear a lot of noise in the town. Her mother would say to her, "Don't go too far up the road. It's where the goyim live." And certainly for the first ten years, she obeyed her mother's words. But every now and again she would see this pretty little girl who had dark hair, black eyes and dark skin who would stop in the middle of the street, carrying her school bag, and would stare at my Sophie, and my Sophie would stare back.

'And they would look at each other as if there was some invisible barrier which stopped them from communicating. At first, it was accidental. They would see each other and stop and look, and then walk on. It happened once a week. Sometimes more, sometimes less. But then Sophie began to time her departure for school with the time that the other girl left her home to go to her school and the two girls would stand and look at each other until my Sophie would wave and the other girl would wave back. After school, Sophie would rush home to see if the girl was standing there, and sure enough, often she was there and they would wave and smile. Eventually they started to shout words to each other. "What's your name? Where do you live?" The usual things. But when they shouted Sophie's mother would come out, look at the other girl and bustle Sophie into the house, telling her not to be silly, that the girl wasn't Jewish and that she wasn't to play or go near.

'Well in those days, you couldn't tell Sophie what to do and to this day nothing has changed.' The congregation burst out laughing. They all knew Mrs Dub. A heart of gold but you couldn't tell her.

'So Sophie contrived one day to tie a message to a ball, and to throw the ball at the little girl. The minute the ball had left her hand, Sophie rushed indoors and greeted her mother with hugs and kisses. Today you would call it overcompensating; in those days you called it hugs and kisses. The next morning the two girls looked at each other and the Christian girl threw the ball back with a note attached which read:

My name is Gosha. It's short for Margoshata. I have three brothers. My father drinks too much vodka. My mother cries a lot.

'When Sophie went to school that day, instead of going into the playground to play she read and reread the note and then she wrote another one telling the girl about her own father, her mother and her brothers and sisters. Then she rushed home and threw the ball back.

'Now the little girl went to a Polish Catholic school which was in the middle of the village and after they had exchanged notes for about three weeks, never daring to speak to each other, one of the nuns in this little girl's school found the note and beat her black and blue. The nun took her home, pulling her by the ear, and threw her through the doors of the house, shouting at the girl's mother that Jews were the enemies of Christ, that Jews were in league with the devil and that for the good of her eternal soul she must have no contact with Jews. That night, a policeman knocked on the door of Sophie's house and spoke in urgent and whispered terms to Sophie's mother and father. Sophie was upstairs in the bedroom she shared with two of her brothers, cowering under a blanket. It was the end of the world and Sophie's life was over. Her brother Izzy, who never liked her, was goading her, telling her stories about Polish gaols and how she would rot and be eaten by insects.

'Well, the beating that Sophie got from her father was such a blessed relief from the horror of Polish prison that she almost thanked him as her bottom stung black and blue. She swore to her parents that she would never ever communicate with the little girl up the road again. Her promise lasted about a week. As she was walking out of the house, a ball landed at her feet. She snatched it up and, too scared to look up the road at the little girl, ran to her Jewish school where she surreptitiously opened it.

Did you get into trouble? My ear is still stinging where the nun pinched it. I hate nuns. I hate school. I hate my mother and father. I hate you.

'Sophie was terribly hurt and wrote an urgent note back explaining that she too had been beaten for daring to communicate, but that she didn't hate the little girl and she was terribly sorry that she had caused problems.

'Now three streets away from where Sophie lived was a fountain and it just so happened that the fountain was outside of the shtetl area and not quite inside the main Christian town of

Tomaszów. One Saturday afternoon when Sophie had been to shul she saw the little girl up the road. Their eyes met and Sophie had this overwhelming desire to speak to her, just to listen to her voice, to find out if she was still hated. Sophie nodded and smiled at the girl and then pointed in the direction of the fountain. Gosha gaped in astonishment at the audacity of it, but a wicked smile came over her face and she nodded enthusiastically, checking that nobody was looking. Gosha and Sophie walked away from their homes, crossed the road, crossed another road and then slowly met on opposite sides of the fountain.'

Mr Dub looked at his audience to see if they were still captivated. And they were. Even the rabbi's jaw was slightly ajar, eager to find out what happened next.

'The first one to speak,' said Mr Dub, 'was Gosha. "You're a horrible bitch and a stinking cow!" she told Sophie aggressively. "You got me into trouble. I hate you and I never want to talk to you again." Sophie was shocked by their first encounter. But the thing which surprised her most was that Gosha's voice was higher than Sophie had remembered. Maybe it was because she hated Sophie so much.

'Sophie put her hand in the cold water and wiped her brow. "I've already apologised," she told Gosha. Her voice sounded deeper than she thought, especially in comparison to Gosha's. "If you don't want to continue sending the notes, let's not. If you don't like me don't write to me."

'"But it's fun," said Gosha. "I like doing it. It's naughty. I like disobeying my parents. My father drinks too much. He smells of vodka all the while, he smokes and the house smells. And when he's in a bad mood, he blames me, and beats me."

'"Then why are you so angry with me? What's it got to do with me?" Sophie asked.

'Gosha shrugged and said nothing.

'"What's it like to be Christian?" Sophie asked.

'Gosha laughed and said, "It's good. Nobody hates you, just so long as you keep telling everyone you love Christ. Did you know that the Jews killed Christ? They did. They hunted him down and killed him like an animal and they put his body on a cross. They nailed him and taunted him. And he was a God. I wonder how you scratch yourself when your nose is itchy if you're nailed to a cross?"

'Sophie shrugged. "I don't know. Maybe it's all part of the punishment." Sophie had never heard of a person called Jesus at that stage of her life, and didn't really know what Gosha was talking about.

'"Tell me, what do Jews believe in? Are you really the devil? Do you have horns? Do you have a tail?"

'"We don't have any of that," said Sophie. "We just go to shul and pray and keep the house clean."

'"But you do drink Christian blood, don't you?" Gosha asked. "I mean, everybody knows that. That's why Christian children disappear. I've been told by my father, and by the nuns, that if a Jew ever speaks to me, I've got to tell the police."

'"Are you going to?" Sophie asked in apprehension.

'"That depends on whether you do the things I tell you to do. But you didn't answer my question. Do Jews drink the blood of Christians?"

'"I don't think so," Sophie replied, shaking her head. "I've tasted my blood when I cut myself and it tastes salty, and the wine we drink isn't like that at all. In fact, it's very sweet."

'Gosha ran away and shouted back, "I've got to go. I'll meet you here tomorrow but I still hate you. And remember, you've got to do everything I tell you."

'After that, the two girls met regularly at the fountain until they were fourteen. By then they had become the closest of friends. They shared all their secrets. They went for long walks together in the country. They even said they loved each other. It was 1938 and the Polish army was on manoeuvres just outside the town. The Polish High Command knew there was going to be a war but they thought that their horses and gun carriages would easily turn back the Germans. They had never heard of the word blitzkrieg. There were hundreds of soldiers in town and one night in the pub Gosha's father got into an argument with a drunken sergeant and was killed.

'Now, you would think that when a husband and father is killed his wife and his children would be grief-stricken. But no. Because he had been a very violent man his sudden departure from the house come as an immense relief to his wife and indeed to the children. So much so that two months after the funeral, Gosha's mother remarried a man she had been secretly seeing for the previous few years. This left Gosha much freer and she and my wife Sophie developed their friendship to the point where they were open about it. Gosha's mother changed from being closed and suspicious to being open and liberal. And it was all thanks to her new husband.

'You see, unlike Gosha's real father, her stepfather was one of those socialists who participated in the strikes of 1936 and 1938 and helped to establish the PPS or Radical Worker's Party. He was a follower of Stanislaw Mikolajczyk, but he wasn't just a socialist. He also had a deep commitment to equality for all people and was concerned that Polish anti-Semitism would eventually rise up and destroy the country. So he positively encouraged the friendship between the two girls and the mother reluctantly withdrew her objections.

'A year later, the Polish army showed how well prepared they were and within days, the Nazis moved in to occupy the whole of Poland. Now, the Nazis had been told that the Poles were Slavs, and that Slavs were subhuman. But worse than subhumans were the Jews. So wherever the Nazis went they gave the Poles eight hours to settle their differences with the Jews. The eight hours in fact invariably turned into several days during which Jews were beaten, robbed, and killed in a bloodbath of anti-Semitic hatred. And the town of Tomaszów was no different. Jews in all the main Polish towns, and in every shtetl were taken into the streets and beaten with clubs and sticks. Shops were looted, sacred scrolls and books were torn and burnt. Rabbis were forced to take down their trousers and urinate on the holy books. It was a hideous nightmare, but only a prelude of what came later.

'And then the Germans brought order, typical Germanic order, to the riots. Again, my friends, I won't go into what the Nazis did because you know it well enough. All I'll do is relate what happened to my dear wife. Unfortunately like three million other Polish Jews, her family was swept up and taken to concentration camps. And that would have been the fate of my beautiful Sophie had it not been for her friendship with Gosha. Because two days before the shtetl of Tomaszów was emptied by the Nazis and everybody carted off to Auschwitz or Bergen-Belsen, Sophie went to Gosha's home to kiss her and to say goodbye.

'But Gosha's father was having none of it. The girls were then fifteen and they knew exactly what transportation meant. Rumours were coming back even in those early days that torture camps were being built and that the Jews were being rounded up for slave labour, even the infamous Dr Mengele was being talked about, though nobody really knew what he was doing. So when

Sophie came to kiss Gosha and her mother and her stepfather goodbye, there were floods of tears, even from Gosha's mother who had begun to look upon Sophie as a daughter. Sophie and Gosha went up to Gosha's bedroom and Gosha said, "My stepfather says that your life is in great danger, Sophie. He says that the Germans have no real interest in destroying the Slavic races, but want them to work as slaves for the master race. But for you Jews, it's a different matter. He wants you to take my identification cards, so that you can go away from here, and pretend to be me."

'Out of a drawer Gosha removed her citizen's identification papers which contained an old photograph. The resemblance wasn't good. Sophie frowned. "I don't understand."

'Gosha whispered urgently. "You must take these papers and you must go away. Don't turn back. Just leave."

"'But what about you?" Sophie asked.

'Gosha shook her head and said, "Don't worry about me. I'm a Pole. We'll be all right. There's a strong Polish resistance movement, we'll overthrow the Germans and get them out of our country. But it isn't your country, Sophie. It's ours. And the Nazis want to see you all dead. Or so my stepfather says. It's the Jews they're after, not the Poles, so you must take this and go quickly."

"'I can't leave my parents," said Sophie.

"'If you don't, you'll die with them. My father says that we can't help your parents, but we can help you. I love you. You're my friend. You'll die if you don't do what I tell you."

"'But . . ." said Sophie.

"'No buts," said Gosha as she kissed her on both cheeks. There were tears in both girls' eyes as they said farewell.

'Gosha stood in the doorway and watched Sophie reluctantly walk away. When the Nazis came the following day to round up all the Jews and transport them to concentration camps, Sophie had already kissed her parents and her brothers goodbye and was five fields away as the petrol fumes from the lorries made the warm August wind grey and polluted. She watched in fear and desperation as the long convoy of lorries snaked its way out of Tomaszów carrying her family, her other relatives, her friends, the rabbis and the town leaders to their unknown destination and certain deaths.'

At this point, Mr Dub stopped talking. The congregation looked at him in concern. His voice was quivering, and his lips seemed to be repeating silent thoughts. He swallowed, and continued, his voice weaker than before, 'All alone, my Sophie trudged across fields, avoiding roads wherever possible, until she came to the nearby town of Piotrków, where she found work as a servant in the home of a rich man. She used the papers of her friend, and adopted her name of Margoshata. She told the rich man's wife that she had been raped by her father who was a drunken escapee from the Polish army. Horrified by her story, they gave her shelter and Sophie spent that night, the first night in her life she'd ever been separated from her family, sleeping close to the stove in the kitchen. Nobody, not even for one moment, suspected that Sophie was Jewish.

'On Sunday, the first Sunday that she was with her new employer, there came the time to go to church. At eight o'clock in the morning, the rich man and his wife proudly came into the kitchen and stepped down into the larder where my Sophie was scrubbing the surfaces. "Margoshata," said the rich merchant. "You won't do any work today. This is Sunday. Even though the Nazis are in control of our country, the churchbells still ring. My wife and I have brought you this dress. Wash yourself, put it on and come with us to church."

'Speechless, Sophie did exactly as she was told. The dress didn't fit well and was rough, but it was new and for that she was grateful. But when she walked behind the rich merchant, his wife and their four children, and entered the church with the other servants, a feeling of strangeness came over her. Instead of the cheerful shul where she spent Friday nights, and Saturdays, where everyone knew each other, and where there was the comfort of prayer and belonging, here was a huge, alien, cold building. Images of death were everywhere — crucifixes of Christ dying in agony were on all the walls, and pictures of Him lying dead in Mary's lap were in all the stained-glass windows. There were pictures of dying saints and statues of Mary, weeping. The whole church was enveloping Sophie in images of sadness and death and cruelty.

'Poor Sophie. She didn't know what to do. But that wasn't the only problem for her. She had no experience of Christianity. And suddenly, her life depended on knowing what all the other people in the congregation had known from birth. She knew she had to cross herself but she didn't know what hand to use. Do you touch your forehead first, then your heart, then your left, then right, or what? She sat in the church and knelt on the stool when the others did and stood when the others stood and sang lusty hymns when the others sang — always a fraction of a second behind their words as she listened and repeated what they were singing. She wondered whether they had a Kiddush after the service — a small glass of wine and biscuit — but there was nothing like that. The priest called everybody forward for Communion and for the first time in her life, my wife accepted the body and blood of a Jewish rabbi who had died 2000 years earlier, killed by the Romans in excruciating pain. As the wafer touched her mouth and she sipped the wine, she wondered whether God would send a thunderbolt to strike her dead. But nothing happened. The wine was thinner, a bit sharper than our Kiddush wine, and she tried not to grimace. She followed the other servant girls back to her seat and sat there until the service was over.

'But that wasn't the end of the problem for her, because after the service the rich merchant whispered in her ear, "When did you last confess?" Sophie opened her mouth and shook her head. She didn't even know what a confession was. He smiled and held her hand and took her to the little cubicle where the priest sat on one side of the grate and poor Sophie had to sit in a curtained-off area to say her confession.

'The priest said something in Latin which she didn't understand, and so being a smart girl she didn't respond. She could feel the priest looking at her so he asked her in Polish, "How long is it since your last confession my child?" Well of course she wasn't going to tell him the truth so she started to make up these incredible stories. She told him it was a long while, and recently she'd been very busy doing things for the resistance, like putting sugar into the petrol tank of a Nazi motorcyclist so that as he was heading out of the village, his motorbike suddenly shuddered to a halt and threw him over the handlebars. The priest could hardly contain his laughter and it impelled her to embellish the stories of even more daring adventures she had had fighting the Nazis.

'Now,' said Mr Dub looking at his audience, 'You may think that that was a foolhardy act. After all, we all know that many priests in Catholic Poland collaborated with the Nazis. She was fortunate because he was one who didn't. In fact, the Father who she spoke to turned out to be a bit of a Resistance hero who met his death along with many Jews in Auschwitz. He loved the way she told the story and he forgave her her sins immediately. Now you may think it was a bit of a breach of ethics but he happened to mention a few days later to a local Partisan leader that he should look out for my Sophie for here was a girl with real courage. He didn't tell the Resistance leader what she had done because that was a breach of the laws of confession. He just said, "Keep an eye on her. She's a good girl."

'And so that was how my Sophie joined the Resistance. For two years she worked as a scullery maid for the rich merchant and his wife during the day, fought with the Resistance at night, and on Sundays confessed everything to the priest. The only thing she didn't tell him was the truth about who she was.'

At this the congregation burst out laughing. They were loving every moment of Mr Dub's story. Even the rabbi; but he looked at his watch. Another few minutes and Mr Dub would be going over time and that wasn't good. The rabbi tried to signal Mr Dub but the cabinet-maker was so caught up in his narrative that he either didn't see or maybe he didn't want to see, so Mr Dub continued.

'And then came the end of the war, and the defeat of the Germans. That was when the Russians moved in. And my Sophie feared the Russians more than the Germans, for she knew that they were animals whereas the Germans were only madmen. She moved west to escape the oncoming army and she found herself in an American Red Cross camp where for the first time in five years, she gave her proper name and called herself Sophie. Her other self, Gosha, was completely forgotten as Sophie resumed her old identity and eventually became a refugee aboard a ship where we met travelling to this wonderful land of ours, this new country, and where we got married and established our lives.

'Now for twenty years, Sophie never once told me the story of how she had taken on the identity of Gosha. She felt an incredible sense of guilt that she had taken this girl's identity, for reasons I can't even begin to imagine. I knew there was something wrong because every few months she would lock herself in her room and write a letter and then surreptitiously post it. And every few months a letter would come back from Poland or the Ukraine or America which she would open behind the locked door of our bedroom. After reading the letter she would be sad for a couple of days. I didn't know what it was all about until one day I decided to open the letter before I gave it to her. Yes, I know you'll be angry with me but twenty years is long enough to keep a secret,' said Mr Dub banging the wooden rail of the bimah.

'And the letter told me what I wanted to know. It said that there was no trace in any of the Swedish dispossessed person's registers of a Polish Catholic girl called Margoshata Poniatowski. And so I confronted Sophie and tearfully she told me everything. Do you know what her shame was, my friends? Her shame was that she had turned her back on Judaism. That for those five years of the war when she was using another person's identity she had become a Christian. Oh no, that's not true. I'm sorry. I lied. She never became a Christian in her heart. She was always Jewish but she pretended. And she cursed the Jews in front of the Polish merchant and his wife, and like them, she blamed the Jews for the misery that Poland was suffering.

'Well, let me tell you friends, I forgave her straightaway. Not that it was my business to forgive her. After all, she hadn't harmed me but I felt she needed forgiveness and that's what I gave her. And then I started to help her look for Gosha. I said to her that there was no point in writing to those organisations, that we had to go but she told me I was crazy. She told me she would never go behind the Iron Curtain, not while it was ruled by Moscow.

'We had to wait another twenty-five years before Sophie felt safe enough to leave our home, and to go behind enemy lines. We had to wait until the fall of the Iron Curtain just a few short years ago. You know, we were one of the first people to go back to the village of Tomaszów after Gorbachev took down the Iron Curtain? The people of Tomaszów had hardly seen any Jews since the war. Of course, much of the shtetl was gone and in its place were the usual tower blocks of Stalin-type grey flats and apartments for the workers. Where my Sophie had once played in a beautiful valley outside the village were factories belching filthy smoke into the air, and the old fountain had been knocked down and replaced by a statue of Lenin. That too had recently been knocked down when the townspeople were celebrating the overthrow of communism, and we found it lying there in ruins.

'Well, Sophie and I. We walked down the main street of Tomaszów and stood outside the house where she was born, and where she had lived for fifteen years until the Nazis came. We knocked on the door and there we found an old lady and her family who looked at us with great suspicion and told us that they had lived in that house all their lives and we couldn't come in. They were scared we were trying to repossess it. They had heard the stories about how the Jews had returned and were taking back their property, though God knows why any Jew would want to live again in Poland or Germany. In a way, my Sophie was glad she couldn't walk into the house because the memories she had of it were the memories of a fifteen-year-old girl, and some were very happy memories.

'So we walked, hand-in-hand, up the hill to where Gosha had lived. This time there was no dividing line, not even an imaginary one. This time there was no difference between the upper and lower town because all the Jews had gone. We stood outside the gate and we looked at the house. Somehow it was more emotional than looking at Sophie's own house because Sophie knew that all her family — mother, father, sisters, brothers — were all dead. Killed in Auschwitz and Bergen-Belsen. But she had no knowledge of what happened to Gosha. Would she still remember her? Would she still live in the house? We just didn't know.

'So Sophie and I knocked on the front door and a fifty-something-year-old man opened it. He looked at Sophie and me and he asked what we wanted. Sophie asked if the family Poniatowski still lived in the house. The man shook his head and said, "No, we've lived here forty years." Did he have any idea where the family went to? "I have no idea," said the man, "but the woman over the road," he pointed to a house, "she's lived here all her life, she might know." And so we went trudging over the road, a road which my Sophie was always frightened to walk on when she lived in the village, and we knocked on the door. A middle-aged woman answered and when we explained what we wanted she took us into the back where chickens were running around the yard and two snarling dogs were tied upon leashes.

'Sitting in a chair was an old grey-haired woman. She must have been eighty, ninety, I don't know. We introduced ourselves and we told our story. The old woman — thank God, her hearing was still good — nodded and said, "Yes I remember like it was yesterday. The stepfather was a Communist. Gosha's father, he was a drunken evil man. He got killed you know. Good riddance. The stepfather, he was a decent man, so the Nazis knew he was a Communist because they were told by informers and they came and took him. And they arrested the mother as well, and that left Gosha and her sisters and brothers. One day Gosha was walking in the street near the fountain and a Nazi patrol demanded her papers, but she didn't have any. And so they arrested her. I think they took her to Auschwitz. And then they came for the rest of the family, and I suppose they were killed as well."

'The old woman shook her head. And then lay back in the chair and closed her eyes. She couldn't tell us any more. There was nothing more to tell. We left the old woman and went back to Warsaw and flew out of that hellhole.

'It wasn't until we returned home, that my Sophie cried for her friend, for Gosha who had died for her. And every year, on the very day that Gosha gave Sophie her papers, I come to shul, and I say a Kaddish for Gosha and her family. And before any of you question my right to say Kaddish for a Christian family, well, they were righteous gentiles, and I'll go on remembering them until the day I die.'

Mr Dub realised that he was sounding angry, even militant. So he excused himself, and finished up with, 'And that, my friends, is the story of how my wife became a Christian.'

Sunday and Monday passed without incident. Mr Dub's story resonated in the mind of the rabbi. He was amazed that the old man had had such a command of language that he was able to stand up for ten minutes and deliver a story of such complexity with such eloquence. And the rabbi got to thinking, maybe there are more people who can tell stories. Maybe I should phone up a few of the congregants and suggest it to them.

The phone played an active part in Rabbi Teichmann's life. Not on Friday night or Saturday of course. Then, by law, he was forbidden either to use or to answer the phone, but for the rest of the week, he was always busy answering enquiries, talking to people, phoning and making arrangements.

Life was very different in a big city to the sort of life Mr Dub's wife Sophie had lived in her youth. Then in the shtetls and Jewish villages in Europe, if you wanted to talk to somebody they were next-door or at worst across the road. These days it could take people an hour in the car to visit somebody they needed to talk to.

On Tuesday, Rabbi Teichmann's phone rang. He was upstairs in his study when his wife Rivka called him down. As he walked down the stairs, his expression asked 'Who is it?'

She held her hand over the receiver and said 'It's Charlie Finburg.'

'Who?' he asked.

'He comes to the shul occasionally. I think I know him.'

The rabbi answered the phone politely, listened carefully to the enquiry, nodded several times and said, 'Six o'clock. I look forward to seeing you there.' He put down the phone and said to his curious wife, 'Another one for Friday night. The way things are going, I should charge admission.'

But on the following Friday, at six o'clock, it wasn't just Mr Finburg and Mr Nathan who were new members of the minyan. At the back were their wives who had come specially to listen to the stories, and three new people walked through the door looking inquisitively around to make sure they were in the right place. People who came more often than three times a year, but were still relative strangers.

At the appointed time, the rabbi stood. It was the middle of the service — the part the newcomers had come for. It was time to listen to another of the rabbi's stories. Well, again he would disappoint them and again he hoped that there was another Mr Dub in the congregation who would stand up and tell a story.

'Friends,' said the rabbi. 'Again it's time for what is becoming something of a tradition in this shul, a tradition of storytelling. Before I hand over to one of you who I'm sure would like to tell his story ...' Again there were murmurs in the congregation, people looking at each other quizzically. 'Let me tell you a very quick little tale, something which is based on a story I heard as told by one of our great rabbis. You'll see the relevance in a minute. Once there was a community not dissimilar to ours. And this community was headed by a rabbi who was known far and wide for his piety and his brilliant mind. This rabbi would answer the most detailed and technical questions on Jewish law. People came from all over the area just to seek his advice. But within this community there was a group which was growing in opposition to this rabbi's assistant.

'Now in all fairness the rabbi's assistant was a fairly lazy man. He would take the service but that's all he would do. Rarely did he attend communal meetings, almost never did he prepare a sermon and he was always too busy to teach little boys their bar mitzvahs. So the rabbi was forced to do more and more of the day-to-day work around the congregation, until the group who opposed the assistant became so furious about their beloved rabbi's exhaustion that they decided things had to change. And so they went up to the rabbi one day and they said to him, "Rabbi we need your advice. You have too much work to do and your assistant doesn't have enough. No matter how much we've tried to persuade him to work he always finds an excuse. Frankly, he's lazy. You know it and we know it."

'"And your question?" asked the rabbi.

'"We want to suggest that your assistant moves to another community. It's not right that he should be taking a salary when you're doing half of his work. Our decision is for the good of the shul and our whole congregation. So the question is, are we right to do what we're thinking of doing?"

'Well, the rabbi thought about it. He pondered the amount of work he was doing compared to the amount of work his assistant was doing and he thought, yes it is right to get rid of him, which is what he told this group of people.

'A few days later, a delegation went to see the rabbi's assistant and they said to him, "We think you should move to another shul. We don't think you're suited to this one. You're not doing nearly enough work to support our rabbi. We don't want to fire you because that would cause us serious problems with the Beth Din, so we want you to do the right thing, and resign."

'Let me tell you that the rabbi's assistant was shattered. It was a beautiful community. He enjoyed the work and he had plenty of time to relax and go fishing. To go to another community would make life difficult. It would mean he would have to uproot his family and, when eventually he got another post, he would have to work much longer hours. He didn't know what to do, so he went to see the rabbi.

'"Rabbi," he said, "I've been asked to resign. A delegation thinks that I'm too lazy. They think I should pack up and go. But then I won't be able to fish, and in my new community, much will be expected of me. And I don't know whether I'm capable of it. What do you think I should do?"

'The rabbi walked to his study window. He looked out across the town and stroked his long white beard. He pondered his assistant's question very carefully and he turned and said, "No. I don't think you should resign. I think you should stay."

'And that was the answer that the assistant gave the community leaders. He said, "I've decided to stay. The rabbi advised me to and that's what I'm going to do."

'Well, they were stunned and immediately went to see the old rabbi. They said to him, "Rabbi, we don't understand. You have given us advice to get rid of him and you've given him advice to stay. How can you do that?"

'"It's easy," said the rabbi. "I always try to give the right advice to people and never put a stumbling block in front of them. That's the law. For you the best thing is for him to go. For him the best thing is to stay." The rabbi shrugged his shoulders. "Easy," he said.'

Much was expected of Rabbi Teichmann by his community. He was always at their beck and call. He loved his work but the more he did, the less the community expected it should do itself. Maybe this little homily would explain that even though he was the rabbi, God expected everyone to be a partner in the service; that prayer was a two-way process. The more effort you put into your faith, the more you got out of it.

Rabbi Teichmann looked at the congregation who were smiling. Some had heard the story before but to others, it spoke of the age-old conflict between doing what was right and doing what was proper.

'So, my friends,' said Rabbi Teichmann, 'which one of you will delight us tonight with a story?'

DR JOSEPHS' STORY
OF THE KIBBUTZ HERO,
AND HIS DAUGHTER

At first nobody moved. They just stared vacantly ahead. Rabbi Teichmann looked at the expanded population of his Friday-night minyan and realised that soon it would contract back to the former number, the basic ten, and that his problems would return. How could he have been so arrogant, so close-minded. What a fool he had been. He should have come armed with a dozen stories. He was on the point of continuing the service and was composing a small apology that would be called *mea culpa* if he were a Catholic priest, when, God blessed him and Dr Josephs stood and said, 'May I ask you a question, Rabbi?'

'Certainly.'

'Does the story have to be of a religious nature?'

'No, not at all, so long as it's appropriate to be told in a synagogue.'

'One more question, Rabbi. Does the story have to be personal? Because the story I have to tell happened not to me but to somebody that I know and who must remain nameless.'

'Dr Josephs,' said the rabbi. 'There are no rules. These stories are meant to amuse, enlighten, teach. Rules simply don't apply except they must be fairly short because we have a meal to get home to.'

Dr Josephs stood in his place for a moment or two. Something coalesced within him and he said, 'Very well, I'll tell you a story,' and he walked up to the lectern. As the rabbi sat down, Dr Josephs, a former general practitioner in the area who had retired some years earlier and who was now spending his leisure years travelling and reading, began to address his lifelong friends.

'Before I begin, this is not a story about me. Even though it might sound like it is about me, it's not. It's a story about a very good friend of mine, and before you start trying to guess his name, he didn't live in this community. In fact, he lived overseas. It was a story he told me just before he passed away last year. My wife and I went to visit him when he was in hospital dying of pancreatic cancer. He had lived a long life and a good life he was a man satisfied with his lot when he died, alav ha shalom.

'My friend's name doesn't matter, but I'm going to call him Jack for the sake of the story. His real name was Aaron, but that's strictly confidential.' The congregation tittered good-naturedly. They knew Dr Josephs as a good raconteur and were looking forward to hearing his story.

'When he was a young man of twenty-one, Jack had left the home where he had been born and had lived all his life, and decided to emigrate to Israel. Now in those days, the early 1970s, Israel if you'll recall was in the valley of despair. And it had only taken a few short years to make it so. In 1967, Israel had swept aside all of the Arab armies which attacked her in the Six-Day War. It was a monumental piece of military magic and an example to the world of what happens when righteous and fanatical zeal clashes with a proud peoples' determination to hold on to the land of their forefathers. And in case you haven't realised it yet, the Arabs were the fanatics and the proud people were the Israelis.' Again, the shul burst into laughter.

'But you know the old expression, "to the victor the spoils". Well, there were no spoils for Israel after she won the Six-Day War. Sure, her borders became secure and she was toasted as a David who had beaten the Arab Goliath. But the underdog was soon seen as the aggressor and, with the growth of the refugee camps on her borders, Israel was seen as tough-talking, intransigent, arrogant and militaristic. By 1971, when my friend went to live in Israel, the gloss of the Israeli 1967 victory had already worn off and there were rumours that the Arabs were re-arming themselves for a final push which would forever send the Israelis out of what they considered were rightfully their lands.

'Jack was a typical Diaspora suburban Jew. He had been bar mitzvah, he had been educated in the language of his country, he knew enough Hebrew to get by in shul, he was Zionistic and passionate, and he was suffering a crisis of identification. He believed he was the stuff of which Israeli settlers are made. His room at home was full of books about the great Israeli pioneers — Jabotinsky, Ben-Gurion, Weizmann — and the growth of the Palmach, the Haganah and the Irgun. At night he would close his eyes and fantasise about himself dressed in desert boots, khaki shorts, a camouflage tunic with the sleeves rolled up and knife-edge creases cutting his biceps, wearing a paratrooper's beret with field binoculars strapped around his neck. There he was, my friend Jack, in his suburban bedroom, riding in the gun turret of a tank across the sand dunes of the Negev, leaving clouds of dust in his wake and pushing back the relentless Egyptian foe as military jets screamed overhead strafing and bombing the fleeing army.

'It was in this mood that Jack decided to emigrate to Israel. But he found the reality of life in the Promised Land somewhat different to what he'd imagined. After he kissed his parents goodbye and went by train to the south of France and then caught a boat from Marseilles to Haifa, his heroism took a downward plunge. Oh! The train journey was pleasant enough. He enjoyed telling the other travellers in the carriage about his decision to join one of Israel's elite army regiments ... possibly even fly one of their French-built Mirage jet fighters. This gained him enormous prestige amongst his xenophobic fellow travellers. But when he arrived in the maelstrom of Marseilles, where everyone looked like a hit man in the Mafia, and later when he was on board with young men and women of every nationality sailing towards Israel, his confidence began to desert him. Especially when he saw the size of the young Jewish men from America, South Africa and Scandinavia who were making the same journey. Eating his meals beside them, the heroic stories he had told on the train journey became somewhat more muted in their bravado.

'His confidence returned somewhat as they neared the Israeli coastline, but disappeared again as the ship entered the bay. For when he arrived in Haifa, he thought there would be bands to greet his immigration, but instead, there were thousands of people on the dockside, a broiling hot sun and queues everywhere. The harassed officials could only just keep up with examining and stamping everybody's papers and telling people in a hundred different languages to stand in this queue or that queue and to wait patiently until they could be processed.

'As he stood on the Haifa docks, Jack looked towards the distant hills, and there, like a beacon welcoming ships from all over the world into the end of the Mediterranean, gleamed the vast golden cupola of the Baha'i temple. Up there it was a paradise, but down on the docks was what Dante must have envisaged as the outer levels of hell. The dust, the noise, the petrol fumes, the stink of the ships, the shouting, the excitement of the police and immigration officials as they tried to marshal the thousands of people who had arrived in Israel that day were overwhelming.

'Eventually Jack was put on a flat-bed truck with canvas walls and an aggressive engine which coughed rather than roared as it struggled out of the dock and up the long winding path into the hills overlooking the Jordan valley. There he and the four others destined for that kibbutz were unceremoniously unloaded off the truck into a dusty central area, something like a parade ground. They were greeted with indifference by the kibbutz director who told them that they were part of the 26th learn-to-speak-Hebrew group that the kibbutz had entertained since the War of Independence, and that they should expect no special favours. They must work hard, contribute to the kibbutz, and in return, they would be taught to speak the language of their new land.

'Then the director told them where to go to find their rooms and to assemble later that day in the dining room for an hour of orientation.

'Now Jack came from a comfortable middle-class home with reverse-cycle airconditioning, a furnace in the basement to add warmth in winter, and his own bedroom with a personal television and stereo set. Imagine his feelings as he stood with his suitcase outside a barrack hut. A part of him was ecstatic. This was just like being in the army, just what he had imagined. But another part, and dare I say an even bigger part of him, saw his heart sink in trepidation at living in such squalor when life up until then had not only been comfortable but bordering on the ideal. In fact, it was only this hankering after another self which impelled Jack to contemplate emigrating to Israel. But now wasn't the time to exhibit the duality of his mind, so Jack walked into the hut with two other young men and commandeered one of the bunks as his own.

'Yes! I said "commandeered". But it was more than that. He actually demanded it, as though it were a challenge to a fight with the other two young men who had been allotted space in the hut. He was a lion, marking out his territory. Now you see, all his life through school and at university, Jack had been a follower. Nobody had ever paid particular attention to him. He had never been one of the elite whom schoolboys follow admiringly around the playground. Instead he had been one of those who follow the sporting hero, or the school bully.

'But this was Israel. He had put his former life behind him. He was on his own, and now he was determined to be different from the follower he'd always been. This time he would be a leader of men. So, having commandeered the bunk he then turned to one of the other young men in the room and said, "So tell me. Where are you from?"

'It was much more aggressive than he intended but that didn't matter. Until one of the other young men turned around, and sneered, "What's it to you?"

'The accent was deepest South African, the stance that of a prize-fighter, and before he had even had a chance to show his manhood to the world, Jack sank back into his normal state of deference. He shrugged his shoulders and said, "Sorry. Just interested."

'The young South African man unpacked his suitcase and took off his shirt. Jack saw his muscular back and broad shoulders, and realised that this South African had come straight out of the army. This wasn't a man to be messed with. Boy, had he picked on the wrong one to try to dominate.

'The other young man in the room was taciturn, to say the least. His head was closely shaven and there was little difference between head and shoulders. His neck was almost non-existent and like the other young man, he also stripped off his clothes in order to change after the long journey. And when Jack saw his body he realised that here too was another muscular, tough character. It turned out that this second young man had fought with the Americans in Vietnam and his mind had been scarred by the battle of Khe Sanh. Before that, he had been relatively normal. Afterwards, his response to the horrors he had seen was to withdraw from the world, telling everybody by his restraint and economy with words that it was better to leave him alone.

'If Jack could have drawn up the characteristics of the worst people with whom he could be sharing a room for six months, then he couldn't have done much better than these two. Strong, silent, aggressive, powerful. All the things Jack wanted to be but never was ... all the characteristics which held Jack in awe.

'And so the days turned into months on Jack's kibbutz. In the morning he would be wakened at three thirty for a light breakfast before jumping onto a tractor trailer to be carried out into the fields where the hundred or so young volunteers would work in the cold early-morning hours. They spent their time digging weeds, planting potatoes or carrying the blue plastic bags of unripened bananas — or bunches of grapes which were called eshkols — on to tractors to be taken to the sheds for sale to the merchants. The work would last until nine when they would have another breakfast. This one consisted of hard-boiled egg, herring, sour cream, slices of cheese and lots of hot sweet tea. Then they would work again until twelve when the tractor would carry them back to the kibbutz, exhausted and filthy, where they would wash in communal showers, rest for an hour, eat in the cheder ochel — the dining room — and then from two till five, spend their time learning Hebrew in the ulpan.

'Most of the young men and women — whether from America or England, South Africa or South America — found the going tough. They were city-bred and pampered and not used to the rigours of a rural existence. Their initial enthusiasm quickly died and was replaced by the grinding awful monotony of hard labour. All except the two young men with whom Jack was billeted. They were like automata. They would work unceasingly, carrying the heaviest loads without even breaking out into a sweat. They worked and retired to their room to read, and then they worked, and retired again. They never participated in the occasional frivolity of the ulpan, nor the exuberance of young people away from home and restraint for the first time in their lives.

'The other youngsters on the ulpan seemed to be having a wonderful time ... all except Jack, who found the company of the two laconic roommates enervating and distracting. He complained about it to anyone who would listen, but nobody was really interested, and certainly nobody wanted to swap.

'So the putative soldier, the saviour of Israel, the tank commander, the fighter pilot quickly regressed once again into the follower of men, the periphery of the crowd, the shadow. To say that his first few months on the kibbutz were a disappointment would be to commit a major understatement.

'Now you would think, wouldn't you, that this was the way it was until the end of Jack's time on the kibbutz? You would think that he would have regressed and become a nobody. One of the millions of people who have a dream but never go that extra step to fulfil their goals. But with Jack, it was different. You see, Jack felt very deeply about his dream. About his need to find his own personal fulfilment, a better life and a stronger sense of identity in the land of Israel. And what was holding him back? As he lay on the bunk in his shared room, he realised it was his two roommates who were holding him back. Not that they said more than half-a-dozen words to him all week. Not that they physically restrained him. In fact, they were quite intimidating to lots of people, but Jack was so uncomfortable with them that it soon became obvious they were his alter ego, his other half — the quiet, menacing, desperate characters who once ridiculed him, who lived in his former land, and whom he hoped he had left behind when he emigrated to Israel.

'Now there wasn't much he could do about them. They were tougher, bigger and stronger than him. So what he started to do was to write notes about his life on the kibbutz and the notes of course turned into little stories which he sent back to his mother and father. These were stories of his heroism, of his bravery, of the little victories he scored; a story about the time he saved the kibbutz from a Palestinian raid; the time when he rescued an Israeli pilot whose parachute was trapped in a tree; and the time he cleared a kibbutz field of landmines using a broken stick and the instincts which he had developed. Jack's mother was so fascinated by the stories of her son's heroism that she sent them to the local newspaper with a curt little note, saying "You have kids roaming the streets and vandalising properties, but have a read about my son who went to Israel and he has become a hero".

'When the first story appeared, Jack's mother bought fifty copies of the newspaper which she sent to friends in the local community and relatives in other cities and countries, and of course, she sent the paper to Jack, saying how proud she was. Jack read the story on his bunk and felt his legs turn to water. How could she? he thought. Everybody would read it and everybody would know he was a liar and a cheat. He spent that night secreting the paper in a dozen different places to make sure that nobody on the kibbutz read it. It would be his ultimate ridicule, his final downfall. He would destroy it in the morning, take it into a field and set fire to it, or tear it into a million pieces and eat them with his morning cereal. But when morning came and he reread the article for the fiftieth time, he found he couldn't destroy it. It was what he had always wanted, an affirmation of himself. Only he of all the thousands of people that read the story, only he knew that it was a web of lies, a Walter Mitty fantasy.

'And so Jack continued to work in the fields and to walk in the umbra of all the others in the kibbutz, until a real-life incident happened and a terrorist attack was foiled by one of the real kibbutz guards. Jack rapidly wrote the story as if he was the hero and sent it off to his mother. For the next three weeks he waited breathless to see if she would send it to the newspaper, and sure enough, it came back with the caption, "Local man — Israeli Hero", with Jack's photograph and the full details of how he had singlehandedly saved his kibbutz from extinction. Jack realised that he was running into danger. All that the Israeli Embassy had to do was to look up the facts and then he would be exposed as a liar and a cheat.

'So he did what newspaper reporters have done since newspapers first came on the scene. He made up a false identity and he made up quotes. This time he didn't need to pretend that he was the hero. This time Jack wrote under the pseudonym of "A Modern-Day Hero". The first stories he wrote were very much like *Boy's Own* comics, full of desperados and derring-do, which were rejected by the newspapers to whom he sent the stories. But then he found his métier and when his first story was published and he received a small cheque he realised for the first time in his life that words were as much deeds as were the actions of those around him, that while he didn't have the strength of his roommates or the courage of the guards or the tenacity of the kibbutzniks, Jack's heroism would come through his words.

'Three more stories followed in quick succession until the newspaper wrote to him and asked whether he would be able to provide them with regular stories of the heroism of those around him. Apparently the large-scale Jewish readership revelled in these vicarious thrills. And that's precisely what Jack did. Everyday, he would wake at four o'clock and work in the fields until midday. Then he would shower and attend Hebrew classes and in the evening, when everybody was outside playing games or fishing or making love, Jack would be in his room, pen in hand, imagining a world which only his courage inhabited.

'After a while, his roommates began to treat him differently. It was subtle at first. They were curious about what he was constantly writing. For the first time in all the months they had been living together, the South African actually said to him, "Eh man, what you doing?" to which Jack responded, "Nothing that you would be interested in", and went back to his writing. But he saw the two of them talking one day, looking over and nodding in his direction. And then later when Jack was in the dining room, sitting alone as usual, the young taciturn American man walked in, got his food and sat opposite Jack. Others in the kibbutz looked in his direction in curiosity. The American had made a point of finding empty tables wherever he could. The last thing he wanted to do was speak. And now he was seeking Jack out. This was something unusual.

'It was compounded when the South African walked in, his face set in a scowl, his jaw muscles tense as always. And when he had filled his tray full of food he also walked over to Jack's table and the three of them sat there. Jack could hardly eat from the tension. He was being sought out by the two people on the kibbutz to whom everybody gave a wide berth. The South African asked, "All this writing you're doing man. What's it all about?"

'Jack said, "I'm a writer. I write for newspapers. I write stories."

'"Yeh," said the South African. "No kidding? I've got stories I could tell you. Stories that you wouldn't believe."

'"Why don't you?" asked Jack. "You tell me. I'll write them. We'll get them published."

'"Yeh?" said the South African.

'And instead of sitting in the sun or going to the library, the three of them sat in the dining room, the American telling Jack of his experiences in Vietnam, the South African of the horror of border patrols. Jack remembered every detail, every nuance and when he wrote them down and showed them to his roommates, they nodded in appreciation. Naturally he changed the stories somewhat to make them more heroic, but the heroes didn't seem to mind. Slowly other people began to accrete to the group as it became known that Jack was a writer of heroic tales. Most people didn't have heroic tales to tell. Most people were like Jack. But it was amazing how many people wanted to hear Jack reading his stories out loud after he had written them.

'By the middle of their stay in the ulpan, their allotted time to learn the language before they became full citizens, things really began to improve for Jack. His back strengthened, his arms became broader, his stomach flatter, and his legs developed a shape. He found that the back-breaking work was no longer as exhausting and he could manage a full-morning's labour in the banana plantation or the orchards without sneaking off and finding a tree to sit behind, out of view, and cry.

'At the end of their stay, the students in the ulpan put on a play to show how much they had learnt. Those who shone in Hebrew or those who were outgoing and gregarious were given lead roles. Those who were quieter and more withdrawn were appointed to be chorus or extras. Jack was one of the three people behind the scenes who handled the props. It was a role he had come to accept — as an assistant rather than a performer.

'Jack left the ulpan and went into Jerusalem to follow his profession. He left his storytelling behind. The life was austere and tough and when in 1973 the Yom Kippur War nearly destroyed the nation of Israel, Jack realised that it was time to return home. There he married and established a family and became quite successful in his local community.

'I haven't told you what Jack's profession was because it really doesn't matter. He could have been a jeweller, a butcher or an accountant; but what did matter to him were the stories. Jack was removed from the source of his inspiration. Those stories had given him the self-respect that he had sought all his life, and now he was back to being just Jack. But the one thing he did remember was the feeling he had as he had mixed with the real-life heroes of Israel. The ordinary men and women who had established the kibbutz, dug up the stones in the ground with their bare hands, worked from sun-up to sundown without a break and trudged their long way home from the fields singing Israeli songs and thanking God for their freedom. The further he was from his time in Israel, the more the images became real.

And so when his working day was done, Jack sat down and wrote stories, sketches about the people whom he had met, the things he had done and the places he had seen.

'By now Jack's mother had died so it was his wife who read of her husband's heroism and his deeds of valour. And it was his wife who begged him to seek a publisher and have the stories made into a book. He fought her long and hard but her demands eventually made him send the manuscript to a literary agent, who read it and told him she thought it was marvellous. The book was published the following year and became a minor success. Jack denied that he was the subject. When he was interviewed he said that he had written about an archetypal hero, not about himself. But nobody believed him. Everybody knew that Jack was the real hero of the story.

'The book sold in America and South Africa, and of the many hundreds of letters Jack received, two he kept until the day he died. One was from the young American man who had shared his room on the kibbutz. It arrived fifteen years after they had last seen each other. It was a letter begging for money. The young man had become a drug addict and was dying of tuberculosis. Jack sent him as much as he could afford.

'The other was from the young South African man who had returned to South Africa and become a fighter for the ANC. When Nelson Mandela became the first President of a multi-racial South Africa, this young man, now married with a family, became his adviser on Middle Eastern affairs. The letter from the South African told Jack that he had read the stories and that they brought back memories of the most difficult and traumatic time of his life. He went on to add that if it hadn't been for Jack bringing out the problems and forcing him to confront them, he may never have recovered and reached the position he held today.

'And when his daughter was old enough, Jack would sit her down and recall for her his tales from the kibbutz. He would tell her about how he had carried a gun and guarded the perimeter of the kibbutz from terrorists; of how it had been him that warned the Israeli army of an attack by the Syrian army late one night; of how he and a group of others had crept across the Lebanese border and stolen two Mars Bars from a Lebanese shop which they paid for with Israeli money. And of course, it was Jack and a group of others who roused the entire kibbutz community with a glorious Shakespearean play at the end of their time on the kibbutz. From time to time, his daughter would ask him to tell her the stories of his time on the kibbutz again and as he told them, he embellished them with a detail here or a bit extra there until for Jack, the tales became a reality. This is what had actually happened. This is what he really did. These were his escapades.

'And in the way of things Jack's daughter grew to adulthood and announced one day that she was going to go to Israel as part of her Zionist Youth Group and that she would live there for a year before returning to go to university. And she further told her parents that she had asked for and been accepted on the very kibbutz that her own father had lived in when he was about her age. Her mother was ecstatic, but Jack wasn't so pleased. In fact, he had severe misgivings and he did everything in his power to stop her from going. He refused to pay. He refused to sign the forms. He refused to go to the meetings in the shul where the Israeli leaders explained to the parents what would be happening to their children.

'Jack's daughter couldn't understand why her father was so reluctant. Even to this day he was an arch-Zionist and contributed heavily to the United Israel Appeal. But by force of argument, her mother overcame her father's objections and the day came when Jack's daughter left to go to Israel. Her letters back home were read avidly first by Jack and then by his wife. In terror, Jack looked for the words, "Liar! Cheat! Duplicity. Untruth. Fraud." but nowhere could they be seen. Indeed, in all of his daughter's letters there was not one mention, not even once, of Jack having been on the same kibbutz. It was a mystery which, thank God, his wife didn't recognise.

'That year went by very quickly and in no time Jack and his wife were at the airport to welcome back the young men and women who had gone over to Israel as children. Naturally, there were hysterical scenes at the airport, much crying and kissing and hugging. Israeli songs were sung through the airport concourse to the amazement of the other travellers who were going to America, Asia or Africa. Eventually Jack and his wife got their daughter back into their car and, holding their hands, they travelled home where a banner outside read "Welcome Home Darling".

'She kissed her brothers and sisters and sat exhausted in the lounge room, surrounded by kit bags, sleeping-bags and rucksacks which she refused to allow anybody to unpack, especially her younger brothers, because they were full of presents. After force-feeding her tea and cakes and biscuits, and after her initial blush of contentment at being home, her mother asked, "So what was it like being on your father's kibbutz? Your letters gave away very little."

'The daughter smiled and said, "It was just wonderful." She looked at Jack but Jack couldn't look at her. Not once. In fact, he looked down at the floor waiting for his cowardice to be revealed. His heart was pounding, he could hardly swallow, the lump in his throat was so enormous he thought he'd asphyxiate, and he felt a horrible prickling in his armpits.

'"Tell me all about it," said her mother. "Did you come across people who remembered your father?"

'There was a pause. Jack was too mortified to look up at his daughter. He just stared down at the carpet but his daughter put her hand on his head and then around his shoulders, and said, "To this day, they remember him. The wonderful things he did — his exploits — are still talked about. Dad," she said digging him in the ribs, "you were a real character over there. A hero. Why didn't you tell us the truth?"

'And all Jack could do was shrug.'

Dr Josephs finished his story, nodded politely to his audience, and returned to his seat. The rabbi returned to his place, thanked him profusely, and continued with the service.

And for the rest of the evening, everyone glanced surreptitiously at Dr Josephs, trying to decide whether or not the story was really about him, or whether there really was a man called Jack.

At the end of the service, the rabbi was folding his tallis in order to walk the few feet to his home and enjoy his Sabbath meal with his wife and children when a lady approached him. She was one of the women who had come into the shul, somebody who only ever came three days a year, but he knew who she was. It was Mrs Finburg; he seemed to remember her name was Geta.

'Good evening, Rabbi,' she said. 'Shabbat shalom.'

'Shabbat shalom,' replied the rabbi, not shaking her hand because in the Orthodox Jewish tradition, men don't touch any woman who isn't a wife or daughter.

'So tell me,' she said, 'these stories that the men are telling. They're very interesting.'

'Yes,' said the rabbi. 'It seems to have attracted a few more people to our little erev Shabbat minyan.'

'Good. Very good,' said Geta Finburg. 'And tell me. Is it exclusively men who can tell the stories?'

The rabbi thought for a minute and stroked his beard. 'I don't see why. If you wanted to tell a story, provided it was fit and proper of course, you could tell it. With one proviso — you couldn't go to the lectern. That is for men only.'

'Sure,' said Geta. 'Next week perhaps,' and she smiled and walked away.

Now Mr Dub was listening. He was standing in a corner of the shul, putting away the Kiddush cup that they had used to drink a blessing to the start of the Sabbath. And what he heard didn't please him. It didn't please him at all. Now there was no malice or ill-will between him and either Charlie or Geta Finburg, nothing at all. They hardly knew each other and if it was Charlie who wanted to tell a story that would be fine, provided it was appropriate. But Geta! That was another matter. Not that she was known to have a caustic tongue, an evil temper or a loose mouth. No, nothing like that. It was because she was a woman. And in Orthodox Judaism, women didn't take part in the running of the service. Not now. Not in the past. Not in the future.

Let's examine that for a minute. What does Mr Dub mean by 'take part in'?

Obviously the women pray, sing the blessings and recite all the prayers that the men recite, but they don't lead the service. Between the men and women is a mehitzah, a sort of a transparent structure, which physically separates the men and the women. This is so that neither disturbs the other while they're praying ... no surreptitious glances between husband and wife, or young man and young woman.

Look! Don't blame me. You're probably a modernist. You're probably thinking to yourself, Oh for Heaven's sake, that's ridiculous in this day and age. Well, that's up to you but the story I'm telling you about is a story about Orthodox Jews, not Liberal Jews. Liberal Jews have women rabbis, and men and women sit beside each other and pray, and women come up onto the bimah and participate in the service. But I'm telling you about an Orthodox shul where there is a clear separation between men and women. One from the other. And before you get angry and self-righteous, think about how many women priests there are in the Catholic Church or how many women mullahs there are in Islam. And the Church of England hasn't exactly got a proud record of elevating women into the priesthood, has it? So, don't come that arrogance with me. Every religion, except for the most modern, have traditions which to us might look old-fashioned, but they're there for a good reason and it would take somebody much cleverer than me to come up with a convincing argument to overthrow them.

So I'll just carry on with my stories and if you don't like it, well I'm sorry. I was telling you about Mr Dub overhearing the conversation between Mrs Finburg and the rabbi. Now Mr Dub went home and the conversation between Mrs Finburg and the rabbi disturbed the normal peace of his Sabbath. Mr Dub didn't like what he heard. He couldn't argue against it because the rabbi, of course, was right; but it wasn't the way it was meant to be. During the night Mrs Dub noticed that her husband was a bit ... how can I say this ... fidgety. Every now and again he would shake his head, tutt and mutter inaudible imprecations under his breath. She asked him what was disturbing him and he told her not to worry about it, that he would sort things out. And taking his advice, she didn't worry any more.

But Mr Dub did. He phoned a few people and like him, they felt uncomfortable with what was going to happen but they couldn't formulate a rational argument against it.

And so the week went by until Thursday night, the day before the beginning of the Sabbath when Mr Dub and Mr Dayan the butcher knocked tentatively on the rabbi's door and were ushered into his study by his wife. Now the rabbi had no idea that a revolution was brewing in his community. And these two men in front of him were not revolutionaries, so he didn't expect what happened next.

'Rabbi, let me tell you something. If Mrs Finburg stands up and tells a story, Mr Dayan and I are not going to come to shul on Friday night. I'm sorry but we've given it a lot of thought. It's a hard decision but it's one that we're committed to.'

'Explain,' said the rabbi surprised.

'What's to explain?' said Mr Dayan interrupting. 'You know as well as I do that women can't lead the service.'

'But she isn't leading, my friends. She is merely telling us a story. What's so bad about that?'

'I'll tell you what's bad, Rabbi. It starts with a story, then it continues with a prayer, and in the end there will be no end, if you see what I mean.'

The rabbi stroked his beard. Mr Dayan stroked his beard. Mr Dub scratched his whiskers, and the three men sat quietly, pondering, until the rabbi said, 'Let me tell you a story. One day in Vilna a wise man came to speak to the congregation. The main thrust of his speech was about how important it was to observe the laws of the Sabbath, to constantly review what they were and make sure that each and every member of the congregation was fulfilling all of their obligations. But when he had left, the congregation was unsettled, and many were puzzled by the content. So some people went up to the Rabbi of Vilna and said to him, "Why did the wise man speak to us about observing Sabbath? It doesn't make sense. Everybody here observes Sabbath. He was preaching to the converted, so to speak."

'And the rabbi of Vilna thought and then said, "Look, it's like this. When there's a little fire, the firemen put out the flames. But if it's a huge fire, if it's a massive conflagration, there's no point in putting out the flames. It's a waste of resources, especially if water is scarce. You have to allow the flames to burn the building. But what a shrewd fireman will do is to spray water onto the adjacent buildings so that the fire won't spread. You see, it's all to do with protecting what hasn't yet been damaged by the flames. That's why the wise man spoke to us about observing the Sabbath, even though he knows we all do. Because he wanted us to ensure that we, in this synagogue weren't going to be influenced by those outside who were less observant."'

Well, Mr Dayan and Mr Dub shook their heads and shrugged their shoulders. 'I don't see what that has to do with it,' said Mr Dayan.

'Simply this,' said Rabbi Teichmann. 'We all know that there's a conflagration outside this little synagogue of ours. A huge movement away from Orthodox Judaism into Liberal and Reform ways. I'm pouring a little water on Mrs Finburg and all the other women in the congregation so that they're not attracted to and damaged by the fires of Liberalism. I'm giving her a little bit of rope so that she feels more a part of what we are. It's not so bad.'

Mr Dub and Mr Dayan left Rabbi Teichmann's home. They weren't completely satisfied but now they had a man's understanding of what was going to happen the following night.

MRS FINBURG'S STORY OF THE BUDDHIST'S TREE

Whenever Jews come together to pray in the shul, their faces are always turned to the Holy Ark, the Aron Hakkodesh, which itself always faces towards Jerusalem. There is only one occasion on which they avert their eyes from the Holy Ark, and that is when the priests, the Cohanim, mount the steps, cover their heads with a prayer shawl and intone a blessing over the congregation. Tradition has it that the congregation looks away so that it will not see the blessing taking place. It's a tradition which harks back to the Second Temple, the temple of King Herod, which was destroyed in 70AD.

So when Mrs Finburg was invited by Rabbi Teichmann to stand and tell the congregation her story, the men who were in the front of the shul were forced to turn their backs on the Aron Hakkodesh, the Holy Ark, and listen to her words through the mehitzah. All except Mr Dub and Mr Dayan. They stayed in their place, staring at the Ark, mumbling an occasional prayer and imprecation under their breath, whilst the rest of the congregation turned in their seats and looked at a somewhat nervous Mrs Finburg.

Now, Mrs Finburg had been perfectly happy to stand and tell this story when she woke up in the morning but by lunchtime she was already suffering misgivings, and as the clock ticked towards the time when she should leave and go to shul, her stomach was knotted. Part of the reason was that Mr Finburg believed that he, not she, should tell a story. Not that he sided with Mr Dub or Mr Dayan about a woman's role in Judaism, but if he wanted to go to a Liberal synagogue where women actively participated in the service, then that was his option. He and Mrs Finburg had been brought up in an Orthodox tradition and though they weren't particularly observant, they certainly didn't believe in the loose interpretation that the Liberals followed. So it was Mr Finburg who was partly responsible for Mrs Finburg's crisis of confidence.

Until, that is, the rabbi said, 'And now it's my great pleasure to ask Mrs Finburg to tell us her story,' and that was that.

Suddenly she was on her feet, people coughed, cleared their throats, blew their noses, turned in their seats and listened expectantly. All except two rude men in the front row nearest the steps that go up to the bimah. All she could see of them was the back of their balding heads. Rude!

When she started speaking, her voice sounded distant, almost as if it were in echo. Mrs Finburg almost never spoke in public and so there was a certain timorous tone but it disappeared as she got into the swing of the first few minutes of the story.

'This is a story which has nothing to do with Judaism or our synagogue or what happened to people in history who are Jewish,' she said. The words were a bit strained, the syntax difficult. Speaking aloud in public was harder than she thought.

'This is a story of what happened when I first went travelling through Asia when I was young and then later when I went back with my daughter Rachel. When I was twenty-five, my father paid for a trip which I took around the world. Before I tell you about the trip, let me tell you about my father. He was a very generous, loving man, a man who was incredibly well-read in everything to do with philosophy. Now, you all knew him as a scrap-metal merchant when he came to this country after the war and thank God he did very well, though it was hard work. But why, you may ask, was he so interested in philosophy? Good question. Let me tell you.

'Before the war in Germany my father had been a real live philosopher. He had attended university at Wittenberg where many great men taught. Men whose names may be forgotten today but who in those days were a household word. Not like philosophers today, their names are not well-known. But in the era before television, when people used to read articles in newspapers and when ideas and philosophies were discussed on a regular basis at dinner parties, then the names of the philosophers were well-known. My father knew people like Heidegger, Hannah Arendt, Martin Buber and of course he knew Wittgenstein before he went to study with Bertrand Russell in England. Such a cultured society in Germany. Always split down the middle though, between the incredible intellect, music, philosophy, art and literature on one side and the horrible, hideous aggressive militarism on the other. It was like night and day; hot and cold.

'Of course I don't remember it because I was a very young girl before the war. All I remember is my house which was opposite a park in Wittenberg and a constant procession of people coming and being treated with great honour by my father, and long dinner parties where I would listen in amazement to incredibly complex words that I didn't understand.

'And being Jewish and a philosopher and hating every single thing to do with the Nazis, my father watched the growth of

Adolf Hitler from a bar-room bully to the Reich's chancellor. When he saw Hindenburg hand over control to Hitler and swastikas being painted on the windows of Jewish shops, he had, thank God, the foresight to gather me, my brothers and sisters and my mother and the rest of her family, and leave that horrible place and turn his back on it forever.

'As it was, he was only just in time because the following year, the Jews were kicked out of their places at universities which were taken by second-class and horribly jealous minds. When my family arrived in this country, my father couldn't speak the language and so couldn't teach philosophy. It was different for Einstein when he went to Columbia. He spoke the universal language of mathematics as did the other great German Jewish scientists, but for a philosopher, if you can't explain the nuances and the subtleties to your students, then you're of very little use.

'My father was a philosopher without a voice and so in order to feed the family, he got a job in a scrap-metal yard. Over the years, he built up his position to foreman and then he bought into the partnership until eventually he owned the place. He used to say he was the cleverest scrap-metal dealer in the world, and there wouldn't be too many that would disagree. The only person cleverer, I think, was a certain porter in a London hospital during the war. He was Wittgenstein.

'So where did this leave me?' said Mrs Finburg, clearing her throat. Already she no longer heard her voice but was confidently weaving the thread of the story in and out with little anecdotes and asides. A part of her mind thought that this storytelling business wasn't nearly as difficult as the men seemed to make out, but then Mrs Finburg was a putative feminist and she often thought those sorts of things about tasks which were traditionally male-centred.

'My family grew in relative comfort and certainly in very great peace and harmony in this wonderful country of ours. We wanted for nothing and my father ensured that all of us got a good education in the arts, the classics, the humanities and the sciences. We all enjoyed learning and my father became our teacher when it came to philosophy. He guided us through the intricacies of the minds of Plato, Aristotle and Socrates and then he taught us the beauties of the more recent philosophers such as Descartes and Spinoza. When we all had professions, I made the decision that I wanted to travel and my father agreed to pay for a trip around the world. Being the oldest, he thought I was entitled but one thing he begged of me was to spend more time in Asia than in Europe. For even though I had not been to Europe since I was a child, I had an understanding of the European mind whereas I had no understanding at all of the philosophies of Tao, Buddha or Islam.

'And it's here that my story begins, because when I went to Bangkok twenty-five years ago, I travelled beyond the city into the countryside in order to experience the simplicity of Thai rural life. I travelled north, close to the border with Laos, and there, not far from a place called Udon Thani, I came across a Buddhist temple where monks wearing saffron robes spent their lives sitting at the feet of Buddha and chanting songs. It was a large encampment with a beautiful temple built on a hill and beside the temple was a magnificent tree, a tree which the Buddhist monk who spoke to me told me must have been at least 300 years old, for it was planted by the first Buddhist monk who founded the monastery. He told me that the leaders believed that while the tree lived, the Buddhist monks knew that the community would survive in strength and in prosperity. He told me so much about Buddhism and about the peace and harmony of the Buddhist mind that I was overwhelmed.

'But even more, I was overjoyed. There's so much in Buddhism which has its parallels in Judaism. Its value of the individual and the nature of the spirit. I left there feeling a much wiser and calmer person and the rest of my trip through Europe and America was an anti-climax. Oh, I know that sounds odd. I saw all the great museums, went to fabulous shows which I still occasionally think about and saw incredible sights; but the most powerful memory I have to this day is of that Buddhist community in the beautiful verdant hills of Thailand and the huge tree which dominated the life of the village.'

Now by this time everybody was beginning to wonder where Mrs Finburg was going with her story. She was speaking beautifully, it was eloquent but it was a travelogue and they were wondering what it all had to do with her father who had been a prominent member of the community until his death fifteen years earlier. Interestingly though, nobody, not one person in the congregation, knew that he was a philosopher. They only knew of him as a scrap-metal dealer. Undaunted by the now fidgeting audience, Mrs Finburg didn't have the rabbi's ability to galvanise an audience with a sudden phrase or mannerism, she continued.

'The story ends where it began. When my beautiful daughter Rachel was a young woman and had finished her university course, she decided she would like to travel around the world. My husband and I thought it was a great idea and we agreed to pay for her ticket. But there was one condition which we imposed on her, which my father never imposed on me. And that condition was that Rachel and I travel to Bangkok and then continue our journey by train and road to the Buddhist community outside Udon Thani. I begged her to let me do this. I said that after we'd visited the community she was free to go anywhere in the world. All the way over on the plane I told her about the community and especially about this huge 300-year-old tree and the part that it played in the community. The merging of nature with longevity and the eternal continuity of humankind.

'We landed in Bangkok and travelled by train and bus to the community. It was much as I had remembered it, though there were a few more buildings. There were still monks with saffron robes and shaved heads and the ever-present sound of chanting. There were more cars in the area than I remembered, but that was to be expected. I talked to one of the monks who was the leader of the community who told me that the wonderful monk I had met when I was Rachel's age had died many years earlier. I was sad because he was a beautiful man, and with him died part of my memory, but the thing I most wanted my daughter to see was the tree. We walked hand-in-hand through the huts and houses that comprised the village until we entered the central clearing. Up on the hill was the Buddhist temple and to its right ...'

Mrs Finburg waited a moment. She looked at their faces. They were riveted. Good. Even the two rude men with balding heads had turned around to look at her.

'The tree had gone. In its place was an empty space, a hole in the sky. I couldn't believe it. It was such a huge beautiful mahogany. It seemed to climb forever towards the sky. I remember feeling dwarfed by it, of touching its eternal bark, of trying to put my hands around its huge girth, and yet it was no longer there. I couldn't believe it. I grabbed a monk and asked him, "Where's the tree?"

'He replied, "Oh that was cut down many years ago."

'I said to him, "But it was so tall and strong. I didn't think it would ever die."

'He looked at me strangely and said, "But it's still alive."

'I said, "What are you talking about? It's no longer there."

'And he laughed. He said, "Yes it is," and he pointed to three or four buildings which were nearby, "in Buddhism everything is reincarnated. We're here forever — animals, insects, plants, trees, you and me. We have many different levels in our lives. When this tree died and we had to cut it down because we were in danger of it falling, we first cut down the biggest branches. These we then cut into shingles for the roofs of the houses. The smaller branches we used as protection against the rain. Then we took down the trunk, a huge trunk, which was very difficult for us to do. And we stripped the trunk of its bark and we used part of the bark as medicine and the other part we daubed around huts to keep them protected from the storms. The wood was treated and we cut it into long planks which we have used to build the houses. As you can see, the tree still lives but in a different form."

Mrs Finburg looked at the congregation and said simply, 'Thank you for listening to me.'

She sat down but people kept on staring at her, especially Mr Dub and Mr Dayan in the front row. As they turned slowly back to the rabbi who mounted the steps of the bimah, the philosophy of her words began to make themselves plain. It was a very beautiful story and one with a real message.

With the exception of prayers and studying the holy books, nothing happens in an Orthodox Jewish house during the Sabbath. But as soon as the sun goes down on Saturday night and three distant stars are visible in the sky to signify the end of Shabbat, the activity begins again. As soon as Rabbi Teichmann returned to his home after the Saturday-evening service and the lighting of the habdalah candle to signify the beginning of the working week, his phone started to ring. Some of the callers were members of the community who had heard about Mrs Finburg's story of the

Buddhist's tree. Others were just checking the times of service the following week and still others were phoning to wish the rabbi a good week, something which they rarely, if ever, did.

Sunday was no different, except for one important call from a neighbouring rabbi. 'So, what's this I hear about these stories you're telling on erev Shabbat? I hear you have your congregation flocking to your service.'

Rabbi Teichmann smiled and shrugged. 'Flocking is an exaggeration, but we are certainly seeing a lot more faces. In all the time I've been here I can't remember when we've had more than a bare minyan on a Friday night. Suddenly, we have people to spare.'

'Good,' said the other rabbi. 'Just make sure you don't lose out on the Saturday-morning service.'

Rabbi Teichmann laughed and hung up the phone but the thought stayed with him for the rest of the day.

During the week several people phoned and asked what the story would be about on the following Friday night. Not that they believed Rabbi Teichmann when he told them that he had no idea, that these things weren't preordained, that they just seemed to spring up out of nowhere. A journalist from the local Jewish newspaper contacted him and asked if she could reprint one of the speeches. 'That's difficult,' Rabbi Teichmann told her. 'You see, they're not written down. It's an oral tradition.'

'Then maybe I could come to the shul on Friday night?'

'Certainly you would be welcome,' said the rabbi, 'but of course you can't write and I won't allow you to play a tape recorder, so I hope you've got a good memory.'

The lady reporter thought it was all too difficult and decided to tell her editor that there was nothing in the rumours he had been hearing.

And so Friday night came around once again and the rabbi found that before he entered the synagogue after a busy day visiting those who were sick or distressed within his community, he would be adding a special prayer to the prayers he normally said before he entered the shul. This prayer was asking God to shine a light in the minds of one of his congregants, so they would remember a beautiful story and would happily recount it to the congregation. So far he had been lucky, unbelievably lucky. Excluding his, there had been three beautiful stories told by three of the congregants. And all of them were more than just a tale. In each one, there was a universal message which made everybody think beyond the details which they were told. Rabbi Teichmann knew what he was going to say when he stood and prayed that somebody else knew too.

This time there was a hubbub in the shul. Even though it was small, it normally echoed on a Friday night and the congregants normally sat sporadically making the place look even more empty and less hospitable. But this time there were whole groups of people sitting there, talking, smiling and nodding. It was just like a Saturday morning and the words of the rabbi from the neighbouring shul came back to worry Rabbi Teichmann. There were five ladies in the women's section behind the mehitzah including Mrs Finburg, Mrs Dayan, Sophie Dub and a couple of others. And in the men's section ... boy! He needed four hands to count them. There were of course the usual faces that he knew so well but sitting alongside or behind or in front of those dedicated men were at least another ten, maybe twelve people. Some were fathers with sons, some older men and many who came just the three traditional times a year. Rabbi Teichmann nodded to each and every one of them and thanked them for coming, before he mounted the bimah and began the Friday service to welcome in the bride, the Sabbath.

And at the appointed place and at the appointed time, the rabbi turned to his congregation and said, 'My dear friends, it's wonderful to see you all here celebrating the arrival of our bride, the Sabbath. Now I know that many of you are here because we've developed the tradition over the last couple of weeks of telling stories and this tradition, I hope, will continue tonight. But before we do, something occurred this week which has moved me very deeply and which I would like to recount in a parable; a beautiful tale told to us by a great maggid, a very wise man. Now many of you won't know what a maggid is. It means a person who narrates an incident or event, though recently, during the last few hundred years, it has come to mean someone who acts as a preacher. But in Eastern Europe, it also meant a man who used to go from town to town encouraging and raising the spirits of the downtrodden or undermining those of us who were arrogant in order to improve the quality of our lives through our religion.

'This story which I'm going to tell you relates to an incident in Lithuania many years ago. A Jew was being held in the local gaol. He had been falsely accused by anti-Semitic neighbours who just wanted to get hold of his property and the anti-Semitic court had found him guilty on spurious hearsay evidence. Now he was facing his execution. Well, the rabbi of the town knew all about this and had pleaded the man's innocence but to no avail.

'And on the night before the man was due to be executed, the local chief of police, following the law which said that before execution a condemned person must be visited by a clergyman in order for him to confess his sins and lighten the burden he carried to his death, came to the rabbi and demanded that he follow him to prison to hear the condemned man's confession.

'But the rabbi refused outright. He told the chief of police, "He is a murderer, thief and liar. I won't go to hear his confession."

'"What?" said the chief of police. "You are a rabbi, and you won't help out somebody who is going to die tomorrow?"

'"No," said the rabbi, "the courts found him guilty. It's good enough for me. I wouldn't waste my time helping a murderer."

'Well the chief of police became angry and cursed the rabbi. But the rabbi stuck to his guns and the chief of police left in a bad mood. So he went to the Catholic priest and told him what had happened. The Catholic priest willingly said that he would go and hear the man's confession but when he entered the cell where the Jew was held, the Jew adamantly refused to confess to anybody but his own rabbi.

'Of course that left the police chief in a quandary. He couldn't break the law and yet the following day as the sun rose and it was time for the man's hanging he couldn't carry out the direction of the court. Again, he went to the rabbi but this time he was no longer angry and demanding. This time he asked simply how a man of God could leave a Jewish soul in such torment.

'"Please," said the rabbi. "You have your responsibilities, I have mine. I've told you. I will not deal with this evil Jew." Well, this went on and on, backwards and forwards for a week and soon became a celebrated event. Another rabbi was brought in from another town but when he went in to speak to the rabbi of the local community, he too was horrified by the man's deeds of which the court had found him guilty and he too refused to go to bless the criminal.

'The stand-off continued until the government in Lithuania was overthrown in a revolution and all political prisoners were released from gaol. Thank God, the Jew was released as well, even though you could hardly call him political. You see, the rabbi was doing his duty. And even though the country's sense of justice was offended, the moral sense of justice was upheld by the rabbi. If we follow the law of the land when the law of the land contradicts the moral laws of humanity, then we are all doomed,' said Rabbi Teichmann. 'And now, dear friends, let me hand over to whoever it is that would like to regale us with a story.'

MR DAYAN'S STORY
OF THE BEAUTIFUL TWIN
AND THE UGLY TWIN

Mr Dayan stood quickly in his place to prevent anybody else from standing and claiming the right to tell a story. It was more a challenge to the rest of the congregation, or an establishment of his authority within the shul. Suddenly, there were many newcomers, people whom Mr Dayan felt didn't have a right to stand up and speak because they weren't part of the regular minyan which had supported the synagogue every Friday night without fail. These people were parvenus, not that he minded of course. He was delighted to see so many new Jewish faces in the shul, but that didn't give them the right to tell a story. Only people like he, Dr Josephs, Mr Dub and the other regulars had the right to tell their stories.

Of course, when it all began, Mr Dayan had no intention of telling his story. After all, he was a butcher, not a storyteller. But he was so dismayed by what happened the previous week when Mrs Finburg (who, let's face it, only came to shul three times a year) took over the service, that he decided 'Enough is enough' and said to himself, 'I'll show them what should be done.'

ALAN DAVID GOLD

Not that he was alone in this view. During the week, while
the rabbi was on the phone to dozens of new voices, Mr Dub and
Mr Dayan had been talking about what should happen on this
coming Friday night. Out of the blue, Mr Dub told his wife that
he would buy the weekly meat this Thursday and so he made a
special point of closing up his cabinet-making workshop at four
o'clock and driving to the butcher's shop where he knew Mr
Dayan would be. When he had bought the veal for roasting and
some brisket for Sunday lunch, he said to Mr Dayan, 'You know,
it worries me that someone other than one of us will get to his ...
or her ... feet and tell a story this coming Friday night. You know
what I think? I think that you should tell a story.'

And that's precisely what Mr Dayan decided to do. So, here
he stood in the shul on Friday night and he walked confidently
up the steps of the bimah, not even bothering to look behind him
to see if any other members of the congregation had stood and
wanted to tell their story. It was his right to do so and he would.
Anyway, he had been practising the story in front of a mirror for
the whole of the morning, and knew it pretty well off by heart.
What he didn't know he would make up because now he was no
longer a butcher ... today he was a storyteller.

The rabbi and Mr Dayan shook hands and the rabbi went to
sit down. Mr Dayan faced the community. Amazing! thought Mr
Dayan. It was just like a Saturday-morning service, the
synagogue a sea of faces. Very different to a normal Friday night.
It was working, the rabbi's little plan. It was good.

Now everything seemed to be all right, up until the time
when there was the silence of anticipation and Mr Dayan opened
his mouth to speak. Suddenly, he was attacked by a rush of fear.
Except for barking orders at staff or talking to customers in the
shop, Mr Dayan never made speeches. Well, that's not quite true.

In the past, he had made a speech at each of his son's bar mitzvah and when his daughter was married he had everybody in hysterics telling jokes, but three times in your life isn't much, is it? It's not enough to be practised, just like three-time-a-year Jews pretending to understand the order of the service. But there was no going back.

'The story I'm going to tell you,' he said, his voice sounding as faltering and high-pitched as Mrs Finburg's the previous week, 'is about two boys who were born to a mother in Eastern Europe. Where and when? It doesn't matter. Let's just pretend that it was the Pale of Settlement ...'

He looked at the congregation who looked quizzically back at him. Suddenly, he felt the need to explain a little bit of Eastern European Jewish history.

'... that's the area which Catherine the Great created for the Jews in 1772 when she took lots of land from Poland, and then by the nineteenth century it had grown to include parts of Bessarabia, the Ukraine, the Crimea and Lithuania ...'

The rabbi looked up in concern. One of the problems of letting people speak was that everyone, given a suitable forum, had a tendency to become didactic. He hoped that his look would remind Mr Dayan that he wasn't supposed to be giving a lecture, but telling a story.

Seeing the rabbi's frown, Mr Dayan quickly continued, 'Let's also pretend that it was before the time of modern medicine and doctors driving Mercedes cars and playing golf on Wednesday afternoon.' The congregation burst out laughing, giving both Mr Dayan and the rabbi a lot more confidence.

'The mother of these two boys lived in a shtetl with her husband and a maid who did work around the house. Now the husband was a butcher, like me, but unlike me he was doing very

well because in those days, in that shtetl, everybody ate kosher.'
Again there was titters of laughter but this time peoples'
consciences made the joke somewhat less funny.

'The whole town used to buy their meat from him. His wife,
of course, didn't work. What wife did in those days? But she kept
a beautiful home and with a maid to do the hard work she spent
much of her time making sure that her husband's social position
in the village was well supported.'

Mr Dayan looked up at this point, and stared into the far
horizons of the shul. People looked at him in wonder. 'Ah,' he
said, 'those were the days when a butcher was an important
person in the village. Not like today, when butchers are merely
tradesmen. In those days, we were craftsmen ...' Then he saw
that people were staring at him — not least the rabbi — so he
decided to continue with his story.

'Now for many years this couple tried desperately to have
children, not that they were like Abraham and Sarah, because
this man was only forty-two and the woman was thirty-seven. But
God heard their prayers, and, miracle upon miracle, the woman
announced that she was pregnant. Well, the whole town, of
course, knew within minutes. A butcher can't keep a secret. A
butcher has to tell every customer everything that happens in his
life, as well as where the government is going wrong and why the
price of meat is low compared to other commodities.'

The rabbi's confidence returned, and he settled back to enjoy
yet another good story. He turned and looked at the rest of the
congregation. Most of them were smiling. God was blessing him
yet again. So long as Mr Dayan got to the point soon, everything
would be all right.

'The nine months of the pregnancy went by very quickly and
the doctors who came to examine the woman said that she was

so big she was probably going to have twins — a double blessing. The time came for her confinement and before long the first child was born. It was a hard struggle to get him out but when the midwife delivered him, he was such a perfect little boy she could hardly believe her eyes. She had never seen a child that beautiful. His skin was fair and smooth, his mouth a perfect harp shape, his legs and arms sturdy, and his voice when he took his first breath and cried, was lusty and strong. The midwife handed him to the mother who kissed his eyes and wiped his mouth so that the midwife could attend to the birth of the second twin.

'This one came out much easier for he was far smaller than the first twin, so much so that he looked horribly premature. On closer examination, it was seen that this second boy had a large head and one of his arms was deformed. It was twisted around in its socket at the shoulder where the other brother had crushed it in his growth. This alone was enough to make the midwife say a little blessing against the evil eye as she held him in her arms. But her whispered prayer became a wail of horror and dismay when she examined the rest of this little baby. Because if his arm was misshapen, then his hips were grotesque, like a splayed-out chicken. And when she lay him down on the bed to get a good look at his entire body, she saw that his left foot was hideously twisted, almost at right angles from where his brother twin had fought him in the womb and eventually gained a supremacy in the confines of their mother's body.

'The midwife's revulsion grew as she wiped the second baby down and cleared its mouth. She was glad to hand the ghastly, ugly little thing to its mother. When the mother took him, her face twisted from the joy expressed at the birth of the first child to the depths of horror which only a parent can experience as she saw the reality of the other. She looked at the second twin in despair — it was like holding beauty and the beast in her arms. When she had properly composed herself, she kissed the beautiful twin and said to the midwife, "Tell my husband to come in".

'The father greeted the two children with overwhelming pleasure until he was shown the deformed limbs and ugly twist of the second twin. His reaction was like his wife's. He pushed the deformed child back into the arms of the nurse, raised his head to the ceiling, and cried aloud, "How can God mock me by giving me such pleasure with the one, and such desolation with the other? Can they both have come from the same womb, from the same mother and be children of the same God?"

'The parents took immense joy from the one child, and steeled themselves to a life of prolonged agony with the other. Secretly, though God forbid he would ever admit this, even to himself, the father prayed that the second son would die. But when he saw the way in which his wife paid equal attention to both children, and was ashamed of her initial thoughts when she was given the child from her womb, the father's attitude also changed, and he learnt to look at the second child with feelings which weren't altogether those of horror.

'And so the children were breast-fed and at the age of eight days they were circumcised into the Jewish community. And as they were wheeled around the town by the nanny, people peered into their pram to admire the one but always seemed to turn away from the other. As the two boys grew in strength and health, the good-looking twin grew stronger and broader and even more handsome, while the ugly twin never seemed to grow very much at all. He was always shorter and more twisted than those around him and was ridiculed in school, so that he grew to hate appearing in public. His mother and father, of course, encouraged him and supported him but one look in the mirror told him how very different he was to everybody else.

'The town's children ridiculed the ugly twin although his handsome bigger brother spent most of his time defending him and fighting off the taunts. You see, the dominance he exhibited in the womb didn't translate itself into aggression against his brother in life. In fact, it was quite the opposite. It was almost as if the good-looking twin realised that inadvertently he had been the cause of the other twin's misfortunes. And so from the time when they were both at school, the attractive twin acted as a white knight, defending his brother from the attacks of others who were repelled by his ugliness, and who exhibited their repulsion by aggression.

'The ugly twin found refuge in the strength and good nature of his brother. But the remorseless and ceaseless condemnation of the school society was too much for the deformed twin to bear, and every day after school, instead of staying in the playground and running amok with the other children, or playing ball in the street, the deformed boy would withdraw into the house and into the world he had created for himself in the security of his own room. A world of books, scholarship and searching for a reason why he had become the butt of God's joke.

'And so the years went on and the two boys grew into men. The beautiful twin was sought after by girls and always had lots of friends. But no matter how much his mother and father encouraged him to go out and try to be normal, the other twin preferred to come straight home after school and lock himself in his room where he would eat his meals and study his books.

'Fortunately, the parents had the money to ensure that neither boy needed to earn a living, and the father ensured that when he died, there would be sufficient money to look after the children for the rest of their lives, as well. Again, I must repeat that butchers in those days were very unlike butchers today.'

As a necessary relief from the horrors of the story, the congregation burst out laughing. Mr Dayan waited for them to come to order before he continued. 'So what did they do with the rest of their lives, these boys who were like the sun and the moon? Well, the good-looking twin announced that he was going to become a rabbi. He had always had a love of God and a joy in the Bible and he and his brother spent hour after hour, night after night, debating the intricacies of Jewish thought.

'Did I say debating?' asked Mr Dayan. A few of the people in the congregation nodded, not realising it was a rhetorical question. 'There was no debate in the little room at the top of the butcher's house where the two brothers used to spend their time. You can't call it a debate,' said Mr Dayan, 'when one brother teaches and the other listens in admiration. And which brother do you think it was that was the natural teacher? It was the deformed brother of course, because in the time he spent alone, rejected by society, he went to his room and studied his books and became more and more of a thinker than, like his brother, a doer. So the ugly brother developed the most beautiful mind, and became a wondrous scholar. Not only had he read the great books but he had read them many times. He was intimate friends with the holy sages and mighty philosophers of Judaism. He knew the thoughts of the rabbis in the Talmud, the Mishna and the Gemara; and what he didn't know about the thoughts of Moses Mendelssohn or Baruch Spinoza wasn't worth knowing.

'Now normally, as we all know, Talmudic matters are learnt in a yeshiva where great debate takes place between students as to what this rabbi said or what that rabbi meant. But there was no debate in the attic at the top of the butcher's home. Instead the good-looking twin listened to the distilled, almost crystalline essence of the original thoughts of a miraculous mind ... but a mind trapped in a hideous body. A beauty beyond compare.

'So our handsome young man went on to take all the examinations which are required to become a rabbi. And because he had learnt so much from his brother, he passed his exams with flying colours. And nobody knew that this young man had not been to a great yeshiva, but had been taught everything he needed to know by his brother.

'Shortly thereafter, the handsome twin married a beautiful young woman from the community. And on the first occasion when the rabbi, with his glistening black beard and jet-black curly hair, had to stand and deliver a sermon, the words he used were the words of his brother. And people listened in awe at the brilliance of this young man, the complexity of his thoughts and the simple, almost musical way in which he expressed them. But, because of his modesty, the young rabbi told his congregation that these were not his words, but the words of somebody much wiser than he would ever be. But do you think that the congregation believed him? No! Not on your life. They listened to the clarity of expression, and knew in their very hearts that the modest young man had written the words himself, and that they were the distilled essence of his spiritual soul.

'Well, on the day in which he delivered his first sermon the very first thing he did was to return to his parent's home and climb up to the attic where his brother was waiting. And he told his brother how the people had listened to his words and how they had been amazed by their brilliance. Then the beautiful brother threw his arms around the ugly brother and kissed him on his withered cheeks and told him how grateful he was. And he told him how he had tried to convince the community that they weren't his words, but nobody believed him.

"'Please come to the shul next week. Please let me introduce you to the community," said the good-looking brother. "You haven't been out of the house for years now. You must come out."

"'Why should I come out," said the other brother, "to face the ridicule and contempt of people who see my deformed body? Do you think I like it when I walk down the street and people avert their eyes from me? You don't understand. I'm happy in here. I'm surrounded by the wisdom of the ages and if I can help you to help people, then I'm content."

'And so they argued and argued but it was of no use. The deformed brother refused to leave his room. And so on the next Saturday and the Saturday following and every Saturday for the next two years, the new rabbi delivered sermons which were of such exquisite, almost frightening, brilliance that people began to come from other synagogues just to hear the joy of his beautiful words and to look at the extraordinary beauty of the man, and to revel in his modesty, because each time he spoke, he insisted that it was another who had written the words, one far greater than he.

'And so it went on until one day the beautiful brother was walking through the woods when he saw a sight which made him reel back in horror. He was thinking about his brother's sermon the previous week. He hadn't fully understood its enormous complexities nor the subtleties of the twists and turns in the logic, but nonetheless he appreciated that they were the words of genius ... But I'm wandering, I was talking about the sight which confronted the beautiful rabbi. What he came across was an old deer whose leg was caught in a hunter's trap. The deer was nearly dead through the pain and the suffering caused by this hideous contraption which had bitten into the bones of its leg, but that wasn't the worst part of it. As the rabbi stood there wondering whether to put the deer out of its misery by smashing its skull or to use a rock to prise open the vicious teeth of the trap, a pack of wild dogs burst into the clearing and, snarling and yapping, began to attack the deer. They tore at its throat, its stomach and its eyes until the deer died from its wounds. But that wasn't the end of the scene. Not content with tearing the beautiful beast to death, the dogs, with the taste of blood in their mouths, began to growl and flash their fangs, snapping and clawing at each other over which one would eat the dead animal's flesh.

'Horrified by the cruelty of nature, and the way in which a beautiful beast had been trapped, then torn apart, the good-looking brother turned and ran back to the town. It was a sign from God. He didn't fully understand what it was but he knew that it had something to do with the way in which the community was treating his brother.

'And so the following Shabbat he went to the attic room where his brother lived. And he just stood there.

'Now his ugly brother had spent the entire week writing the most beautiful sermon and had proudly finished it just in time for the Sabbath. He flourished it with pride, telling his brother to deliver it to the congregation when he stood in the synagogue that morning.

'But the rabbi shook his head and said, "No I'm not taking it. Not this time. For years, people have thought that I was the one creating these marvellous words, and no matter how much I begged them to believe it was you, they wouldn't believe the truth. And you, my brother, you made matters worse by refusing to show yourself. All you've done is to compound the lie which I've been living. Now is the time for things to change. This time I'm fighting you. This time I'm going to force you to put on your best Sabbath clothes and come with me to the shul where you will deliver your words of genius and beauty."

'But the brother shook his deformed head sadly and said, "You know I won't. You have no idea what would happen if people listened to these words coming from my mouth. Don't blame yourself. God has chosen an ugly fellow like me to write beautiful words for a beautiful man to speak. Trust me, dear brother. I just can't come out and give a sermon."

'Now normally the rabbi would acquiesce but this time, especially after witnessing the death of the trapped deer, he fought with his brother. He took his brother's clothes out of the wardrobe and despite his protest, forced his brother to wear his jacket, trousers, shoes and a hat, and said to him, "You will come with me or I'll break the laws of Sabbath and carry you."

'"This is a mistake you will regret," said the brother kindly, knowing what would happen.

'And so they walked downstairs and out the front door, surprising the servants in the house. They walked slowly down the path to where people were already gathering to go into the synagogue. The congregation beamed at the rabbi as he walked towards them, but then their faces became fearful as they looked at the deformed little man hobbling beside him, a man supported by the rabbi and treated by him as a pupil assists his master. In the synagogue the rabbi sat his brother down in the front row without introducing him to a congregation which had all but forgotten he existed.

'Until the time when it came to the d'rashah, the sermon. The rabbi turned to face the congregation and he said to them, "My friends, for all the years that you have come here and listened to my words of wisdom, I have tried to convince you that it wasn't me who wrote them, but one far wiser, one touched by the very essence of Almighty God. Yet you have sought to disbelieve me. You have made me keep the existence of the real writer of my sermons a deep and dark secret, for which I feel an eternal shame. For the words that I have spoken to you these many years have been words that were written for me by my brother, a sage, a spiritual man, a man whose mind is more beautiful than any others that I know. I now call upon my brother to stand up here and to preach to you the sermon that he had written for me to preach."

'And with that the rabbi walked down to the floor of the shul, helped his brother stand and helped him climb the stairs until the brother was standing on the bimah facing the congregation.

'Well, you should have heard the reaction from the people. It was like watching an acrobat at a circus. There were "oohs" and "aahs" and gasps. The brother turned to the rabbi and shook his head sadly. And the rabbi realised that all along, the brother had been right. That the people could not accept beauty out of the mouth of a beast.

'So there he stood. Of course, there was no need for the ugly brother to read the speech for he had written it, and knew it word for word. And so he began to deliver the sermon that should have come from the mouth of his brother.

'But the people didn't listen. They didn't want to know. They fidgeted in their seats. They coughed. They whispered words to each other and when it was over the rabbi said "Amen" but he was the only one. And the deformed brother walked sad and unaided back to his seat for the rabbi to carry on the service.

'And afterwards, not one, not two, not ten people, but the whole community gathered around the rabbi and shook his hand and congratulated him and told him that if they thought he was a great man before, now they thought that he was even more marvellous, that he was saintly, that he was the voice of God.

Because to have given the kavod, the honour, of such beautiful words to his pathetic and deformed brother was the highest act of nobility. To actually pretend that the deformed brother had been capable of writing the words was the noblest of all noble acts, and no matter how much the rabbi protested, nobody would believe him; all walked away smiling and nodding and saying, "In our presence we have the finest man who lives".

'And the brothers walked home from shul, one to return to his attic never again to leave, and the other to return to his wife and family, much wiser now about the cruelty of the world.'

Rabbi Teichmann was very satisfied with Mr Dayan's speech. It was strong. It had a good moral fibre to it. There was lots to think about. He was amazed by the depth of intellect in his little community. Until very recently, until the beginning of the stories in fact, he hadn't recognised the amount of knowledge in his congregation. People had only ever come to the synagogue, prayed, laughed a bit, talked during the service and then gone home. It wasn't like the old days when so many of the congregation were learned of the ways of Judaism, when the men would sit around long tables for hours on end, in heated discussion about the intricacies of the Talmud.

When he had tried to introduce Bible study to the community, the usual ten people had turned up. But now people whom he had only ever known through the ritual of prayer were suddenly taking on an entirely new being. He was seeing aspects of personalities that he had never known existed before. It gave him immense pleasure, and this pleasure stayed with him for the rest of the Sabbath, and into Sunday ... in fact, all the way until the time of the telephone call from the chief rabbi of his city, who asked him to drop by the following day for a cup of coffee.

Now rabbis, like all other clergymen, are answerable to a number of different institutions. In the case of a rabbi, the Beth Din is a body based on the court which used to control the Temple and religious affairs of ancient Israel. Today, each major city has a Beth Din, a house of the law which is composed of rabbis who judge divorce applications, and other religious and spiritual matters. Chief amongst these rabbis is the chief rabbi who determines the moral code and spiritual correctness of the rabbis in his jurisdiction. So when Rabbi Teichmann sat down in the study of his boss, Rabbi Mendel, it was a bit like an employee having a chat with an employer; friendly, open and warm but tinged with an I–Thou relationship.

'Rabbi Teichmann,' said the chief rabbi somewhat formally, 'I'm hearing some very interesting stories about your shul. People are telling me that you've introduced a new element to your Friday nights. Instead of you preaching a sermon, it appears that one of your congregation is telling a story.'

Rabbi Teichmann put down his coffee cup and stroked his beard. 'That's what's happening, but it's not like you've just described it, Rabbi Mendel,' he said. 'It all began because the sermons I was preaching weren't exactly setting the world on fire.'

'Is that the fault of the sermon?' the chief rabbi interrupted. The implication was obvious.

'When I told the first story about my grandfather who came to settle in England ...'

'Is this the one that involved the prostitute and the pot of honey?'

Rabbi Teichmann tried not to show surprise. There was a spy in the shul. Somebody who reported what was happening to the chief rabbi. He was very distressed. Who could it be? Mr Dub? Mr Dayan? Surely not Dr Josephs?

But he continued as though unaffected, 'That's the one,' he said. 'Anyway when I had told the story, the reaction was very positive, so I can only assume that it's not me or my ability to preach a good sermon. I'm not sure that people want to listen any more to fine points of Bible analysis or to a moral code that was valid in the days when the rabbis were writing the Talmud.'

The chief rabbi shook his head in sorrow. 'But my friend, these are the eternal truths of Judaism. Turn your back on these and there is no religion.'

'I'm not turning my back on them,' Rabbi Teichmann said defensively. 'I'm merely using the lessons which they teach us in a different format. And anyway, the reason I'm organising storytelling isn't to supplant a traditional sermon so much as to find a way of bringing people back to shul on a Friday night. You see, my attendances used to be rock bottom, just the bare nine and me. One cough or cold and we haven't got a minyan.'

The chief rabbi nodded. 'I know. Attendances are falling in all the shuls. But we have to find a different way of bringing back our congregations. I'm not sure that doing it with guitars and rock songs and stories about prostitutes and pots of honey is the right way.'

Rabbi Teichmann sipped the last of his cup of coffee and put the cup and saucer down on the table. 'Are you telling me I can't do this any more?'

'No,' said the chief rabbi. 'I'm not trying to interfere in the way you run your shul. I'm just asking you to bear in mind that no matter how modern your idea, Judaism has seen many modern ideas come and go, and yet we remain intact holding firmly to the words of God, which were given to us by Moses.'

Rabbi Teichmann nodded. He understood the lesson.

The following Friday night, Rabbi Teichmann greeted everybody who came into the shul. The first in was Abe Flaxman, the beggar who was a guest of Rabbi Teichmann, having just come out of the hospital, his tuberculosis brought under control with the use of strong antibiotics. Next, of course, were the regulars and then faces that the rabbi hadn't seen in many a long month. They sat at the back, they sat at the sides, and some in the front. They came with their wives and children. Twenty, twenty-five, and by the time he mounted the bimah to begin the service there were thirty-seven people in the shul that night. Thirty-seven! Amazing. It equalled the normal Saturday-morning service. Would miracles never cease?

Before he began his service, he said a small prayer to himself. He hoped that the words of the chief rabbi wouldn't come true. But logically he couldn't understand why what he was doing was so very different to what other rabbis were doing in other shuls. All of the stories that were being told had a strong moral foundation. Perhaps the difference was that the other rabbis directed what they wanted the congregation to learn whereas he trusted his congregation to do the right thing.

It was already halfway through the service and, even though he had his back to the congregation as he said the Friday-night prayers, he could feel the buzz of excitement as people wriggled in their seats, waiting for the appointed moment when he would turn around and ask for a storyteller to come forward.

When eventually he turned to face his congregation, six or seven people including two women, were looking up at him eagerly, and smiling. The message on their faces was 'Please Rabbi. Please choose me. I have a great story to tell.'

The question of course was whom to choose. By taking one, he would offend all the others. Perhaps the chief rabbi was right.

Perhaps things were being too modernised. Maybe now was the time to pull back. He took out notes for a sermon which he had prepared. He unfolded and flattened them and placed them on the lectern.

He looked up, and again studied his congregation. So many faces that he hadn't seen before on a Friday night, and he knew with absolute confidence that they would disappear, each and every one of them, if he went back to giving a sermon. So he folded the speech and he said, 'Who today is going to reward us with a beautiful story? A story which will touch our hearts, will teach us a lesson and which will amuse and entertain us, a story fit to be heard in a house of worship.'

A little boy who was bar mitzvah the previous year, and who hadn't attended the shul since shot up in his place. The rabbi knew him well. He also knew that he was precocious and would use the event to show the community how clever he was. He, unfortunately, wouldn't do. Mr Bohm at the back nodded and smiled and tentatively raised a finger but he was already eighty years of age and the rabbi knew him to be slow of thought and even slower of speech. He would lose the audience within the first few minutes. But his eye was attracted to Professor Rivkin who had only been in the congregation since moving to town four years ago. Professor Rivkin taught at the university and rarely came to shul. This was an opportunity not to be missed.

And so the rabbi said, 'Friends, there are so many who want to tell a story that I have to be a judge, and I judge at random. I know I'm disappointing many of you so perhaps the fairest way is on Sunday for you to put your names into a hat and then I'll draw out the name of who is to speak next, but in the meantime I would ask Professor Rivkin to come up and tell his story.'

PROFESSOR RIVKIN'S STORY OF A MODERN-DAY ADAM AND EVE

Now Professor Rivkin was a tall and elegant man. He was a historian and the learned articles which he wrote appeared from time to time in the newspapers. These articles provided a reflective background to some conflict or other which was happening somewhere in the world. The perception of the newspaper editors was that just because he had the title 'Professor' before his name, and held the Chair of History, he must know the history of everything.

So when a dispute arose between the Eskimos and the Canadian Government, or when Russia and Japan disputed the ownership of a lump of rock in the middle of the sea between their two countries, an editor somewhere would say, 'Get an article about the history of the dispute from Professor Rivkin'. And the professor would oblige by going to the university library, looking up the origins of the dispute, and rewriting the details into an eloquent 750-word article.

So for the synagogue, he was something of a local celebrity. So much so that the previous year he had been invited by the Ladies Committee to give a talk to a Sunday-afternoon discussion forum, attended by the rabbi's wife. And she told the rabbi that Professor Rivkin's speech was sympathetically and beautifully told. As the rabbi sat, he looked forward eagerly to hearing what Professor Rivkin had to say.

And from the very first moments of his story, the congregation was washed by the warm fluid beauty of his deep melodic voice. 'Firstly may I thank the rabbi and all of you for giving me the opportunity to tell a story. This is one of my favourite stories and I hope you enjoy it. It's a story told to me by my father who I believe was told the same tale by his father before him. You know, storytelling is one of the most ancient and revered of professions. Unfortunately, since the advent of modern mass communication, storytelling as an art has lost its place of honour within most communities. If you trace the history of storytelling, which, of course, is very difficult because it's an oral tradition, it's safe to assume that storytelling is the oldest form of art ever to have been created by humankind.

'Going deep back into ancient history, it's quite conceivable to think of Neanderthal and Neolithic men sitting in their caves or under the overhang of a rock, warmed by the glow of a fire, while the important men of the tribe told the clans and families all the ancient tales of the vicissitudes of the gods, or the heroic details of the hunt, or the reasons why physical phenomena like rivers or volcanoes or the sun, stars and the moon, exist. It's amazing to think that the tradition of narration, or storytelling, was continued by the great blind Greek storyteller, Homer, whose narration of the *Illiad* and the *Odyssey* formed the very basis of our Western tradition of literature.

'But I'm not here to give a lecture on storytelling. I'm here to tell you a story. It's not a Jewish story, for which I hope Rabbi Teichmann will forgive me. It's a universal story which deals in universal themes. It's the story of a man whose name was Augustus. Now, Augustus lived many centuries ago in a town in Europe. He was the son of very rich parents. His father was a merchant who travelled far and wide. His mother was a great socialite who was occasionally asked to the court by the local duke. Augustus grew up surrounded by books, rich tapestries, beautiful art and the whole panoply of his society. His mother wore dresses of brocade, the tapestries which adorned the walls of their home were sewn with the finest Flemish silks of reds, golds, greens and yellows. They had servants who looked after their every need and Augustus was destined by his position in his society, as well as by the demands of his father, to follow his father as a merchant and to maintain the family's wealth.

'But Augustus was a difficult boy. When he grew into manhood a change came over him. For reasons which neither he, nor any of his family or friends could comprehend, he rejected the wealth of his father and mother. But, more than that, he rejected the lifestyle which they led. He found the clothes which he wore to be ugly, the beautiful tapestries on the walls repulsive, and the shimmering silks which his mother wore he found to be rough and crude.

'Augustus looked around him and saw the artifice in his own world, but when he looked at natural objects, he saw the soft beauty of the animal world, with its innocent creatures living happily in the forest. And he saw the timeless solidity of the world of the forests, growing tall and majestic towards the sky. Whenever he came home from wandering the forests and fields which surrounded his home, Augustus' heart fell as he entered the town where he and his family lived. When he saw his parents dressed in the finest silks while the servants whom they employed dressed in rags and lived a life little better than those of brutes, he became angry. When he went into the streets of his town, he saw beggars hobbling on crutches and women lying in gutters desperately trying to breast-feed starving children. And he became even angrier. He saw taverns full of drunk and dehumanised men and serving wenches being abused and beaten by their masters. And he became angrier still.

'Poor Augustus felt alienated from the world in which he lived; a world in which those who were poor and destitute eked out a meagre existence. Now some who felt like Augustus found refuge in religion; others in works of charity. But the refuge which Augustus sought was in the forests; the beautiful, cool, quiet, peaceful, pure forests. Forests unspoilt by the brutishness of humankind.

'The oppression of the town became so all-encompassing that one day, having sat in a sylvan glade since early in the morning, Augustus realised that no matter what, he couldn't return to his home. And so, knowing well that his parents would be horribly distraught, Augustus decided to remain where he was. He gathered leaves and twigs and branches and plaited them together as a blanket, and for a pillow he found a moss-covered stone. Before it became too dark to see, Augustus gathered nuts and berries which he ate as night fell. And he lay down to sleep, breathing the pure air of the woods, and slept longer and deeper and more peacefully than he had ever slept before in the whole of his life.

'Augustus woke up the following morning to the gentle scrapings of a deer which had wandered into the clearing looking for new grass and leaves from a nearby shrub. The deer looked at him and Augustus looked back. The deer had never seen a thing like Augustus before. Normally the humans which the deer saw from afar through the forest were loud and aggressive and scared him but Augustus simply lay there. The deer trotted over to Augustus and sniffed him, and Augustus slowly sat up and rubbed the neck of the animal and kissed its long and dolorous face. Gently Augustus tore up a fistful of grass and fed it to the deer. When the animal had finished, it bounded happily away.

'Augustus wanted to cry with joy, because for the first time in his life, he was truly at one with nature. He had become part of the community of the wood. It was now in his blood, in his soul, and he realised from that moment onwards that he could never go back to his home. Of course he had severe misgivings about how he would survive. A man like him, brought up on meat once a week would have to kill in order to survive, but more than that, he would have to learn how to be a hunter and a gatherer. His food, his clothes, his basic needs, had always been provided for him without his ever having to think about where they came from, or how they were prepared.

'And so, he took himself deeper and deeper and deeper into the woods where the sun only rarely shone. And there, beside a river, he suddenly emerged into a clearing where trees had fallen across the banks and where the sun shone down brightly, as if God Almighty Himself had ordained this as a light in the darkness of creation. And there he built a small hut for himself from dead branches and mud from the river bank, and supported it with moss-covered rocks which lay strewn near the river.

'Now it was not a well-constructed hut and the first good rain or wind would have blown it down, but it was what he needed for the time being. A place to return to after he had been deeper into the forest to explore and find himself food. A place he could call his own. And he went in search of food because by now it was the middle of the morning and he was hungry. All he had eaten since the previous morning was some bread and cheese which he had taken from the house, and then the nuts and berries from the previous night.

'The first thing he did was to go in search of dry twigs and stones that he could knock together as flint to make a spark. Then he wandered deeper into the wood where he found mushrooms and more berries. He filled his pockets and wandered back, crossing the river by one of the fallen trees. And there he sat in his makeshift hut, eating the mushrooms and the berries and the nuts which he had found until his hunger was abated.

'But Augustus realised that he couldn't survive on a diet of fruit and nuts. He drank huge drafts of the fresh clean water in the river and saw trout swimming in a deep pool close to the opposite bank. His heart sang as he realised that nature had provided him with sustenance at his fingertips. He had to catch the fish. Without a net or hooks, this wouldn't be easy.

'He sat by the riverside, pondering the problem, until the answer became obvious. Crossing the river, he slowly lowered himself into the water, which came up to his rear end. Naturally, the startled fish swam away, but Augustus remained standing there like a statue, his legs, arms and hands in the water, his eyes peering into its depths. And slowly the fish returned to their deep pool. And with the swiftness of an eagle, as a trout swam across his cupped hands, Augustus heaved it out of the water, and watched it land and flop around helplessly on the river bank. He left the water, and put the trout out of its misery, bashing its head against a rock.

'Lighting the fire was more difficult than he thought, because neither of the stones he chose were sufficiently hard and flint-like. But eventually he chose the right ones, and within an hour of catching the gleaming, metallic fish, Augustus was picking its flesh off the makeshift spit. It, and the cooked mushrooms, were the best food he had ever tasted in his entire life. He lay back after his meal, looking up at the thin blue smoke climbing into the forest canopy, and realised that he could live like this for the rest of his life.

'And so it was the next day and the day after and the day after until he felt confident enough to fashion a stone flint into an axe-head which he used to cut down branches enabling him to build a proper hut.

'The weeks became months and the months became years but not for Augustus, because with the exception of the changes of season, Augustus had no knowledge of the passing of time. Time was a measurement for busy people whose life was an existence in the town. In the forest, time was measured by the rising and the setting of the sun and by the warmth of summer and the cold of winter. Although Augustus had made many friends in the forest, he was forced by his very nature to track and kill animals in order to use their fur for warmth and their meat for sustenance.

'But not everything in his life continued to be glorious. As Augustus grew older, he began to see deficiencies in the life he was living. As he would wake up, faced with the same monotony of gathering food, repairing clothes and mending his habitat, he occasionally thought back to the days of ease of his childhood. And when this happened, he found life in the forest somewhat less satisfying. Increasingly, as the sun went down, and his small encampment was lit by the embers of his fire, Augustus would look back at the life he once lived in the town and think of the many glories that he had experienced or the comforts he had enjoyed.

'And the feeling became increasingly stronger that if he was only to acquire some of those comforts his life would become infinitely happier. Comforts? Books to read, for Augustus had been a scholar when he lived in his parents' home. But more than books, Augustus also yearned for candles to light the dark nights so that he could read before he became tired. And then there were his dreams of again wearing the clothes made of silk because the animal skins he wore were so rough to the touch. And while he was musing, he decided that life would be so much easier with farming implements with which he could expand his arena of life and plant seeds. This would give him some greater control over his environment.

'And so, after much soul-searching, Augustus overcame his fear of returning to the town and began to look for things that he could trade. Casting his mind back to those first few days of his new life, Augustus clearly remembered the feeling of liberation when he became a creature of the woods and had taken silver coins out of his pocket and thrown them into the bottom of the river. Now, he realised how useful those coins would have been.

'The only things he could trade were the products of the forest, and so he gathered together a crudely fashioned basket full of mushrooms and attractive acorns which he tied together with twine as a bracelet. Then he set out from his encampment to the distant edge of the forest which bordered the town where he had grown up as a boy.

'He didn't want to go into the heart of the town where the market was, and so on the periphery he knocked on doors in order to sell his products and gather a few coins to buy the implements he needed.

'But what he didn't realise was how much he had changed. When he knocked on the first door, the woman who opened it looked at him, gasped and closed it immediately, shouting for her husband to come and assist her. Augustus, who had been isolated from human beings for so long, was even more frightened than the woman.

'He ran away, and hid behind an outbuilding. He put the basket down, and gazed into a nearby water barrel. He had not seen his face in many years, because the river near his home, far from being a gentle stream, was fast flowing, and its surface was constantly rippled. When he saw himself in the water's surface, like the woman, he received a terrible fright. For facing him was a wild man, whose face was hidden by a mass of hair, and whose skin was rough and nearly blue. He reached into the water to touch the face, but it disappeared. So he put his hand to his face and felt his beard. It was huge and bushy. He decided to return to the house to apologise to the lady. But instead of her, the man came to the door, opening it aggressively and shouting words at him. In a harsh and rasping voice, Augustus begged forgiveness. He hadn't heard his own voice in years. It was harsher and deeper than he remembered and he listened to what he said in amazement. He told the man that he had been living in the woods for many years, but that he needed some implements to use, and so he was here in town to trade. He asked whether the man would like to buy some of his products. Augustus had forgotten many of the words that he knew before he entered the woods and he found explaining what he wanted somewhat difficult.

'As it happened, the man was in need of mushrooms for a stew that his wife was making for their dinner that night and so he took the mushrooms and gave Augustus a handful of copper coins. Augustus thanked the man and walked away, still carrying what remained in his basket.

'Before he decided to undertake any more trading, Augustus took from his pocket the crude stone knife which he used to cut the hide of animals and grasped his rangy beard, cutting it as close as he could to his face. He did the same with his hair at the side, the back and in the front, where it had grown down bushily over his eyes. He continued to trim as best he could with his rudimentary implement until his hands, rough as they were and callused from the hard work, told him that once again he looked like a human being, the same as those who lived in the town.

'And so he picked up his basket and went from house to house until his basket was empty and his pocket contained a handful of coins. In the market he traded the coins for candles, a proper flint and wick, and two books, translations from the Greek of the great philosophers which he knew he would be able to read given enough time. And finally he purchased some digging implements.

'With a sense of enormous relief, Augustus returned to his clearing hidden deep in the massive forest. But the smell of the town, the acrid smoky human smell was still there in his nose as he lay on his bed of reeds and looked around his crude hut in the light of the candles. It took the next day and the day after for him to lose the smell but with the implements he had bought, he was able to dig deeper furrows into the ground than he could using the stone implements which he had fashioned. Quickly, with the iron implements, Augustus was now able to clear whole areas which the crude stone tools had never enabled him to do. In these furrows he planted seeds and using a crude vessel shaped like a gourd and formed from the bark of a tree, was able to carry water from the river to ensure that the new seeds were well-bedded down.

'But a gnawing ache began to grow in his stomach. He found that he became depressed and ill-at-ease as the candles which had brought him so much pleasure burned down to stubs, and he had to ration their use to one hour of dark each night. So a month later, Augustus returned to town with more produce from the forest. Again, he was able to improve his crude surroundings with the new implements which he bought. And these unnatural possessions became the focus of his life.

'It was on his fourth visit nearly a year after his first, that he was followed back to his home by a young and particularly unattractive woman whose name was Helga. Now Helga was the tenth daughter of a local charcoal-burner and his wife. She was crude-looking with scars on her face and hands from where burning wood had fallen on her. Her hair was thin and wispy from malnutrition, yet she was fat in her legs, arms and thighs from an inadequate diet of lard and tubers. Helga had seen Augustus on his last three visits and occasionally looked towards the woods in case the mysterious Nature Man came out to trade. People had begun to talk in the marketplace about the strange woodman with his animal clothes who carried with him the dank smell of the forest. He became the stuff of folk legend, with stories invented about him being the devil spawn of bears, or a lost child who had been brought up by wolves who taught him to run on all fours and sniff the scents of the ground. People became scared of him whenever he emerged from the forest, partly because of the stories which were circulating, but mainly because he had a wild unnatural look in his eye. Yet Helga wasn't scared of him. Quite the contrary, he fascinated her and she determined that the next time he came to town, she would follow him back to find out who he was and where he lived.

'And so it happened. Augustus emerged from the forest, with his pathetic basket of mushrooms and nuts, traded the money for iron or wax, and returned from whence he had come. And Helga followed him all that day, and late into the evening until it was dark. She had no idea of the time or distance she had been following him but she knew that she was exhausted and that he lived deeper in the forest than anybody from the village had ever travelled. At last, she came to the clearing where he lived, and found his encampment. There she saw a substantial hut built of timbers and bark and wattle and daub. There were small fields where crops grew in the muted light of the day, but which at night became cold, black and unwelcoming. As the gloom enveloped her, Helga felt frightened and alone. She was never the bravest of people but she had no idea that the woodman lived this far into the wood.

'All alone in the oppressive quiet of the primeval forest, she gathered her shawl around her, and prepared to wait through the night. But when she saw the single welcoming light of a candle glowing inside the woodman's hut, she felt an overwhelming desire to enter the house, and to be safe from the beasts which roamed the forest at night. She saw the strange woodman moving around inside and she smelt the delicious aroma of a mushroom and meat stew which he was making. Ravenous with hunger, cold from the night and frightened of the dark, Helga didn't know what to do. If she was to try to find her way back to the town, she would undoubtedly get lost and die in the woods, and so tentatively and fearfully she walked across the clearing and knocked softly on the wooden door.

'There was a yell of surprise from inside, a feral cry of terror which made Helga draw her hand away and move from the door. It was suddenly flung open. The woodman stood there, his chest naked, wearing a pair of skins over his legs. He was brandishing a crude stone knife at whoever stood in the doorway. Helga leapt backwards screaming and fell onto the ground. But when the woodman saw that it was a woman and that she was alone, he came and helped her up and took her into the hut where he apologised, and ensured that she felt safe. Then he fed her some of the stew from a crude wooden bowl.

'It was the most delicious stew that she had ever eaten — venison, mushrooms, berries and aromatic spices. It was warm and glowing in the hut as she tried to tell the woodman that she had been passing by but had got lost. She knew then that he didn't believe her and he told her so.

'"Why did you follow me?" he asked.

'"I wanted to see who you were."

'She thought he would be repelled by her ugliness as were all the rest of the townspeople who called her Misbegotten Helga. But Augustus no longer knew ugliness, because he hadn't lived amongst townspeople for many years and had only briefly seen them as he traded. Physical looks, beauty or ugliness, were no longer something which played on his mind. All he saw was a woman. He looked down at her breasts glowing in the light of the fire and felt a long-dormant desire sweep over him that he had not known for many years. He put his hand on her shoulder and drew her to him. Helga stayed with him that night and for many years afterwards.'

It was at this point that Mr Dub and Mr Dayan who were sitting in the front of the shul, began to squirm in discomfort. Not that they weren't transfixed by the beauty and eloquence of the story, nor by Professor Rivkin's extraordinary command of the art of the storyteller, but the mention of naked breasts and heaving bodies and whatever else he was going to get onto, weren't suitable subjects for a synagogue. They looked at the rabbi, anticipating his condemnation but Rabbi Teichmann was staring up at the tall, lean, ascetic figure, revelling in every word. Mr Dub shook his head. Mr Dayan stroked his beard, both of them concerned about the falling standards of the rabbinate.

But if Mr Dayan and Mr Dub wanted the rabbi or the speaker to notice, then they would have been disappointed. Instead, staring at a point midway in the shul, Professor Rivkin continued without censure.

'During those years, Helga became Augustus' boon companion, his workmate, his helpmate, his bedmate. The Eve to his Adam, both living in a latter-day Garden of Eden. And it would have continued in this way, an idyllic if somewhat primitive way of life, had not Helga suddenly become anxious to see her parents again.

'Now many of you may know the most famous passage from Thomas Hobbes' great work *Leviathan*, in which he describes the life of man as solitary, poor, nasty, brutish and short. Well, that's how most of us these days view the lives of our ancestors. But in many cases it just wasn't so. Life in the forests and in the fields was hard but fulfiling. Yet, hard as it was, it followed the cyclic rhythms of nature, and there was as much rest during the long dark nights as there was work when the sun rose. Furthermore, the rural peasants knew how to enjoy themselves, as many painters, musicians and writers have pointed out over the centuries. No! I believe that what Hobbes was referring to by solitary, poor, nasty, brutish and short, was life in the new towns and cities, for there, in the absence of the pacifying hand of nature, life was indeed inhuman for the poor.

'But for all her happiness at being with a man who protected her in the peace and serenity of the forest, it was this urban existence which Helga began to miss. And so, after many years, and bearing her man three children, she told Augustus that she was going back into town to visit her parents. Accepting her decision, he said goodbye and asked her to hurry back. The moment Helga finished her long and arduous trudge through the forest and emerged into the periphery of the town, people crowded around her, recognising her and wondering where she had been all these years. In the intervening period, her mother had died in childbirth and her father, weighted down by the burdens of hard work, collapsed and died one night while he was stoking the fire to burn the charcoal. The family was struggling on as best it could and in despair at their plight, Helga went to see the priest to ask for his help.

'When he saw her and listened to her tale, he was amazed beyond his wildest dreams, for here was a wild woman returned to civilisation. He introduced her to his bishop who introduced her as a curiosity to the ducal court which was in the upper part of town, where the air was clean and the houses large and expensive. As soon as the court heard that there was a curiosity, a wild woman returned to civilisation, they were all agog. They clustered around, fêted her and demanded to hear her story. This she told not once, but a dozen times to a dozen different people until eventually she was called to an audience with the duke himself. For this, of course, she had to be bathed by the women of the court. Her hair was combed and washed, her body was scraped of its dead and grey skin, ointments were rubbed into her sores and eventually she was dressed in the finest silks, in just the same way as in Tudor England, monkeys, bears and Negroes were dressed in silks as a parody of the European form.

'And standing there before the duke this wild woman of the woods told the story of her five years living on the floor of the forest, suckling deers for milk and acting like a squirrel or a wild boar rooting for truffles. She told the court how her home was anywhere where she found herself and her blanket was the wild forest floor, of how she was woken by deers who licked her ear and how she had learned to swing from tree to tree using creepers and vines. And the more fantastical the stories, the more the court believed her and wanted to hear more.

'Until one day, when she had told the story for the second time of how she had rescued a squirrel from the jaws of a wild lion, the court began to get bored of this latest attraction. For a troop of players had come to town offering new entertainments which they had learnt in Paris and London. Helga was escorted from the ducal apartments where she was given her old rags to wear and sent back out onto the streets as yesterday's curiosity.

'Helga was deeply depressed to be removed from the luxury of the ducal court. For implanted firmly in her mind was the feeling of the silks, and the smell of the perfumes and the touch of skin which didn't grate against her fingers. She looked at the scars which had once been suppurating sores and which were quickly getting better. But foremost in her mind was her memory of the comfort of the beds in which she had slept. Their perfumed sheets and the downy mattress which seemed to envelope her body rather than fight it.

'So Helga walked back to her crude old family home where she became yet another of the many orphaned children in the dirty and cramped surroundings. And she compared the crudeness of these surroundings with the richness of the palace on the hill, and she felt great sadness.

'But Helga had children of her own and so within a week, she said goodbye to her brothers and sisters who, if truth be told, were glad to see the back of her because her's was yet another mouth to feed. And she walked the two days through the lowering forest until she came to the hut which she shared with her mate.

'The week following was one of joy and happiness to see her children again and her mate, but secretly her joy was tempered with great longing for the riches and luxuries of the court. As she slept, visions started to come to her. Visions of silk and perfume and expensive soaps and softness. She told her mate of these visions, and Augustus was intensely curious, for it was now many many years since he had been away from the forest and into the town. Tempted by her descriptions he took himself, like Helga, through the forest and into the marketplace in order to see his rich mother and father, just to see what it was like.

'Now they were much older than they had been when Augustus had first left. They viewed him at first with intense suspicion, for after so many years they believed that their son was dead. But when he convinced them of who he was and why he had left them, they shaved him and pampered him and treated him with great love and affection. The smells of the perfume returned to his nose and the dank heavy scents of the wood were quickly lost to him. Slowly his parents introduced him back into their society and there he met men and women whose lives had been pampered by the riches of the town. He saw them in their fineries and he felt a deep sense of shame at the way he looked. One young woman especially attracted him. Her skin was as white as cream. Her hair as yellow as autumn leaves. He looked at her with curiosity and longing. And he told her he would like to mate with her, because one of the many things which he had forgotten was the art of artifice and circumspection. She was horrified and repelled by him, for no matter how hard his parents tried to expel the crudeness of the forest, it was bred into his skin.

'From then onwards, he began to feel a distance, an antipathy to the town and its people, and two months after he returned, the sound of his children crying for him came to him through the distant forest. With much regret and longing, he kissed his sleeping mother and father goodbye, left the house, and took himself back into the woods. It was a long and arduous journey and as he walked deeper and deeper into the forest, his mind was fixed on the beauty of the young woman from the town who had rejected him. Her smell, her softness, her beauty stayed with him for the days which it took him to traverse the forest, and to return to his home. He was unable to forget the colour of her skin, or her hair, or the smell of her body as she had once sat close to him. And when he came into the clearing and saw how crude his home was compared to where he had once lived, his heart sank. For the first time since he had gone to live in the forest as a boy, his heart felt heavy. Suddenly he felt as if he was returning to a dreary and unfortunate life from which, for a short and glorious time, he had been released.

'But the agony for Augustus didn't end there. Because when he saw his mate Helga standing at the door, fat and scarred, her face crude and rough, her hair thin and wispy, her skin red and patchy, her arms and legs heavy, and her clothes little more than rags, he realised that he was a different man from the one who had left the forest. He had seen the seductive pleasures of the town. And they had opened up for him desires which he had long suppressed.

'And the realisation dawned on Augustus that he must leave the forest and Helga forever because he now saw his home and his mate in a way that he had never seen them before.

'Before he entered his crude and unlovely hut, Augustus sat on the ground. Helga looked at him in surprise. But the more she looked, the more she understood what was affecting him. Her heart fell as she realised that from this moment onwards, she would be left completely alone in the woods, alone to raise their children as spirits of the natural world, alone to fend for herself, and to perform alone the tasks which she and her mate had once joyously shared together.

'She looked at Augustus for the very last time. He was sitting huddled like a newborn baby, lit from the candlelight of the doorway in the gathering gloom of the forest. But Helga had no time to offer help or sympathy. She had children to feed. So she turned around and went back into the house closing the door behind her. And from the depths of the dark forest, she heard a long, agonised human howl.'

Professor Rivkin licked his lips, and cleared his throat. He bowed slightly, and descended from the bimah. A few sporadic 'Shekoyachs' could be heard throughout the silenced shul. Nobody moved, not even the rabbi. For the twists and turns of the complex story had mystified the congregation who were trying to grapple with its moral.

The rabbi eventually stood, and continued with the service.

A trend was beginning to develop. Of course, trends are the province of statisticians, who look at figures and analyse the future based on what has happened in the past. All very well and good if you're dealing with the sale of baked beans or how many motor cars to produce in the following six months. But not so easy when you're dealing with a religious congregation. Of course you can always rely upon the faithful to come to church or synagogue. Nowadays, they're called the 'faithful few' because of the swing away from religion in these secular times. But take out the core faithful and there's a large population of (what in any other circumstances might be called) swingers. Not the modern use of the word, naturally, but men and women who wake up on a Saturday morning (if they're Jews), Sunday morning (if they're Christians), never forgetting Friday morning (if they're

Moslems), and who say to themselves 'I won't go to sport, I won't go to work, I won't laze around the house, I think I'll go and pray'. Now these people may go twice a year, once a month, even once every decade ... that's the problem for the religious statistician. It's impossible to predict how many are going to turn up to a service. And so all you can do is to look at a trend over a period of weeks.

And it was this trend that was worrying Rabbi Teichmann as the Saturday-morning congregation began to grow noticeably smaller and smaller and the Friday-night minyan grew definitely bigger and bigger. Last week, when Professor Rivkin gave his brilliantly told story, the numbers for the Friday-night service equalled the numbers for an average Saturday-morning service. Saturday-morning faces turned up on Friday night but didn't turn up on the following Saturday morning.

One of the things which Rabbi Teichmann had never done in the years that he had been a rabbi in the small synagogue in the small suburb in the small town in the country in which these stories were taking place was to say to people, 'Why don't you come to shul more?' Now you may think that odd. If a rabbi is a salesman for his religion, then Rabbi Teichmann wasn't much of a salesman. If he was selling insurance or cars or swimming pools he would have been out of business years ago. But Rabbi Teichmann had a problem with trying to persuade people to come to shul. And the problem was simply this: if they felt they were being coerced then they would come along out of a guilty conscience and their whole motivation would be out of kilter. They would sit in the synagogue waiting for the service to be finished, thinking of what else they could be doing (football, work, lazing around the house). So Rabbi Teichmann had always worked on the philosophy that it was better to have a smaller number of people wanting to be there, than a larger number of people who were present under duress. He was about to discuss this problem with his wife when he closed his eyes and instead said a short prayer.

All his life, Rabbi Teichmann had trusted in his closest and best friend, God, to do the right things, to show him the way. In the wonderful stories of Shalom Aleichem, Tevye, the milkman had enjoyed a one-to-one relationship with God, carrying his heavy churns balanced on either side of the yoke over his neck like an ox, and delivering the milk from house to house. And in between houses, Tevye had discussed the problems of the world with God and demanded action immediately when he saw that things weren't going well. On another occasion in a shtetl in Eastern Europe, a group of rabbis, so distraught by the state of the Jewish communities, by the anti-Semitism, by the hatred, by the way in which they were so bitterly oppressed from so many sides, decided to put God on trial. And so rabbis and wise men came from all over Europe to sit and listen as the prosecution and the defence argued this way and that about whether God was guilty for inflicting these hideous punishments upon the Jews. And God would have been found innocent except for one thing — none of the rabbis could excuse God for causing such hideous sufferings to orphans, to the innocents born to women and who, through no fault of theirs, were dealt the same punishment as men and women who had lived a full life.

Rabbi Teichmann enjoyed an intimacy with God which gave him great comfort but there was still a respect there which told him that God was the boss and that he was nothing more than the mouthpiece. Something, he knew, would turn up. And this thought stayed with him as he entered the synagogue on the Friday night, shook hands with Mr Dub and Dr Josephs and the other men and nodded a greeting to the women. He mounted the bimah, turned to the congregation and saw that the thirty-seven from the previous Friday night had now expanded to almost sixty. There was a warmth of bodies in the synagogue that wasn't normally there on a Friday night. It was the sort of warmth that rabbis experience on the high holy days of Rosh Hashanah and Yom Kippur and there was a buzz in the congregation which filled all the spaces, all the nooks and crannies and corners in the normally echoing synagogue.

Rabbi Teichmann shook his head in sorrow. Never did he think he would be so sorry to see so many people on a Friday night. It was a culmination of his wishes, of his deepest desires. Yet because it took away from the glory of Saturday-morning minyan, it was a sight of sadness for him. Mr Dub, Dr Josephs and Mr Dayan knew the rabbi well enough to know that he was not a happy man but they had no idea what was causing his problems.

And so began the Friday-night service. As he was davening, the rabbi kept stealing surreptitious looks at the congregation, wondering whether he had the temerity to make an announcement at the end of the service, begging them to come to synagogue the following day. But he knew in his heart that, though it would work, though it would have an effect, it was the wrong thing to do.

And so the point of the service arrived where rabbis throughout the world turn to their congregations who sit and look up expectantly for the delivery of a sermon. This time, however, Rabbi Teichmann knew who would be giving the speech, for twenty-six people had put their names into a hat and he had drawn one the previous night at random ... Well, to tell the truth, and there's no point in lying, the first three names had been rejected as unsatisfactory. They were nice people but completely boring. Two had thick accents which the rest of the congregation would find hard to understand and one of them was always jumping forward to say, 'Here, I'll do it. Let me do it.' What is known as a glory seeker.

So the rabbi had no hesitation in pulling a fourth name from the hat, which thank God, was a young man of charm and wit and not inconsiderable intellect. A man who had only been in the community since he and his wife had married six years ago and who had travelled to the town to be with her. A young man who was a bookseller by profession and who Rabbi Teichmann knew would have many good stories to tell. And so the rabbi said to the congregation, 'And now it's time for another one of our stories. Looking at the large number of people here, I welcome each and every one of you, I know you're going to be delighted by the name which I took out of the hat yesterday. Mr Jack Roberts, would you please step up onto the bimah and enlighten us with a story.'

JACK ROBERTS' STORY OF THE MARRIAGE OF ROSA AND ZOLTAN

'I want to take you on a journey. It's a journey which will take us back in time through many dark centuries, a journey which is full of danger but also full of great rewards. Not material rewards of course. There are no monetary gains for those who listen to a story. The gain is in the acquisition of a texture that you may not have felt before or the sight of vivid colours in the pictures that I paint in the air as I tell you about times long past and fears long forgotten.'

Jack Roberts, the bookseller, put his hands on the wooden railings of the lectern and leaned slightly forward, balancing on the balls of his feet. The rabbi, for the fifth time in five consecutive weeks — how wonderful life was — settled back and prepared to be amused and entertained by the eloquent young man.

In the note that Jack had sent, which the rabbi had drawn out of the hat yesterday, he had detailed the theme of the story. Although it had nothing to do with Judaism it was a universal message and the rabbi believed it was a proper topic for a synagogue. He looked at Mr Dub and Mr Dayan who were sitting across the way from him. They were the religious police of his synagogue. If things didn't go strictly according to their clockwork, then they would become distressed, and would whisper and mumble. The Rabbi turned away and resumed listening as the beauty of the words washed over him.

'This is a story, ladies and gentlemen, which relates to the time when Europe was coming out of the Middle Ages and the fervour of the Renaissance was in the air. In Bohemia, close to the border of a small Germanic principality, there lived a farmer. His farm bordered a swift-flowing river whose waters were always cold and icy, even in the height of summer. When the snows from the distant Tatra Mountains melted and surged through the land, they gave life to the verdant fields and fertile soils.

'The farmer's name was Zoltan and he was the son of another farmer whose family had tilled the land for generations. Nothing much changed in this valley over hundreds of years. Life was confined and secure. Visitors rarely passed through the valley on their way from the east to the west because the main routes which crossed Europe were further south or further north. But occasionally people did happen by and they would bring news about what was happening in St Petersburg or Rome or in the Ottoman Empire in the earliest days of the rise of the Hapsburgs.

'When he turned eighteen, Zoltan decided that he wanted to get married. Already he was farming more fields than his father had ever ploughed in his entire life. Because he was shrewd and clever, Zoltan had bought fields at bargain prices from men with no offspring who were too old to cope with the workload. Today we would decry this as mercenary opportunism, but in those days, as the Church and the feudal lords were beginning to release their stranglehold on title, people who acquired land, even at the cost of others, were to be admired.

'Zoltan worked hard, and was pleased with the way in which his small estate was growing. But something was not well in his life. He was fed up with returning to his parents' house in the village after a hard day in the fields. He was fed up with his mother's cooking and his father's complaints, he wanted to strike out on his own and establish a home for himself. So Zoltan paid a small amount to a labourer to look after his fields whilst he took a pack of food on his back and walked the six miles to the next village where he would speak to the priest about finding him a suitable bride. For one thing was certain, no matter how many of the girls smiled hopefully at him at church in his own little village, Zoltan wasn't interested in any of them. He had grown up with them — they had played in the village square as children, gone bathing naked in the icy waters of the river in the heat of the summer or rolled in the snow as the village closed down for the winter and waited for the spring. They were like sisters to him.

'Zoltan was a tall and ruggedly good-looking young man and when he presented himself to the priest in the nearby village, he proffered a letter of introduction and recommendation from his own priest telling his brother priest that the young man was a good Christian, rich, hard-working and honest. The priest read the letter and looked up admiringly at Zoltan. Yes, this was a catch! He arranged for Zoltan to stay at the local inn whilst he spoke to the village elders to determine who could pay an appropriate dowry and whose daughter would make a suitable wife for the young man from the nearby village. After only a few days of pondering the thorny subject, a farming couple was asked to come into town with their eldest daughter, Rosa.

'Surprised, but obeying the direction of the priest, the couple left their farm and came into town where they were invited to dinner at the priest's home. There, sitting in a corner, was a

MINYAN

young man, a stranger. He had dark curly hair and although his clothes were the rough tunic of a peasant farmer, he had broad shoulders, a lusty chest, strong legs and he was tall enough for his head to nearly touch the ceiling of the priest's dining room. The priest introduced the young man to the mother and father, though deliberately, for reasons of modesty, not to the young woman Rosa. The priest told the parents that the young man was a guest from the nearby village and this was the first time in his life he had ever been beyond the confines of his town. The mother and father nodded admiringly, and they sat down to eat an evening meal of stew with large chunks of black bread and pots of recently fermented beer.

'During the evening, the somewhat taciturn young man said little, but looked closely at the young woman, who sat in the shadow of her parents. The young woman hardly dared to say a word or to glance up, in case the young man deduced meaning from her look or conversation which wasn't there. For Rosa knew precisely why she had been summoned, and what was expected of her. As they ate, the priest expounded on the growing dangers of liberality, and the way in which the traditional social order, so admired by the Church, was being turned upside down by free thinkers and radicals. The evening came to an end with hardly anybody speaking other than the host and the priest bade the family goodnight and sent them on their way the two miles back to their farm. Closing the wooden door and fixing the latch, the priest said to Zoltan, "So my boy, what did you think of the beautiful Rosa?"

'"She is very beautiful. She has delicate creamy skin and her teeth are all still there. Her hair is too straight for my liking but she seems healthy. She has strong shoulders. I like her. I think she will do nicely for me, provided the dowry is adequate."

"'Good,'" said the priest. "'Then I'll make the arrangements in the morning. In the meantime, you go back to the inn for the night and return to your village tomorrow. Within a week I'll come with the family and we will be guests of your priest when the marriage contract is negotiated.'"

'Now you may be thinking,' said Jack 'that it was all smooth sailing from that moment onwards. Here was a young man in need of a bride; there was a young woman who was modest enough to attract him. But that wasn't the way things worked because this was no mere acquiescent young woman. Rosa was strong-willed and firm of mind and, as I said, she knew exactly why she had been invited to dinner in the priest's house that night. The moment she looked at the crude young man she knew that she was being judged by him like some milk cow he was thinking of purchasing. Under normal circumstances, Rosa would have offered the assembled company her normal conversation, which was direct to say the least, and often contradictory to the views of her mother and father and indeed of the priest and the village elders. But she had been enjoined by her long-suffering father to remain quiet at all costs, and to seem mild and delicate. For once in her life, Rosa decided to acquiesce to her father's instructions and to sit mutely in the shadows, because she hoped that her silence would bore the young man and deflect his interest. Unfortunately the opposite had happened because Zoltan was somewhat taciturn in his nature and the last thing he wanted was an outspoken wife.

'So when the mother and father and their daughter rode their wagon into Zoltan's village accompanied by their priest, Zoltan proudly welcomed them. He was accompanied by his mother and father and the village priest, who blessed the gathering and invited everybody into his small but comfortable house next-door to the church of St Elizabeth.

'Why did Rosa accompany her parents, when she wasn't particularly keen to get married? That will soon become clear.

'But true to form, and to her parents' consternation, as the two parties stepped through the doorway, Rosa surprised everybody (except her parents) by grabbing Zoltan's arm and pulling him aside.

'"I need to talk to you before we go in," she insisted.

'Zoltan was staggered. It was the first time he had heard her voice. It was more melodic and deeper than he expected. Yet it had a delicacy which he found appealing. "Of course," he said.

'"We both know that I'm here in order for you to accept me as a bride. My parents are prepared to offer a good dowry in order to sweeten the exchange and I'm quite happy to marry you. I'm seventeen and I need a husband. And my younger sister is madly in love with a young man from my village and she can't marry until I marry, so it's best all around if we do get married."

'Zoltan's jaw dropped in surprise. This was so direct, so matter-of-fact, that he could hardly believe the words she was saying. He had been brought up to believe that girls were romantic and fell in love, whereas men married for women to bear them sons who could work in the field when they were too tired. He was also brought up to believe that women, being naturally subservient to men, didn't really have opinions of their own, but looked to their husbands for advice.

'"I don't understand," he stammered.

'"Oh for God's sake. It's not all that difficult, is it? I'm telling you that I'm prepared to marry you and that your mother and father are going to get a good deal from mine. But I'm not like some horse or cow to be sold at auction. I'm only willing to marry you if you make certain promises. Refuse, and I'll leave here now and return to my home."

"'I ... I," said Zoltan.'

Jack Roberts looked around to see the reaction from his audience. So did the rabbi, who turned and looked around his congregation. The women were smiling and nodding in admiration. The men frowning. This was wonderful, thought Rabbi Teichmann, a story involving everybody. He wondered whether any of it were true.

Jack continued, 'By this time Rosa was getting fed up with Zoltan's dimness, and snapped at him angrily, "You really don't understand what I'm trying to say to you, do you?"

"'Yes," said Zoltan. "You're telling me you want to marry me."

"'No, I'm telling you I'm willing to marry you on certain conditions."

"'What conditions?" he asked.

"'These conditions. Firstly you expect nothing more of me than you expect of your mother. I'm neither your housemaid nor your servant. Secondly, and this might embarrass you but I don't really care because I want it absolutely clear. Again I remind you that I'm not a cow and you're not a bull. I will meet my wifely obligations to you in our bed but it must be when I want to, as well as when you want to. You have no rights over my body, no matter what vows we take in Church. And thirdly, there's an apothecary of whom I've heard. He's in Prague. He makes a potion which women can take which stops them from having babies. I don't intend to be like my mother and have ten children. It's my intention to seek out this apothecary and to take this potion when we have three children. I believe that's enough. Now," she said challengingly, "do you still want to marry me? If not, don't waste my time or my parent's money."

'Zoltan was in a state of shock. He had never heard a woman speak like this. None of the girls in his village, nor his aunts and certainly not his mother had spoken to a man in this manner! This woman deserved a good spanking in order to put her back into line. No, he wouldn't marry this woman. Not now and not ever. But she stood there unmoving and indeed unflinching. Zoltan thought as quickly as he could. If he rejected her, he would be the laughing-stock of his village, and worse, the next time he went looking for a bride everybody would know about it. And when he thought carefully about what she said, whilst he didn't agree with any of it, he had to admit that much of it made sense.

'He swallowed and nodded meekly.

'"You agree?" said Rosa in surprise.

'"Yes," he said more definitely. "Yes, I think you're right. I could have married any of the girls from my village if I'd wanted someone just to be a servant. But you're different. Why didn't you say these things when I was at your village? You hardly said a word. I thought you were shy."

'"You agree?" said Rosa incredulously. It wasn't what she expected. She'd hoped he'd say no. Then she could return to her village, and the blame would be on him. But one thing she said was true. If she didn't marry, she'd be an old maid, and her sisters would die unwed as well. So she sighed, and smiled.

'The priest came out and said, "My dear young people, please come in. We're ready to begin the marriage negotiations."

'The following morning Rosa and her parents left to return to their village. The wedding day had been set for three months hence. This might seem a long while for a simple, rustic wedding, but a wedding was a communal celebration, and much was expected by the community of the parents of the bride and groom. The bans had to be posted, the animals had to be fattened for the wedding feast, merchants had to be sought to provide linen and knives for the table, a cape had to be made for Rosa in which to be married ... Yes, there was much to do.

'And one of the first things which Zoltan's priest did was to write a note to Count Bedrich, the young and handsome nobleman whose castle overlooked all the lands of the valley and those to the north and east. Count Bedrich had recently taken over the running of the estate from his old father who had been stricken by a stroke. The title had passed to Bedrich who came back from Prague, where he was a courtier to the king, in order to take charge of the lands which now belonged to him.

'It was one of twenty letters which Count Bedrich received that day, letters which his secretary dealt with. But because he was the new count and was hardly known to his people, the secretary, a wise old man, felt it might be appropriate for the count to acknowledge this letter personally. So the secretary, who had been the young Count Bedrich's father's secretary all his life, wrote a letter which he gave to Count Bedrich to sign.

'"Tell me, old friend," said the young count. "Is this a well-known local family? They appear to be two young people from different villages."

'"I know them, Sir," said the old man. "They're a good family, well respected in the area, but no different from many hundreds of others."

'"But they farm my lands."

'"No," said the secretary, "they're freeholders. They pay you a tithe but the land belongs to them. It was an agreement your father came to with people who farmed close to the river. You of course have all the rights of the river in both content and carriage."

'Count Bedrich nodded. "But it would be good for me to go to this wedding. It's only seven or so miles. I can ride out there on the morning and give the bride and groom my blessing."

'"But your father never attended . . ."

'"That was my father. In my reign, I intend to be closer to my people. Is there any reason I shouldn't?" asked the count.

'"None at all, Sire," said the secretary.

'And so the letter of agreement to the wedding was signed; the final obstacle which could have prevented the union of Zoltan and Rosa. And when the priest read it he smiled and copied it out accurately with a crudely drawn facsimile of the count's seal and sent it to Rosa's priest for him to keep in his records.

'The three months went by quickly without Rosa and Zoltan meeting again during that time. And on the morning of the wedding a large party from Rosa's village travelled the six miles along the river bank and up the hill into Zoltan's village. From the other direction, from his huge castle high on the hill overlooking the countryside for miles around, rode Count Bedrich, resplendent in his silver cape, gold epaulettes, yellow tunic and purple leggings. His boots, made of the finest calf skin, had been newly acquired from the bootmaker in Prague. He was recently bathed, his hair newly combed and the morning was warm and luxurious. As he rode his horse down into the valley floor following the directions given to him by his secretary, he smelled the perfume of the wind, an aromatic smell of lilac and lavender which came from the fields. With it was mixed the darker mustier smell of the impenetrable woods nearby.

'As he rode into the village, the people walking towards the church stopped in their tracks and turned and looked at him in awe. They dropped back to allow his horse to pass and he smiled at them and nodded. And they bowed low to him, not knowing who he was but recognising him as a man of great importance and power from the richness of his dress, and the nobility with which he rode.

'Count Bedrich cantered towards the Church of St Elizabeth where he dismounted from his horse and knotted the reins to a post supporting the archway over the door. The area was crowded with villagers and well-wishers who drew back from the exalted presence of the count.

'"Good morning to you," he said gently and smiled. But all they did was mumble and draw back. Here was a sight which had never been seen in the village. A rich and powerful man attending their church. Some, who had been to Prague, had seen men like this from afar. And they had been the toast of the inn as they retold the stories countless times ... stories about the height of the horses, or the way in which they were dressed, or the clothes worn by the noblemen and women. But no one ever suspected that such a noble would visit their impoverished and out-of-the-way little village.

'The villagers stood mutely in awe, staring at the count. They were uncertain and some were even afraid. But it began to dawn on some of the throng that this must be the new count, and the word was whispered from mouth to ear. A relief spread like a comforting blanket over the villagers. Some even smiled. But all were surprised at the visit. Neither the count's own father nor his grandfather before him had ever bothered visiting his villagers. When business was to be done, or announcements made, an official from the castle would ride imperiously into the middle of the village, ring a bell, and summon the villagers to hear what had to be said. Those who worked in the fields were told of the decisions later that night in the inn.

'The priest emerged from the church and gasped when he saw the count. He knew who the stranger was, because he had seen him once before when he and the other clergy had been invited to attend the old count's funeral. The priest bowed and said, "Sire, we are honoured." But the count deflected the honour and said, "I'm only here as a wedding guest. Two of my subjects are getting married and I felt it my duty to come and pay my respects."

'As he said the words a commotion began to grow from the other end of the village — the music of minstrels, and the sounds of laughter and gaiety. Rosa and her wedding party, preceded by the musicians and jugglers employed by her parents, were walking from the outskirts of the village towards the church. Zoltan, who was in the church and who by practice was not permitted to come out before the arrival of his bride, heard but did not see what was occurring.

'But Count Bedrich saw. And what he saw took his breath away. It was the first time that the count had seen Rosa; indeed, one of the first times that he had come face to face with a true, natural beauty.

'In the Royal Courts of Prague, whenever great men and women gathered in Hradcany Castle high on the summit of Petrin Hill, Count Bedrich had surrounded himself with some of the most sophisticated ladies of the day ... and here I use the word "sophisticated" in its true sense, meaning women who had little about them which was natural but used the falsehoods and artifice of heavy cosmetics and luxurious clothes to hide their pallid faces and overfed bodies.

'When Count Bedrich saw the ruddy, fresh-faced complexion, beautiful long straight golden hair and tall, majestic body of the bride as she walked slowly under her golden canopy towards the church, he felt a pang of lust surge through his body, a flood of emotions which he had never before experienced. The girl he saw coming towards him was magnificent. He couldn't take his eyes off her.

'Count Bedrich wondered whether the peasants in the village could appreciate just how truly beautiful she was. Her smile was utterly radiant, her eyes bright and gleaming. There was a delicacy in her step and yet a strength of purpose which he didn't know existed in the lives of his peasants. She almost appeared to be challenging him as she walked closer and closer. But challenging him to what? He couldn't understand it ... until he realised that unlike all the others, she was not casting her eyes modestly to the ground, but was looking at him directly, almost impertinently. Count Bedrich grasped the priest and demanded, "Who is this girl?"

'"It's the bride, Majesty."

'"I know that you fool. But who is she? Tell me about her."

'"She's the daughter of ..."

'"No. Tell me what kind of a girl she is," he said imploringly. Rosa was getting closer to the well outside the church, walking forward in slow and deliberate paces. In another minute, she would be there.

'"I've only met her twice sir. She is intelligent, free-willed and she has a strong spirit. In olden times she would have been called a shrew but these days ..." the priest shrugged.

Rosa stepped closer and closer and all the while her eyes were not on the villagers or on the church or even on the priest who would soon marry her to Zoltan, but on the count. He, in turn, couldn't draw his eyes away from her.

'When he had first arrived, the peasants had shown naked fear. But not Rosa. Even now, as she came close to him, she showed no fear of him. And her very step, her very look, even the way she held her head was a challenge to his authority. And more. To his manhood.

'He felt as if he was in the presence of the most powerful and naked force he had ever known. He felt the same feeling he had experienced when first he knelt before the King of Prague. But this was deeper and somehow more powerful, for with each step she took towards him he felt his body trembling. He felt his heart pounding and suddenly she was level with him. She stood almost as tall as he did. And the closer she was, the more perfect was her skin. There wasn't a blemish on her face, her hair was planted with beautiful petals and her bodice was open so that he could see her delicate throat and the creamy-white skin beneath her dress.

'Rosa stopped for a moment and looked at the count. He knew that she knew who he was but there was no deference in her eyes. Instead, she said to him in a voice which showed complete control and mastery, "Thank you for coming down from your lofty castle to attend my wedding. I hope you won't be disappointed in our little service," and then she walked on. But her aura stayed with him, preventing him from breathing, from comprehending either who or where he was.

'Since he had been count, he had held power of life and death over all and any subject in his realm. And yet, by her few insolent words, she had made him subject to her. He opened his mouth to speak but before he could say anything, and without his permission to leave, Rosa walked on and into the dark entry of the church.

'A harsh, rasping voice suddenly shouted out "Stop". The count was surprised when he realised that the voice belonged to him. Immediately, there was silence. The musicians stopped playing, the jugglers stilled their acts. The crowd looked at him in stupefaction. Rosa stopped and turned. The count realised that he was panting. His mouth was dry, his heart pounding. He didn't know what to say. He didn't know what he had just done. All he knew was that he had to possess this woman. To make her his. In a voice which sounded different from his own, a voice which resided deep within his body, and which was dredged up from the very depths of his carnal lusts and desires, he hissed, "There will be no marriage. I revoke my permission. Have this woman brought to my castle today. Now! Immediately!" he shouted.

'And he untied his horse, mounted quickly and drove the beast through the press of the crowd who scurried out of his way like terrified hens. They looked at him as he rode away. Each and every man, woman and child in the village stood and looked at the count's disappearing form, and gasped in fear and incomprehension.

'The count didn't look back for a moment. Instead, he whipped his horse's flanks and rode like the wind, not stopping until he reached the castle. Only then, exhausted and drenched in sweat, did he fall off the horse into the waiting arms of his groom. Then he fell on his knees and raised his head to the sky and let out a howl of pain and anguish.

'"Oh God. What have I done?"

'Late in the afternoon, the priest, sweating profusely, his face red with concern as well as the effort of the long walk, arrived at the castle. It had been a long and tortuous climb from the valley floor up to the castle and he was forced to stand and rest in the shade of the walls before pulling the bell chain to alert the castle guards to his presence. Recovered, he walked through the courtyard and mounted more steps until he was shown into an antechamber by the count's castellan. The priest had never been into the inner sanctum of the castle before and he was awestruck by the sumptuous tapestries, the collection of crossbows and arrows, the swords and pikestaffs, and the halberds which hung from the walls. But most impressive of all was the view through the archway from the antechamber into the baronial hall. There the priest looked at a vast oak table as long as the tallest tree in the wildest forest. And around the table were tall leather-backed chairs which stood like sentinels guarding the centrepiece: a massive, though delicately carved, solid gold soup server and tureen. Around the high walls of the banquet room were proudly displayed the flags of every province of Bohemia and clustered around the central flag which flew high above the count's own seat was the ancestral flag of the count's family.

'The priest's gaze was disturbed by the entry of the count's secretary. "Yes," said the secretary curtly.

"'I must speak to His Excellency, the Count. I must speak to him immediately."

"'On what matter?" asked the secretary.

'Although intimidated by his surroundings, the priest knew he was on safe ground. "On a matter of delicacy which I will only discuss with His Excellency."

"'His excellency has given me instructions not to admit you to his presence. He demands the girl be brought here by tomorrow night. He revokes his consent to the wedding and he invokes his right of droit du seigneur."

'The priest's jaw dropped in astonishment. He had come assuming that for some reason the wedding of Zoltan and Rosa displeased the count or that there was some impediment of which only he knew. This was such a young and handsome man, such a noble person in spirit and in deed, that the deflowering of a virgin bride was the last thing which was on the mind of the priest.'

At this point, Mr Dub and Mr Dayan looked at each other in astonishment. Neither was particularly familiar with the rights of medieval lords of the manor and had never heard of the act of droit du seigneur. But to use words like 'deflower' and 'virgin' in shul was going too far. Mr Dub, about to stand and cough and ask Jack Roberts to be a little bit more circumspect in his language, looked at the rabbi for approval, but the rabbi was transfixed by the story. So Mr Dub remained in his seat but he was dissatisfied and would take issue afterwards.

Then again, if you came to look at the stories in the Bible like the story of Onan or the murder of Abel by Cain or the number of rapes and deflowerings that took place in far-off days, this story told by Mr Roberts wasn't all that much different. So, he continued.

'The priest felt himself go weak at the knees. Whilst everybody acknowledged the count's right, it was a privilege which had not been exercised in this part of Bohemia for at least two hundred years. It was considered barbaric, a relic of a former age. But there was nothing that the priest could do, nothing except appeal to the Christian values which he knew the count held dear.

'And there he stood, shoulder to shoulder with the elderly secretary demanding, begging, pleading, threatening but all to no avail. And as he left the antechamber the secretary said (and there was a note of sadness in his voice) "I'm further instructed by His Excellency that unless you deliver the girl here as a virgin by tomorrow night, he will revoke the rights of the peasants to grow produce in the fields of the village, to sell that produce and to travel freely upon his roads. Further he will prohibit all fishing and catching of fish from his river and he will charge heavily for all cattle who agist on his land. If this doesn't sway the villagers, then the gathering of wood for fires from his forests will be prohibited forthwith and with the coming of winter many villagers will surely die of cold."

'For once the priest said nothing. He was too stunned by the turn of events. Yet he was convinced that he saw a tear in the eyes of the old secretary who turned and left him alone to ponder the fate of the village and to wonder precisely how he was going to explain things to Zoltan and his parents.

'And so it was decided that for the good of all the communities involved, Rosa would walk with her father and Zoltan up the long hill to the count's castle and there they would wait until the following morning when the girl was released by the count. Zoltan was heartbroken as were his father and mother and Rosa's father and mother were shamed and could hardly look at each other, let alone the rest of the townspeople who gathered around in sympathy — in large measure to convince them that they were doing the right thing.

'Only Rosa kept to herself, walking in the woods near her home and keeping to her room where she refused to talk or eat. The path was clear and indisputable. She could, of course, refuse to go to satisfy the count's lust. After all, it had been her own fault. She had always been too clever for her own good, taunting the village elders and being outspoken on matters concerning the place of women in the home. Yes, she could refuse to go. She could simply pack her bags and flee. But if she were to, the suffering she would bring to her family, neighbours and to the entire village population along the river bank and in the valley would be incalculable. The count was omnipotent. His power couldn't be resisted. His will had to be obeyed.

'Rosa's mind considered all the possibilities until she had finally convinced herself that by closing her eyes and by allowing the count to take possession of her body just once, she would bring happiness and fulfilment to everybody who mattered to her. Not that she was particularly in love with Zoltan. He was just a means to an end. But her use as little more than an animal by the count to satisfy his lusts was something which she found difficult to bear. If only she hadn't been so insolent outside the church! If only she'd done what everybody else was doing, and averted her eyes from his gaze in deference at his magnificence. But Rosa wasn't like that. She never had been. She had looked at him, standing outside the church, knowing full well who he was. And she had felt angered that he was lording himself in superiority over her family and friends, and taking the focus of the day away from her and her betrothed.

'And so she must bear her punishment for her arrogance and intemperance. The following day she walked up the hills surrounding the valley until, like the priest the previous day, her father pulled the bell chain and Rosa was admitted. She kissed her father and Zoltan goodbye; they would sleep outside the castle walls until Rosa emerged, deflowered, the next morning.

'But as daylight came and the two men woke expectantly, the doors of the castle remained closed and by midmorning they pulled the bell chain in trepidation. A guard shouted at them from the top of the castle battlement to go away or they would be sent off the castle grounds by the dogs. The men were mystified and stayed, but their puzzlement turned to horror as the doors opened and twenty guardsmen came out, armed to the teeth, and at the point of spears, forced them down the road and away from the castle.

'Zoltan and Rosa's father ran away from the guards until they were well down the hill. Panting and sweating, they threw themselves into the grass to catch their breath. Zoltan sat up and propped himself against a tree, wiped the sweat from his brow and looked back at the castle. The soldiers had retreated inside and the castle's gates were firmly closed again. At that moment it dawned upon Zoltan's somewhat slow mind that Rosa would not be coming out that day or the one after that or the following. And he raised his face to the heavens and he shouted in anger and hatred, "He's keeping her for himself!"

'When the priest was told, his sorrow at the turn of events quickly turned to anger. From the description of what had happened earlier that morning he realised that his interference would only lead to his own arrest, and so, angry and determined, he assured both families that he would do everything in his power to get Rosa back. He borrowed a horse from a rich merchant who lived further up the river bank, demanding it in the name of God for the sake of a Christian soul, and rode the thirty-eight miles into Prague where he threw himself at the feet of the bishop, begged apology for disturbing his Lordship's afternoon, and told him the whole story.

'When the bishop was told the details of the abuse of this holy marriage, he was both amazed and horrified. He knew the count — a good Christian noble, a man who espoused the highest principles of learning and of the teachings of the Church. The bishop considered him a devout Catholic, one whose scholarship had led him to correspond with the finest brains and the most liberal thinkers of his day. Although the bishop was often worried about the direction of this liberal thought — he himself was opposed to many of the activities of Rome, most noticeably the selling of indulgencies as a way of ensuring everlasting peace — he had welcomed many interesting discussions with the young count. When his father died, it was the bishop who had blessed the young man, and sent him on his way out of Prague with a new copy of the Bible.

'Rising from his throne, the bishop walked to where the priest was kneeling and raised him, saying, "I will personally ride with you back to the castle and intervene on the part of this poor girl. Furthermore I will speak to the King of Prague and advise him to beg the count to release the girl back to her future husband and a Christian life."

'But when they started out two days later, the bishop had a heavy heart. "I've spoken to the king who informs me that both the count's father and now the count himself are amongst his most loyal allies. He further informs me that the count has the absolute right to dispose of this girl as he wishes and in that regard it is now up to us to invoke the moral weight of the Catholic Church against the dishonours perpetrated by this young man. The weight of my authority and office should suffice. Of that I'm sure."

'The following afternoon, the two men arrived at the village. The first thing that the priest did was to organise a special mass in honour of the visit of the bishop. People came from miles around when they heard that the bishop was in the village and the tiny church was overflowing with eager parishioners, hoping to catch sight of a man who had met the Pope in Rome, and so was closer to God than any other person in the country. The bishop was accommodated in the home of the rich merchant and the following day they rode to the castle walls where they were admitted with much panoply. The castellan bowed low and obsequiously as the bishop, dressed in his rich gold and turquoise vestments, walked majestically into the receiving salon where he waited for the count.

'After a few moments, the secretary, flustered and obviously uncomfortable, appeared and bowed low to the majesty of the bishop.

'"I deeply regret your Grace that my master is unwell and unable to receive you. I'm afraid your journey has been wasted."

'Now this would have sent the little priest from the village scurrying but not the bishop who was used to dealing with kings and princes and the artifice which went before them. "I shall stay in this house and pray for his recovery until he is out of bed and able to receive me in the manner to which a bishop of the universal Catholic Church is accustomed. Have rooms made ready for me and my brother priest, and we will begin the passage of prayer," the bishop announced.

'The secretary stood before the two priests, his face a mask of confusion. He bowed low and retired. An hour later, as they were eating refreshments, the count appeared. He was dressed in the finest silks of emerald and royal blue and gold, and he walked imperiously into the salon.

'"My lord," he said without bowing or kissing the bishop's ring, an unheard-of insult, even if it were perpetrated by a noble. Here was a man whose walk and stance and demeanour told them that he had turned away from the sight of God because of the lusts of the body. "I know why you are here and I have to tell you it's of no use. The woman is mine to dispose of as I will. I'll be keeping her. She will stay here."

'"Then," said the bishop, "you are in breach of God's law for preventing her marriage, and I will cause you to suffer as a result."

'"Why are your wasting your time over a mere woman?" asked the young count.

'"She is God's soul and the Almighty's to dispose of, not yours. I'm here to save her soul for all eternity and, I pray God, I'll save yours."

'"Forget my soul, priest," snarled the count. "My soul went the moment I set eyes on her as she entered the church. I've never known a love like it."

'The bishop was staggered by the audacity of the young man's words. "Is your love for her greater than your love for Christ?" he asked.

'But the count turned in anger and walked out, shouting at the flags on the ceiling, "Don't interfere in my business, priests!"'

Jack Roberts looked at Mr Dub who was squirming and sniffing and snorting in the front row. It was obvious that because he was talking about the Christian God, bishops and priests, the elderly Jews on the front row were distinctly uncomfortable. Obviously they found his subject not completely suitable for a lecture in a synagogue. He'd been warned about this by the rabbi, and undaunted he continued.

'The two priests were left alone in the salon. The village priest, his mood black, his disposition in despair, had no idea what to do. He waited while his bishop pondered the options. Their first option was that of excommunication, but that was the greatest and most awful sentence to pronounce, worse than death itself. It was the eternal damnation of the soul. The second was to acquiesce to the count's demands, and leave him and the girl to their fates. The girl would become a martyr and her soul would fly to Heaven, while the young count would have to take his own chances on the Day of Judgement. But as the bishop ate a sweetmeat, an idea came to him. He smiled, but decided not to confide in the village priest, who had shown himself to be something of a clod. He banged his crozier on the floor. A guard entered the room. "Tell the master secretary I wish to see him again."

'A few moments later, the secretary appeared. His face was still ashen with fear for the soul of his young master, for he knew that after his lord had insulted the bishop so sorely, the prelate must surely order his immediate excommunication. But the bishop asked the count's secretary, "Do you believe in the eternity of the soul?"

'"Of course," replied the secretary, a deeply religious man.

'"Then for the sake of your eternal soul, I wish you to be a witness to the marriage of the count to the girl Rosa."

'The secretary's jaw dropped as he heard the unthinkable words. "Marriage?" he said shrilly. "To the girl upstairs? But ... but ... she's a peasant woman. She has no station ... no lands ... no ..."

'"Will you do as I tell you or will I excommunicate you along with your master?" the bishop said forcefully.

'The secretary remained silent for a long time, his mind weighing up the pros and the cons. He could never disobey his lord and master. Nor could he do anything which would frustrate his wishes ... but the idea, the very notion of disobeying a lord bishop, a man touched by the Pope ... it was unthinkable ... absurd ... impossible. Reluctantly the secretary gulped and quietly acquiesced. "Of course I'll do as you command, Lord."

'"Then gather witnesses and we will walk towards the bedchamber where I will perform a marriage service joining forever the two young people."

'Now, if the secretary was bewildered by the bishop's manoeuvrings, then the village priest was stunned into incomprehension. Marriage? It was impossible. The house they were in was one of the most opulent and richest in all Bohemia. The count one of the most glorious nobles. Yet the girl, Rosa, was the spawn of farming folk, a peasant and impoverished.

'But within a few minutes, servants and guards had been gathered and placed in jeopardy of their immortal souls if they refused to accord to the bishop's wishes. So they walked behind the bishop and the priest who were following the castellan and the secretary, all of whom walked slowly and fearfully in a morbid procession, as if they were going to their execution. They walked down the hall and up the huge staircase to the bedchamber where the castellan knocked tentatively on the massive oak door.

'"Go away," shouted a voice from inside. But the bishop raised his crozier and banged heavily, the sound reverberating through the entire castle. "Go away or I'll have your heads," screamed the voice.

'The bishop stepped boldly forward and threw open the doors. There, in the centre of the large bedroom was an unkempt bed. Lying across it was the semi-naked figure of Rosa, her hair strewn, her face smeared with tears. Still draped in his finery, the young count stood at the window looking out over his estates. He turned in astonishment at the intrusion and when he saw the bishop and the gathered company, he lost control of his temper, and screamed, "Get out or I'll have your heads. All of you."

'The bishop said, "You may have no fear for your eternal soul, Bedrich, but these people answer to a higher authority than anything which you can imagine. They are protected by my See, and any recrimination against any of them will lead to your excommunication, and my imposition of an interdict over your lands and estates. You will forever be a non-person, unable to leave your home, unable to take your place in society, and spurned by the rest of the world."

'Count Bedrich looked at the bishop in astonishment. Pressing his advantage, he continued, "I'm here to marry you to the girl Rosa and even though you may object, Your Excellency, you can't stop the marriage service from proceeding. For despite your denials, this marriage will be made both in Heaven and in this bedchamber, it will be binding upon you forever and, until the day of this girl's death, you will be prevented from marrying any other. Furthermore, I will order that half your worldly property be given to this girl on the day of your death, which she may dispose of in any way that she wants. These are the consequences of your action, young man. Consequences which will not only see your lands cut in half but your eternal soul damned in purgatory. Now, Bedrich, before this company of Christians, and for the last time, will you give this girl up and return her to her betrothed?"

'The count's jaw sagged as the awful meaning of the bishop's words sank into his fevered brain. Though he was deeply in love with Rosa, she was a peasant without lands and income. Yet he, being young and the most eligible bachelor in the whole of Bohemia, anticipated marrying into a family of equal or greater wealth, perhaps even giving him the power one day to oppose the king for the crown of the country. But marriage to this girl, no matter how much he loved her, would preclude all of this and all of his plans for his future. He shouted, "You can't do this to me. I'll petition the Pope in Rome to overturn your actions."

'"You have no choice," shouted the bishop. "I will marry you and these people will be my witnesses. Unless you give this girl up."

'Now while the shouting and threats had been going on, Rosa had managed to stop crying and dried her eyes on the sheets. Being a very smart young woman, Rosa understood exactly what was happening and quickly started to weigh up the consequences in her mind. For the first time in the week that she had been held captive, she spoke without sobbing. "I think my marriage to the count is a good idea," she said to the amazement of the bishop. "He has had his way with me. I'm no longer a virgin. He keeps telling me he loves me. Let him now prove it. I think that marriage is right and proper. And I think it should happen immediately, Your Grace," she said addressing the bishop. "I'm ready. Please perform the marriage service now."

'"What!" screamed the count. "I'm not going to marry you."

'"But, you've been telling me all this time you loved me. You forced yourself upon me. In the name of God, you have to honour me and all you've said or you will be branded a liar."

'Fury took control of the count's actions. Suddenly he drew his sword from its scabbard and marched towards the bed. But the bishop was prepared and turned to the guards saying, "Although this is your master, you have a greater overlord in God Himself and through me, God commands you to resist the count or you will be damned into eternity."

'The captain of the guard looked at his men and shook his head. He feared crossing his master more than he feared God. But two of the men, both fervent Catholics, pushed through and with their halberds barred the count from approaching the bed. At that moment, Count Bedrich knew he was defeated and drew back. He knew that he couldn't fight the greater power which impelled his men.

'Softly, he said, "Let the girl go".

'The village priest smiled and mumbled a silent prayer of thanks. The bishop pushed through the press and walked towards the bed.

'"Oh no," said Rosa. "Wait! I don't know who you think I am. This man has taken my honour. Bishop, you said you were going to perform a marriage service. I now demand in the name of Christ that you perform it."

'"You can't demand, my child," said the bishop. "You have no rights. This is your lord and master. He has given you your freedom. That is enough. Now go."

'But Rosa gathered the bedsheets and pulled them to her throat. "I've been dishonoured. I've been treated like an animal. I demand that you carry out the marriage service."'

There was a murmur from the women in the back of the synagogue, who nodded in delight. Even Mr Dub and Mr Dayan, who found the constant reference to Catholicism objectionable in the synagogue, were waiting for the outcome. Nobody knew what was going to happen. Was she going to be married? Would she win? A pin could have dropped somewhere in the shul and people would have jumped in surprise.

Jack Roberts licked his lips and could hardly contain his smile. He cleared his throat for the denouement. 'In the count's bedchamber all was confusion. The girl adamantly refused to leave, and resisted attempts by the guards with screams which rent the peace of the castle. The priest and the bishop wanted her to return to marry Zoltan. And the count, who had once professed his undying love for her, now saw her as a hideous embarrassment and wanted her to leave his castle as soon as possible. Of course the count knew that all he had to do was to summon reinforcements and he could remove her by force but to do so would be to lose face in front of his servants. This needed to be performed with decorum. And so he went to the casket on his escritoire and opened it. From it he took three gold coins, more money than Rosa's family could earn from their farm in a year. And he threw it contemptuously on the bed, saying "Now go". Even the bishop smiled at the generosity and justice of the gesture.

'Rosa looked at the money, knowing its worth and looked back at the count. She gathered up the money in her hand, spat on it and threw it back at him. It clattered on the stone floor and she said bitterly, "You steal my honour and then you believe you can buy back your reputation. You treat me in the way that harlots are treated in Prague. You're not a man. You're an animal. It's not me that has been dishonoured. It's you."

'The count flushed red, but this time it was not with anger, but shame. In those few moments, he realised how different this girl was to the many women he had known in high and mighty society. And he now realised how badly he had treated her and how much he had let his animal lusts conquer his fine scholastic mind.

'The bishop and the priest, the castellan and the secretary, the captain of the guards and all the company held their breath at what was going to happen next.

'The count closed his eyes and mumbled a silent payer. Then he quietly said, "I've behaved in a way which is disreputable and wrong. I've sinned. If not against man's law, then against God's."

'He opened his eyes and looked at Rosa. "Since the moment I took you into my bed you cried as I forced myself upon you. Because of my carnal lusts, I have behaved in a way which is different from the way I have always behaved in the past.

'"Rosa, I now beg you to be my guest and to see me as I really am. I beg you to forgive me. I promise you I'll not touch you again until or unless you want me to. Stay with me for six months. I repeat my promise not to touch you in all that time, and if at the end of six months you still want to return to your home and to the man you were due to marry, then you are free to do so. If not, you are free to return now with these gold coins. If at the end of six months your opinion of me is changed for the good, then I shall make a gift to you and your future husband of double the land which he now farms. But if, at the end of six months, your opinion of me is unchanged, and you still consider me to be a dishonourable man, then I shall make a gift of one-quarter of my estate to the Church in penance."

'The priest frowned, not fully understanding what was happening, but the bishop knew. This young man had not only suddenly found humility but also the true nature of respect. Respect for God. Respect for humankind. Respect for himself. Knowing that the girl was safe, the bishop turned and ushered the company out of the bedchamber, closing the door behind him.

"'I don't understand,' said the priest. "Is she coming with us or not?'"

'The bishop shook his head. "Whatever happens, whether she comes now or next week or in six months or never, the choice will be hers. You see, the count was really in love with her and perhaps one day she will fall in love with him. Who knows what will happen during the six months. Maybe he will give up all his ambitions, and want to marry her. Then it truly will be a marriage made in Heaven.'"

Jack Roberts nodded to the congregation and walked down the steps of the bimah. Mr Dub and Mr Dayan looked at each other in surprise. Was that the end? The story didn't seem finished to them. And the ladies at the back were equally dissatisfied, because they wanted the gutsy young woman to win, get married, and end up a lady. They weren't exactly enamoured of Zoltan, who sounded a bit too boorish for their tastes. A murmur went up as Jack Roberts returned to his seat. There were a couple of desultory 'Amens', but all eyes now turned on the rabbi. And all he did was to shake Jack's hand and continue with the service ... very unsatisfactory.

All was not well during the week after Jack Roberts' story. There was a disquiet growing amongst certain members of the community, and that disquiet made itself known in a meeting called by the president of the shul, which was attended by Mr Dub and Mr Dayan. Interestingly, nobody else was there. Just two of the stalwarts. It was 10.30 in the morning, and Mr Dayan left his butcher shop in the care of one of his assistants and Mr Dub closed his workshop and walked to the shul. Both men were uncomfortable at the meeting because even though they were on the shul's board of governors, they didn't want what they were about to say to be taken as criticism of the rabbi for his innovations because everybody enjoyed what was happening, especially in regard to the increased attendance on a Friday night. The problem was that nobody knew where things were going and where they would end up.

The president of the synagogue began the meeting informally by saying that he had been called upon by Mr Dub who requested his presence in a debate with the rabbi, but that he had no knowledge of where the problem lay. Rather, he explained, he was there as an intermediary.

The rabbi turned to Mr Dub and also looked briefly at Mr Dayan. He could sense that both were uncomfortable and he felt very sorry for them. 'Do we have a problem?' he asked ingenuously.

'Problem is such a big word, Rabbi,' said Mr Dub. Mr Dayan continued to stroke his beard. 'Problem means anger and tension, and no, we don't have that. And let me say that I really enjoy the storytelling on Friday nights. I think it's wonderful. And the way the minyan is growing is just terrific.'

The rabbi nodded. 'So why are we here, if I may ask?'

Mr Dub breathed out, expelling his concerns. 'I'm not sure I know why we're here, Rabbi. All I know is that things aren't going quite right and I've tried to put my finger on it and I can't.'

The rabbi nodded. 'Maybe Mr Dayan . . . ?'

The butcher looked up and breathed in deeply, about to broach a difficult subject. 'Rabbi, you're a very wise man. You have many years of training. Mr Dub and I, we're not so wise.

We read. We watch television. And we're the first to admit that we don't understand all that much about what goes on. I'm happy in my butcher's shop. He's happy making furniture. And we're happy coming to shul. The problem is, Rabbi, these stories.'

'You don't like the stories?' asked the rabbi.

'No. No, we like them. The problem is we don't understand them.'

'You didn't understand the story about my grandfather?'

'That we understood,' interrupted Mr Dub. 'That was easy. And we understood Mrs Finburg's story about the tree and the furniture and things. And Dr Josephs' story about the hero and the kibbutz ...' Mr Dub laughed. 'You know, I've been thinking about that ever since he told it. And without wishing to sound immodest, I think everybody understood my story about my Sophie, though God knows, it's caused her some embarrassment because people are now talking to her about things she has never spoken of before.'

'Then what's your problem?' asked the rabbi.

'The problem is Roberts' story and Professor Rivkin's story. We just don't understand them. We understood the words but what did they mean?'

Now he had got to the bottom of it! The problem wasn't the storytelling as such, but was with the stories which were told as parables. And yes, one did need a certain degree of insight to appreciate the depth of meaning of the recent stories. And it was a problem because the simplistic stories with which they had begun didn't carry nearly the same moral weight as did the more recent ones. And if he had to admit it, nor were the original stories particularly memorable. Oh, they were nice and pleasant enough, but all they recounted were facts, details. But these later stories, now these were very different. These involved the very essence of humankind's relationship with God, with nature, with morality and with the very meaning of good and evil. These were sophisticated and delicate stories where the depth of meaning was hidden in the layers which the storytellers' wove in the delicate fabric of the tale.

'Please forgive me,' said Rabbi Teichmann, 'if I tell a little story which I think may help you understand the situation a little better. And believe me, this is a simple story. One day, a man was walking through a forest and he saw a target painted on a tree and an arrow which had been shot at the target which had hit the very centre of the bullseye. It was an extraordinary piece of marksmanship and the man wondered at the skill of the archer. He went on deeper into the forest and there he saw another target on a tree and yet another arrow, this one also in the very centre of the bullseye. And on and on, until he found four more targets, each with an arrow in its very centre.

'And then the wanderer saw a young man with a longbow and a quiver of arrows strapped to his back. He said to the archer, "If you're the man who shot the arrows at the targets, then you're to be congratulated. You're a wonderful marksman."

'Modestly the archer shrugged his shoulders and said, "I do my best."

'But the traveller would have none of it and said, "No. I won't accept that. You're a brilliant archer, probably the finest in this country. Tell me, how do you manage to be so accurate?"

'"It's not all that hard," said the archer. "I shoot the arrow into a tree and then I paint a target around it."'

Both men burst out laughing. 'Do you see what I'm getting at?' asked Rabbi Teichmann. But both shook their heads and admitted that they didn't understand. 'According to one of our most famous teachers many years ago who told that story, he said that the world is divided into two kinds of people who try to teach a lesson. Some find a suitable parable to explain their point whereas others believe that every incident in life is a parable and the only question which matters is what lesson can be learnt from it. My advice to you two, if you will permit me, is to listen to the stories and to extract from them whatever pleasure you get. If you listen at the level of a narration, a simple story, so be it. But if you see things which are deeper, then consider yourselves fortunate.'

Mr Dub and Mr Dayan left the meeting and as they walked back to their businesses, Mr Dub said to Mr Dayan, 'Did you understand what he was talking about?'

Mr Dayan stroked his beard and said, 'Not a word'.

MR GRUZMANN'S STORY
ABOUT THE NATURE
OF GOOD AND EVIL

It was late on Wednesday night when Rabbi Teichmann finally decided to ask Mr Gruzmann to tell his story. The rabbi had read a brief synopsis and believed that it was eminently suitable. All his life he had dealt with the nature of good and evil and he was keen to hear the story which would be an expansion of Mr Gruzmann's brief account. Of course, Mr Gruzmann's story wasn't the only synopsis the rabbi received during the week. In fact, his 'Suggestion Box' now outweighed his usual mail by a factor of five to one, but most of the suggestions were unsuitable.

Unsuitable? Not in the usual way. There was nothing about the stories which would offend any of the congregation. But most related to incidents which were highly personal, such as events which happened to a particular family when they first migrated; or stories which were too serious and carried no metaphor or message in the tale. The rabbi rejected some witty little parodies which one of the ladies wanted to tell, as well as melodramatic Victorian tales of Gothic intrigue which, however interesting, would have appeared difficult and mannered and hardly the stuff for a Friday-night synagogue service. He had also rejected a joke-telling session which one of the young bar mitzvah students insisted was both tasteful and appropriate.

And all the time, he had in mind the problem espoused by Mr Dub and Mr Dayan earlier that week. Were these stories becoming too difficult? Too arcane? In some way removed and distant from the very meaning of their religion, the reason for them gathering on a Friday night and a Saturday morning? Judaism and its liturgy, as well as the many commentaries which surrounded and expounded on the Talmud, were replete with hidden meanings and messages which were studied every day by learned rabbis, wise in the field of hermeneutics. Yet when you got down to it, the stories which were being told each Friday night were simple, pleasing substitutes for the dreary and enervating sermons which, after a lifetime of sermon-making, were almost all that the rabbi could dredge up from his bank of knowledge and experience. Not only were the stories which his congregants told entertaining, but they were also introducing an alternative strong moral code. And this is precisely what Mr Gruzmann's story promised to do.

Mr Gruzmann only ever came to the synagogue when he was saying memorial prayers for close relatives or on the traditional two days of Rosh Hashanah and the one day of Yom Kippur. The rabbi had no idea what he did for a profession; but that didn't matter. The story synopsis he had written was compelling and the rabbi hoped that his tale would meet the standards.

Within minutes of Mr Gruzmann beginning his story on the following Friday night, the rabbi again felt himself smiling and rejoicing in another God-given miracle. Short and pudgy with feminine hands and a high-pitched voice, Mr Gruzmann was a lawyer who specialised in the sale of commercial and domestic property and also did minor criminal matters to pay the overheads.

But this wasn't Mr Gruzmann's first choice of legal practice. Rather, it was what he had fallen into by default, precisely because God had given him a high-pitched voice, and somewhat feminine mannerisms, the very antithesis of what a court advocate needed if he was to be taken seriously.

Mr Gruzmann had always wanted to represent people in a court of law, the closest thing to theatre which his overweening parents would allow him to contemplate. He would fantasise about being an advocate, standing up in a court of law and eloquently defending the indefensible, or using his persuasive powers to show a jury that the supposed innocent in the dock had a dark and evil heart. But it was not to be. All Mr Gruzmann ever seemed to handle on the few occasions that he went to court were matters concerning clients who had unresolved disputes about the borders of their properties.

Standing in front of the congregation on Friday night was only the third time in the last two years that he had performed the function which he loved most, that of addressing a captive audience. On one occasion eight months earlier, he had appeared in court to defend the son of one of his major property-developing clients who had been charged with the possession of drugs. His speech to the jury would have made Cicero proud, but unfortunately the young man was found guilty and given a hefty fine. The second occasion that Mr Gruzmann addressed an audience was to a local council on behalf of a group of residents who objected to the erection in their local area of a large hotel complex. For some reason, the council voted in favour of the developer.

But this time, as he stood before the synagogue congregation, he had no such fears of winning or losing because it was not an adversarial situation. (What he didn't know was the mood which had overtaken Mr Dub and Mr Dayan as they sat in the front row, anticipating with some concern yet another speech full of complexities which they would find hard to comprehend. And what Mr Gruzmann never suspected was that Mr Dub and Mr Dayan were determined to tut loudly on those occasions when his speech didn't follow the lines which they considered a good story should.)

'My tale,' began Mr Gruzmann, 'begins with the deeds of a philanthropist. Now this man was beloved by all who knew him. He was aged in his mid-fifties, and every year, he donated huge amounts of money from investments that his parents and grandparents had made during their lifetimes. The family ran a business providing the world's very best marble to the sculptors of the Renaissance who were flourishing in the courts of Milan, Florence, Rome, Padua and Venice. And for centuries, the family of Master Joseph, for that was the philanthropist's name, had enjoyed the right to trade in the world's very finest and purest marble from local quarries which they owned. Wherever he travelled throughout Europe, Master Joseph was welcomed into the most sumptuous palaces where he took delight in seeing the most exquisite statues made from the whitest marble, from the very deepest levels of his quarry. And more, for because of his wealth and reputation, other quarries had made the decision to sell their stone through the agency which Master Joseph had established to bring order to the burgeoning trade. Every year, as the beauty of the marble in which Master Joseph dealt became more famous, so his wealth continued to increase.

'Now this man, whilst certainly not living in a way which could in any sense be described as modest, by a similar token didn't live in such an ostentatious way that he gained a reputation for luxury and indolence. He had a beautiful mansion in the best part of town, many animals and enough servants to look after the needs of him, his wife and their children. With what Master Joseph earned during the year, he could afford his own ducal palace, but much of his money, at least two-thirds, was given to benefit the poor, the sick, widows and orphans. In fact, had it not been for his generosity, the amount of suffering in his city would have increased a hundredfold.

'Now some of us give to charity because of our need for recognition or our feelings of guilt. But these weren't the reasons why Master Joseph gave away much of his fortune every year, for one of the stipulations of his donations was that his name was never to be divulged. Over the years, however, it became known that this merchant was a philanthropist who was supporting many different almshouses, orphanages and hospitals in the region, and the townsfolk would look admiringly at him as he walked to church, or attended a civic reception.

'Now one of the orphans in the care of an orphanage which Master Joseph supported was a boy of twelve whose name was Caleb. Whenever Joseph visited the orphanage, he took a special interest in Caleb. He stroked his head, kissed him on the forehead and surreptitiously slipped a coin into his hand as he left. Caleb looked forward with great anticipation to Joseph's visits, for they were the only contact which he ever had with an adult which wasn't harsh and aggressive, or where he wasn't shouted at and abused.

'Being touched kindly by an adult was a novel experience for the young orphan. It was a blessed relief from the dark and drudging monotony and oppressive life in an orphanage. Caleb began to look upon Joseph as the father he had never known.

'The superintendent of the orphanage recognised what was going on and wrote a letter to Joseph informing him that because the boy was twelve on his next birthday, he would be turned out of the orphanage to make room for those less fortunate and would have to make his own way in the world. Knowing the generosity of Joseph and his family, the superintendent wondered if Joseph could find it in his heart to create a place for Caleb in his household or to recommend him to a wealthy friend. "Caleb," wrote the superintendent, "is an honest, moral, hardworking and loyal boy."

'When Joseph read the letter he immediately sent word for Caleb to be brought to his home where he and his wife greeted him and put him to work in the stables. Caleb worked hard and prospered and was treated in exactly the same way as the other servants. He was given good food, plenty of nourishment, warm clothes and bedding in winter, and clean straw every third day upon which to sleep. Conditions which in those days would have been considered a paradise on earth for a servant.

'And so the years went by until Caleb was sixteen and the master needed to take a journey from his home to conduct business in a faraway land. That very night, Joseph's personal servant fell ill and was put to bed with a strong draft of medicine after the physician had bled him with leeches.'

Suddenly, Mr Gruzmann looked up in surprise at the congregation. Most of the large number in the overflowing synagogue were listening in rapt attention but he was certain that he had heard a loud tutting noise coming from nearby. No. It couldn't be. Not possible. He must have been mistaken. He resumed his story.

'And so Joseph's wife suggested that as he needed a strong young man to carry his cases and to look after the horses when the carriage drew up to an inn, perhaps he should take Caleb. Joseph nodded in agreement but made a special journey into the servant's quarters to explain to the exhausted old retainer that his position was perfectly safe. The old servant smiled, laid his hand on his master's arm and blessed him for his consideration.

'And so the two of them started out on their journey. Caleb had never been beyond the city limits before and he hung on tight while the coachman negotiated the rough and rutted roads. From the roof of the carriage he could see the purple hills and down into the verdant valleys and, in the distance, sparkling rivers flowing swiftly to the sea. He smelt the air. It was much like the master's wine — clean, clear and crisp. He realised just how limited his life was, and how very lucky he was to be in his master's service.

'Having concluded his business three weeks later, the master and Caleb returned home. Both were exhausted from the long journey, the frequent stops and the noise and the bustle of the inns in which they stayed. Unlike the master who remained in bed for a day sleeping and then quietly reading books in his library, Caleb had to return to work immediately. But he had youth on his side and spent the day excitedly telling the other stablehands of the wonders that he had seen and the many towns they had passed through.

'And so the years continued to go by and eventually Caleb replaced the butler as the master's retainer, accompanying his master wherever he went, and the more he knew of Joseph, the more he loved the man. For here was a man of goodness and generosity, a man whose example shone in an otherwise dark world. And to celebrate his new status, the master bought Caleb suitable new clothes for his position as a personal servant to one of the richest and most prosperous men in the country. Caleb no longer slept in the stables but now enjoyed a room of his own in the house, with a bed, a soft mattress, a pillow and sheets which were washed every month by one of the low-ranking female servants. At night he would lie in bed and stare up at the ceiling, wondering how fortune had smiled so sweetly on a boy who was orphaned almost since birth. And so life continued with Master Joseph giving his esquire Caleb authority in the house over his personal matters.

'But a dark cloud crossed the sun one awful day which brought the pleasures of Caleb's existence to an abrupt halt. For on this awful day, when the master was at the quarry supervising the cutting of a particularly important block of marble for one of the brilliant sculptors who lived in Urbino in Italy, Caleb had reason to go into the master's private bedchamber to find papers which related to the purchase of a painting from a young and aspiring artist. The document, said the master's wife, was somewhere amongst Joseph's papers in his study desk, but search as he might, Caleb was unable to find it. And so he took out the drawers to see if inadvertently it had fallen behind them into the well of the desk.

'It was the third drawer down which was the undoing of Caleb's life. For there on the underside of the drawer, completely hidden from view, was a square of parchment. It was obviously secreted so that it would never be found and Caleb at first was loathe to remove it from the clamps which secured it, but curiosity overcame him. When he read the document, his blood froze and he felt his breath being sucked out of his body.

'He sat on his master's bed with a bump, refusing to believe what he had just read. Then he returned the drawers and their contents to the position they had been in before he had searched the desk and, ashen-faced, went downstairs to tell the artist that the document was nowhere to be found and to return the following day for his money.

'The master's wife looked at Caleb in surprise, and asked him if he was all right. She told him he looked as if he had seen a ghost. Caleb shook his head and assured her that he was well. He busied himself for several hours during the day, but unable to believe the evidence of his eyes any longer, he returned to his master's room, locked the door behind him, pulled out the third drawer of the desk and reread the document.

'Much of it he didn't understand because the education which the master had paid for only enabled him to read and write in a crude and elementary way. But he understood its gist. He read again the awful words . . .

Whereas Joseph Steinholtz, merchant, was witnessed by me Frederick Hummell, tavern owner, to have murdered in a fit of uncontrollable and drunken rage two young travellers of no fixed abode, who happened upon my inn last night. And whereas I assisted said Master Joseph Steinholtz in the burying of these two young men, so I hereby promise upon the Holy Bible and swear into eternity that I will keep my mouth shut and never say a word upon payment of five hundred thalers. An oath which I take knowing that in the event of my breach of said oath, I too will be arrested for aiding and abetting said crime.

'At this point there were two scrawled signatures, one he recognised as the youthful hand of his master, the other he presumed belonged to the complicit publican. The words on the ancient parchment swam in front of his eyes as Caleb realised that he was crying. He folded up the parchment, returned it and left the master's bedchamber. He went to his room and lay down, trying to control his breathing and rationalise what he had read. He couldn't doubt the document's authenticity but it failed to accord in any way with the man he had known all these years as the kindest, most generous and most loving man who had ever been born. How could a man who devoted his life to relieving the suffering of others have killed two innocent travellers in cold blood? How could he have so mechanically assisted in the burying of their bodies and hidden his crime against humanity for all these years? Didn't he even consider the constant grief which he had occasioned to their mothers and fathers?

'Try as he might, Caleb could not ignore the evidence he had uncovered. For now there were two grief-stricken voices, voices crying in his mind and disturbing his peace; the voices of two young people, two travellers who had met a vicious and bloody end. And beyond these travellers, there were the voices raised in anguish from their parents and brothers and sisters and aunts and uncles and friends who had not heard from them in thirty years and who to this day must still be wondering what had become of them.

'But who could Caleb turn to? Certainly not the priest who loved Master Joseph almost as much as he himself. Certainly not the mistress who would laugh in his face and refuse to believe a word. Caleb realised the only man he could possibly discuss his problem with was Joseph himself, which was the course he decided upon.

'An hour later, Caleb heard his master's horse clacking on the cobblestones below. He knew he should run down and greet his master, take his saddlebags and his portfolio case, and assist him with his boots. He knew he should bring his master refreshment and do what was expected from the equerry and servant to such a rich and famous man. But a huge force crushing his chest refused to allow him to get up from the bed. Ten minutes later, there were shouts throughout the house, "Caleb! You useless mongrel. Come down here and see to me." Normally Caleb would have delighted in the banter, in the mock rage which his master used to feign, just to keep him on his toes. But now he knew he would be sick to the stomach if he went to see his master.

'And so he stayed where he was. A few minutes later, there was another shout. "Caleb, are you all right?"

'Silence, and then the sound of footsteps through the marble hall, up the oak stairs, along the passageway to his room where there was a respectful knock and his master's voice saying, "Caleb, are you ill?"

'When he received no reply, Master Joseph tentatively opened the door and peered in suspiciously. "What's the matter, old friend? Are you ill?"

'Tears rolled down Caleb's eyes and when the master saw them, he walked over to the bed and picked up Caleb's hand. "For God's sake, what's the matter, Caleb? Let me help you. Do you need a doctor, an apothecary? Can you speak?"

'In a husky voice, Caleb said, "I'm very distressed. I beg you to forgive me and leave me alone. Please allow me to remain here in bed until the morning when I hope to feel better. If you love me, you will do this."

'"I do love you. I love you as I love any of my servants. And for this reason, I'll not leave you until you tell me what's wrong. If you're weighed down by a care or a burden then you must share it with me."

'But Caleb shook his head. "You're the only man I can share it with but you're the only man I can't share it with."

'Joseph frowned. "Shall I summon the priest? He will speak quietly with you. You can open your heart to him."

'"No," said Caleb. Joseph bent down and put his arm behind the young man's neck and lifted him into a sitting position. He kissed him on the forehead as he had kissed him many times before when he was a child in the orphanage. "Caleb, unburden your heart to me. You know you can trust me in all things. Is your grief because you have done something to one of the servants? Or to a woman of the town? I'm a man of the world. I understand these things."

"'No,' said Caleb, somewhat more forthrightly than he wished.

"'Is it money? Have you made a wager? Do you owe people a debt? You know I'll help you whatever it is."

"'If only it was that simple,' said Caleb.

"'For God's sake,' said Joseph. 'You're beginning to frighten me. You're a soul in torment and I can't help you unless you unburden yourself to me."

'Caleb thought for a moment. "What if you truly loved somebody, loved them with all your heart, and then you found out something about them which was so terrible, so awful that ... that ... "

"'Is this person a good or a bad person?' asked the master, having no idea what Caleb was talking about, for the incident which was fresh in Caleb's mind had been muted and forgotten these past thirty years by his master. However it had dominated his mind in the past, today it was dulled into oblivion by a lifetime of charity and good works.

'Caleb responded quickly. "He's the best person I have ever known. Yet his deed is the worst deed I have ever known."

"'If the deed is so bad,' said the master, "then I don't see how it can be ignored. A sin is a sin and must be expiated."

'Caleb nodded slowly, put his arms around his master's neck and kissed him on both cheeks. "I must leave your service, Master. I must leave now. I must never return. But I will always love you and be eternally grateful for what you've made of me and for what I have become."

'And to Joseph's surprise, Caleb stood and walked out of the house without bothering to pack his few meagre possessions and disappeared onto the road which led to the north of the country. Joseph was so stunned that he sat on Caleb's bed for more than an hour trying to make sense of the unimaginable.

'His mind was reeling. He knew all of the people in the household whom Caleb considered to be his friends and associates, and Joseph knew that the young man had almost no society outside of the house. Was it Joseph's wife? Could she have done something, said something? Or maybe one of his own children? Maybe they had been picking on Caleb because he was an orphan. But no, it couldn't be. They were such good and noble children and they were kind to Caleb because he was an orphan. So what could possibly have happened to affect the happy boy that Joseph had left that morning to turn him into a young man chased by spectres and nightmares in the afternoon?

'Joseph thought back to the words that Caleb had used and went over the question the young man had asked, time and time again. And a nagging doubt began to surface. A thought so horrible, so terrifying that Joseph at first refused to believe it. A nightmare of his past that he had managed to expunge had come back to revisit him. He raised himself from Caleb's bed, slowly on shaken legs, and walked to the other side of the house where he entered his suite of rooms, went into his bedchamber and looked at his desk drawer. He couldn't even remember beneath which drawer he had placed the document ... something which he hadn't dared to look at in more than thirty years. Was it the second drawer? The fourth? He pulled each one out and turned them over, and there taunting and mocking him across the ages was the contract he had signed so many years ago with the long-dead innkeeper, the only man to have witnessed his drunken rage.

'It had been very late at night and the inn was empty, save for the innkeeper, the two young men and himself. He had been drinking all night, exhausted after a day slaving in the quarry. His hair was still covered in quarry dust, and he could see the way in which the young men were mocking him beneath their voices. And so he'd picked a quarrel. All of them had had too much to drink.

'In only the most distant and vague way could Master Joseph remember any of the details of the quarrel. He seemed to remember that the young men were students and attended a distant university. For some reason, they were travelling through the region to visit a great professor in Moscow, and they treated the locals as clods and dolts. That much Joseph could remember. The young men were horribly arrogant in their intellect. All the other men in the inn had ignored them and then drifted home to their loved ones. Only Joseph had stayed on, intent on arguing some arcane philosophical point to prove that even though he had dirt ingrained in his hands, he was a match for their brains. He wanted them to know that just because his father insisted he learn the stone masonry business by working with the stone-cutters in the quarry didn't mean he was an uneducated man.

'But the debate got out of hand, and with his superior strength, Joseph rose from his seat with a howl of anger, and crushed the necks of the two young men. He remembered his joy as their arrogant faces turned blue in fear at his might. He remembered screaming into their dying ears, "Well, who's better now, you or me?" And most of all, to his everlasting shame, he remembered laughing and shouting and spitting in their faces as their young lives expired. And as they lay on the filthy floor, the innkeeper re-entered to tell the young people to go home, and saw what had happened.

'Knowing who Joseph was, he assured him that he would take care of everything. Nobody knew the young students were there, and the townspeople would assume that they had walked on to the next village. The innkeeper said that he would help Joseph bury them in the woods, but for his trouble, he would need compensation. So Joseph was forced to steal five hundred thalers from his father's bureau and pay it to the publican.

'When his father discovered the theft, Joseph blamed a young stablehand, an orphan boy whom the publican identified as a young man spending money wildly the previous night. The orphan stableboy was found guilty on Joseph's evidence and was hanged within a week by the local magistrate. Joseph's father's money was never recovered.

'And so for over thirty years, Joseph was burdened by overwhelming guilt, and in order to expiate it, and live a normal life, he had performed deeds of goodness and charity for the entire community.

'But had Caleb seen the document? Yes, he had. For just by its position, by the difference in colour between where the clamp held it now and where the clamp had held it untouched for decades, Joseph knew that Caleb had seen the horrible truth.

'Why, oh why, hadn't he thrown the document away when he heard of the innkeeper's death twenty years before? It was an oversight, an act of stupidity and now it was his undoing.

'Joseph returned to his outer chamber and sat before the fire, his face white as a ghost, staring into a dismal future of exposure, ridicule, punishment and extinction.

'That night, Joseph hardly slept at all. His wife sensed her husband tossing and turning in the bed and lit a candle. In the gloom, she asked him what was wrong but all he did was to tell her to return to sleep, the worries were his, not hers. Of course, this robbed her of any sleep and the following morning the husband and wife raised themselves from the bed as the sun rose over the horizon and descended the stairs to the surprise of the servants who had not yet lit fires nor prepared any food. Unshaven, and with an empty stomach and heavy heart, Master Joseph mounted his horse and did what he knew he must. He rode towards the home of the shire reeve.

'The shire reeve was surprised to see so rich and important a man on his doorstep so early in the morning in such a state of dishevelment.

'"Forgive me, dear friend, for disturbing your morning," said Master Joseph. "But it is my unpleasant duty to report to you a theft from my household." The reeve's demeanour altered immediately and he invited the merchant in to sit at a desk and report the crime in an official way. "I have a servant whom you must have seen me with."

'"Yes," said the reeve. "Caleb. I know him well. Don't tell me . . ."

'Master Joseph nodded. "I took the boy from an orphanage and raised him in status to be the most trusted and senior of all my servants. For years, he was honest, faithful and decent. But yesterday . . ." Joseph stopped talking and stared through the window at the buildings opposite. Beads of perspiration appeared on his forehead and his eyes misted over. Knowing his reputation as a philanthropist, the reeve knew how incredibly hard it must be for him to report the dishonesty of someone whom he had trusted so much.

'"Concentrate on what happened, Your Honour," said the reeve. "You will find it easier."

'Joseph swallowed hard and nodded. "I went to my business in the nearby quarry where I stayed the whole day. When I returned I found that a golden crucifix, worth a great deal of money, was missing. Naturally I searched the house and asked my staff and family but all they could report was that it was there when I left for the quarry and that during the day Caleb was seen carrying it and at night, when I returned, he was gone. I searched the town for him yesterday, hoping to relieve him of it and his sin, but he has escaped and is nowhere to be seen. I am reliably informed that he was last seen on the north road."

"'Don't worry,' said the shire reeve. "I'll send a message to the next town to be on the lookout for this young man and to have him arrested. First and foremost, we have to get your property back for you and then we have to deal with the miscreant. For a crime of this magnitude, I'm afraid, he will be hanged."

'Joseph nodded sadly and left the house. As he walked back to his own mansion, he mused on the action he had taken. In all his life, he had committed four great sins. The first two were committed when he was a youthful boy and in a fit of anger, sins for which he had repented the rest of his life. The third had been deflecting the blame from himself when his father discovered the missing money, and watching an orphan boy be hanged for a crime of which he was completely innocent. But the fourth sin, the greatest of all, was something which had been forced upon him. For the whole night, Joseph had tossed and turned, weighing up the possibilities and realities. The course he most favoured was that of going to the shire reeve and the city burghers, admitting his crime, expiating his overwhelming guilt, and suffering the punishment ordained by the law and by God; for without any doubt, he would be tried before a judge, found guilty when the boys' bodies were exhumed and hanged like a common footpad.

'Yes, that was the easiest and most favoured option but it was one that he knew he couldn't take, because upon the moment of his death as a murderer, all his property would be sequestered to the state. His family could be destitute and all the money, the vast hoards of gold and silver which he earnt every year and much of which he spent upon the upkeep of orphans, the sick and the poor, would go into the coffers of the king and everybody would suffer. His family would curse his name to their graves and, without his ongoing support, the condition of the destitute would become infinitely worse.

'But in order to prevent this, Caleb had to be silenced. And to do so Joseph must of necessity commit the greatest crime of his life. For the murder of the two young men was a momentary lapse of his good nature, the giving in to a dark and evil force which is buried within us all. Even the hanging of the boy for theft had been dulled in his mind.

'But the judicial murder of Caleb was a cold, evil and calculated act for which there would be no redemption and for which God would punish him for all eternity.

'As soon as he dragged himself back home, Joseph's heart grew heavier and heavier from his sin. His groom ran across the courtyard to greet him, but Joseph fell off the horse, and staggered into the house.

'In the house, Joseph crawled up the stairs to his room where he took off his clothes, shaved his head, and went to the fire where the ashes of the previous night were now laying cold. He poured oil from the lamp onto the fire and then, gathering up a handful of the sodden ash, wiped it into his head and over his face. He made the sign of the cross in filthy oily ash over his body. Then naked, cold and suffering, he lay face down on the floor of his room, arms outstretched like the crucified Christ, tears rolling down his cheeks, and howled like a wounded animal.

'In trepidation, his wife and servants ran into his bedchamber to see what was the matter. And when they saw the spectre on the floor, they drew back, crossed themselves and fell on their knees to pray. No matter what they said, or how much they entreated, nothing could be done to make Master Joseph rise up out of the position which he had taken. A priest was called, who read various benedictions, then he sent the people out of the room, and begged the tormented man to make confession. But all to no avail. Nothing, short of force, could make Joseph rise up and resume a normal life.

'For that day, and for the day following, Master Joseph didn't move a muscle. He stayed on the floor, naked, annointed with oil and ashes. By the following night, his wife was beside herself with fear for her husband. She knew it involved Caleb and his sudden disappearance, but she had no idea how. All she could suspect was the worst — that something had happened between the two of them, which had brought about this present terrible situation.

'On the third day, Master Joseph rose slowly and unsteadily onto his legs, and slumped down on the bed. Weakly he gave orders that under no circumstances was he to be disturbed. And so it was for that day, and for the next.

'A week after Caleb's disappearance, a message came for Master Joseph. He had hardly been seen all week, and the food which was delivered up to his bedroom had been returned hardly touched, a morsel taken here and a taste experienced there. Not even his wife was permitted into his room and when the servants surreptitiously climbed a ladder outside his window to see whether he was still alive, his emaciated body, blue with cold, could be seen, hunched and kneeling before the crucifix on the wall as he spent the entire day praying.

'His wife knocked on the door, her voice close to tears. "Joseph," she shouted. "A message has come from the shire reeve. I'm going to push it under your door. He says it's urgent and you must read it."

'She pushed it under the door, leaving a corner exposed so she could see whether it had been taken. Five minutes, ten, twenty and a whole hour went by as she sat there waiting for the message to be taken, and eventually, slowly, it was pulled from under the door. And a howl of agony rose to the ceiling and circulated around the house.

'Joseph's wife was terrified and near desperation. She knew her husband was in extreme agony for reasons which she couldn't understand. She had called the priests, the mayor, counsellors, burghers and people who had been their lifelong friends but nobody had been able to coax him from the room. Now, with the delivery of this message, enough was enough. Now his grief must come to an end or he himself would waste away and die.

'So she went to the shire reeve and explained what was happening in her home. She demanded to know what had transpired between her husband and the reeve which had caused this reaction. At first, the reeve was loathe to tell her because he knew that women should never be involved in the business of men but because of her deep and abiding concern for the welfare of her husband, he decided to give scanty details.

'He told her of her husband's call the previous week, and his distress at reporting Caleb's crime. He told her that he had sent messages out and Caleb had been caught four days' journey away, dining in an inn. The boy had come quietly with the local reeve, saying nothing, admitting nothing. The crucifix had not been found but the culprit was now on his way back to face sentence in the courts.

'When she had heard the full story, she understood perfectly why her husband was so distraught. He had loved Caleb and his grief was not for some crucifix but for the fate which Caleb would suffer. But she was amazed that somebody like Caleb, who had shown such love and devotion to her husband and family, should have been tempted to steal the crucifix. Whenever the boy had wanted money, Joseph had always given it to him. He was always well-dressed and never short of silver coins in his purse. Perhaps he had been tempted by the crucifix, but for the life of her, she couldn't think which crucifix had been stolen.

'The following day word had spread through the town that the man whom the blessed Master Joseph had taken from an orphanage and made into someone like a son, had been brought back in chains having stolen from his master. As the townspeople gathered on the road to look at him as he passed, some picked up clods of earth and threw them at him, some spat, some waved sticks at him, some cried out and asked how he could steal from a man who was so good. But the young man remained stoically quiet, not saying a word in his own defence. Even when he was brought into the town's cellars and thrown into a cell, he remained quiet.

'The following day he was brought before the chief burgher who acted as magistrate. There the charge was outlined before him and he was arraigned.

'"Do you plead guilty or innocent of this charge of theft and absconding from your master's home without leave?"

'The boy shook his head sadly and stared down.

'The magistrate, fat, ruddy and pompous, wearing a fur coat and a fur hat, banged his gavel onto the desk. "Your silence will be taken as an admission of guilt. Tomorrow the court advocate appointed on your behalf will plead for your life, and when I have heard his plea, I will then sentence you to death, and may God have mercy on your wretched soul, you ungrateful fellow."

'Caleb was taken back to the cell where he ate the meagre scraps on the plate. It was the first food he had had in a day. In the time since he had been arrested and brought back in chains, constantly falling on the rutted road as the shire reeve's horse to which he was tethered pulled him inexorably onwards to his fate, Caleb had not said one single word.

'Now you may think it odd that he didn't declare his innocence. But the love which he held for his master had not diminished and he wouldn't say a word which would incriminate a man so good and decent as Joseph, even though he had committed a terrible sin. And now, to add to his sins, Joseph had borne false witness, breaking one of God's commandments, adding to the burden of his already heavy soul. But Caleb knew that he would go to his death not slandering a man who had done so much for so many years for so many people.

'The chief burgher and magistrate left the court and rode on his imperious horse to Master Joseph's house where a servant showed him into the library. At long last, and after a week of solitude, fasting and praying, Joseph emerged from his room in order to find out the fate of his one-time servant. The philanthropist's face was thin and emaciated and drawn. His cheeks rough and unshaven, his eyes hollow and red from lack of sleep, his clothes stained and dirty, but no matter how much his wife and servants begged him to wash, shave and change for the visit of the chief magistrate, Joseph refused. Instead, in a weak state and supported by a servant, he shuffled into his library.

'The chief magistrate who had heard that Joseph was grief-stricken, was taken aback by the change which had overcome the prosperous and elegant man. Before him, the chief magistrate beheld a starving street beggar.

'"My God, Joseph. I had no idea you were suffering so."

'In a dry and cracked voice, Joseph asked, "What did he say?"'

'The magistrate pulled himself together. "Nothing. The boy was arrogant and offensive. He neither admitted the crime nor did he attempt to defend his dishonesty. Naturally I found him guilty and have sentenced him to death. Although the law demands that I hear mitigation from his lawyer, the sentence will be carried out tomorrow."

'Joseph held up a skeletal hand. "No! Don't. You must not. I'm wrong. I made a mistake. He didn't steal the crucifix. It was me. I'm guilty."

'The judge immediately realised what was going on. "Dear friend," he said. "You can continue to protect the unfortunate innocents as you've been doing all your life, but don't waste your time or your good works on somebody who bites the hand that feeds him. This boy isn't worthy of your support."

'"No!" said Joseph weakly. "Please. It was me. Let him be. Free him. Release him."

'But the magistrate walked over and with his gloved hand, stroked the filthy hair of his old friend. "Joseph, get a good sleep. Then wash yourself, eat and in a few days you will realise why the sentence must be carried out."

'Joseph was too weak to contradict any further but collapsed on the floor crying. The magistrate snapped at his servants. "Take your master upstairs, and bathe him. Feed him and put him to bed. Call an apothecary to give him a sleeping draft if necessary but whatever happens, see to him. I shall hold you responsible if his condition worsens." And he stormed out of the house, furious that a man of Joseph's goodness was brought so low by such a rogue as Caleb.

'The apothecary who was summoned forced a small vial of liquid over Joseph's cracked tongue. Servants brought up towels and forcibly washed him as he lay on the floor. His wife and manservant unbuttoned and threw into the fires in the basement kitchen the clothes he had been wearing since the day he had seen the shire reeve; and they put him to bed, surrounded by clean white sheets and soft pillows.

'The draft quickly made him lose his grip on consciousness and Master Joseph sank into the deepest and heaviest slumber of his entire life. He slept for two days and as the cock crowed on the third morning after the apothecary had been, Joseph opened his eyes, licked his lips and looked around him. He was ravenously hungry and desperately thirsty. He drank from the flask by his bedside and tried to get out of bed but he was too weak.

Feeling her husband's movements his wife woke up and put him back onto his pillow, like she used to look after her children. "Lay there my darling," she said, "and I'll get the servants to bring you some broth. You need something in your stomach."

"'Caleb?" he croaked. "Caleb?" but his wife shook her head. "Don't worry about him. He is in the past. Now you must regain your strength if you are to continue with the good works which you have always done. Your family, your servants, your friends, have missed you."

'She got up and threw a robe around her and as she walked out of the door, he tried to shout, "Caleb?" but she had gone. The servants returned with her, carrying a small tureen of broth. It was salty and thin but it tasted like the very manna which God gave to the children of Israel as they starved in the desert. When he had drunk his fill, Joseph lay back on his pillow, closed his eyes and drifted again into blissful sleep. He woke in the middle of the day as the sounds of the household increased. And as he woke, he felt stronger and better than he had felt in many days.

'On shaky legs, he threw a robe over his shoulders and walked unsteadily out of his room, slowly down the stairs and into his library. There a servant was arranging the books. "Has a message come for me in the last few days from the court?" he asked. His voice was still croaky.

'The servant, startled by her master, curtsied and said, "I'll go and ask, Your Honour."

'She ran out of the room and a minute later, his butler came and bowed. He was smiling. "It's so good to see you up, my Lord. Can I get you some meat and some bread? You need to keep up your strength."

'But Joseph put up his hand to stop the man from speaking. "Has a message come from the courts about Caleb?"

'The servant smiled and shook his head. "Don't concern yourself, my Lord."

'"Tell me!" shouted Joseph, startling the servant.

'"Yes," he said. "Caleb was hanged two days ago."

'Joseph staggered back and sat heavily in an armchair by the fire. "Dead," he said. "Did he ... was he ... ?"

'The servant walked across and knelt beside his master. "They say that when sentence was passed on him by the magistrate, he smiled. He said not a word in his defence in court and nor would he agree to representation by the court-appointed advocate." Joseph looked at the servant in astonishment and horror, his mind trying to come to terms with the reality of his crime. "In fact," continued the servant, "the only words he said as he walked up to the gallows and stood there before a throng were 'Tell him I forgive him'. And then they hanged him. Who do you think he could be talking about, Sire? Who did he forgive?"

'But Joseph just shook his head and sank back into the cushions. There he remained despite the entreaties of his wife and doctor and friends, unmoved and unmovable until the light went out of his life and he died, sitting in his chair, looking into the fire.

'After the affairs of the estate were wound up, the business and everything which supported the family were handed down to Joseph's oldest son who, though still grief-stricken, made a vow in church before the entire congregation at his father's memorial service. The vow he made was to perpetuate the memory of his saintly father by continuing to give two-thirds of the family's entire income to the relief of the poor, orphaned and the sick. He also vowed to use some money to commission a statue of his father, standing opposite the entrance to the church, and in which, the right hand would be holding a golden crucifix like the one which the evil Caleb had stolen, and which had brought about his father's death.'

This was the way in which Mr Gruzmann finished his story. He looked up at the congregation in anticipation. His story, worked out during the previous week when he should have been seeing to the terms of a contract, was perfect in every detail. It had a strong moral message, and the twist in the tail would have kept everybody guessing. But the best part, the most brilliant, was right at the very end, when the son planned to erect a statue of his father holding the missing crucifix. That should make the community think long and hard.

But when he looked up at the congregation, what he saw dismayed him. Most of the people had their eyes closed, or were whispering to each other, or were even asleep. During his rehearsals of the speech to his mirror during the previous week, he had envisaged people standing and applauding as he descended the bimah into their midst, crowding around him, and asking to explain the intellectual ramifications of his metaphors. Perhaps even a follow-up talk to deconstruct the symbolism ... maybe even a quick introduction to semiotics.

But this ... this was beyond belief. Nobody except the rabbi had been listening. Mr Gruzmann was mortified, embarrassed, crushed.

He descended the steps of the bimah and met the rabbi on the way up, who smiled at him, and patted him on the shoulder.

'Lovely story,' said the rabbi. 'Very interesting.'

And the rabbi continued with the service ...

That, according to Mr Dub and Mr Dayan, was that. Enough. Finished. Okay, maybe the Professor's story had been of some value; maybe Mrs Finburg's story about the tree had taught somebody something. But this? No! This was too much. And they wouldn't stand any more. And nor would they allow the rabbi to fob them off with tales about archers in woods and arrows in trees. If he wanted them to continue to come to shul, there would be no more stories about Christians and Catholics and crucifixes. Let's face it, for 2000 lousy years, the Jews had been persecuted by the goyim. For most of that time, they had been forced to live in countries where tall church spires and golden crosses looked down on their tiny synagogues, an attempt by Christianity to cower them into conversion. So one of the very few places where they could go to avoid looking at the symbols of Christianity was in a shul.

But what was happening? Suddenly stories about bishops and stolen crucifixes were beginning to dominate the life of their very own Friday-night service in their very own shul. Well not any more. Or Mr Dayan and Mr Dub, and quite a number of regulars, would walk out, and start a minyan in the home of one of their number.

A breakaway. Not something which they wanted to do. Since the arrival of the rabbi, the petty factions which normally infested the shul had been brought under control, and the politics of the place was much more easygoing. But this breakaway had been caused by the rabbi himself and this bee in his bonnet about replacing sermons with stories. Okay, so it had started out as a good idea. When the stories were about Yiddishkiet it was fine. But then people had tried to get clever and introduce messages and hidden symbolism and fancy stuff.

The rabbi knew he was in trouble when he wished everybody a Shabbat Shalom and half-a-dozen of the regulars deliberately refused to answer. And when they held back after everyone had gone, it looked very much like a deputation.

'Rabbi,' began Mr Dub, 'I'm very sorry to have to say this, but the story tonight was not suitable ... not suitable at all.'

But the rabbi was prepared. Many of the non-regulars had come up to him to congratulate him on what he was doing. Nobody had particularly liked Mr Gruzmann's story. It was too dark and drear for their fancy but still people liked the idea of storytelling ... they liked what was happening in the shul.

'Come,' he said to the two men. 'Let's sit down over here and talk.'

Mr Dub looked like a boxer about to spring out of his corner on the attack. As they sat, he said 'Now, Rabbi. You know we hold you in very high regard, very high esteem. You're the best rabbi we've had in years. You've done more for this congregation than anybody else ...' Rabbi Teichmann put up his hand in an effort to bring modesty into the conversation. 'What I'm saying is, Rabbi, that we like you very much and we don't want you to take this personally, but this story tonight and the one last Shabbos and even the one before that,' Mr Dub shook his head. 'Rabbi, it has to stop.'

'What's your problem, Mr Dub?' asked the rabbi. He tried to sound ingenuous, but he knew precisely what the problem was.

'Problem? Look, last time we spoke I tried to tell you what the problem was and you told me a story about some archer in the woods with arrows. This time, forget your stories, Rabbi. Let me tell you a story. Once upon a time there was a small happy group of people coming to shul regularly and then the rabbi started to change the way things had always been done, and so the small group drifted away and were forced to go to another shul. So, Rabbi, now I've told you my story.'

The rabbi looked at Mr Dayan, who was stroking his beard. 'Is this the way you feel?'

Mr Dayan paused for a moment, his hand motionless halfway down his beard. When he had thought the thought, his hand continued in its downstroke. 'I'm afraid it is. Look, Rabbi. We like you. You've done a lot for this community . . . '

'Enough already with what I've done for the community. Tell me what I'm undoing.'

'The fact is that none of the regulars like what you're doing. We want to go back to the old ways. To the sermons, and the service that we all know. We don't feel happy hearing stories about people living in forests and people stealing crucifixes. It's not Jewish enough for us.'

'I can understand your feelings,' said the rabbi. 'I can understand them very clearly and it worries me that you feel like this. But what am I to do, my friends? Since I've introduced these stories, instead of my sermons, attendance has gone up five times. We're getting fifty people in shul on a Friday night. The only time that ever happens is when Yom Kippur falls on

Shabbat. It's a miracle. If I go back to what you want to do, then I'm going to lose each and every one of them.'

Mr Dayan nodded. It was a thorny problem but he wasn't willing to give in to the will of the majority. After all, there had to be some acknowledgement of his position in the synagogue ... some rights of precedence.

'I've been coming here every Friday night, give or take, for forty-seven years, Rabbi. Forty-seven years. Surely that means something.'

'It means a great deal, Mr Dayan. Of course, I know I'm putting you in a difficult position. But let me ask you a question and you mustn't try to flatter me ... you must tell me the truth. You know when I used to give sermons, did you truly listen to what I was saying?'

'Of course,' said Mr Dayan argumentatively.

The rabbi put up his finger. 'Tell me the truth, Mr Dayan. Did you listen to what I was saying or did your mind wander? Were your thoughts elsewhere? Did you fully understand what I was saying or did you say a little prayer of thanks when I came to the end and you said "Amen". Mr Dayan, you're in shul. You must tell me the truth.'

Mr Dayan's beard-stroking now increased dramatically. 'Well, if I have to tell the absolute truth, Rabbi, I must admit that my mind usually wanders. I think about what my wife and I will be doing on Saturday night, or what some of the customers have said to me during the week or how much I should charge for lamb or beef ... if you want me to be very truthful.' The shame of the admission made Mr Dayan look down at the ground.

'So,' said the rabbi. 'Can't you think of lamb or beef prices while you're listening to these stories and let all the other people enjoy them?'

'It doesn't work that way, Rabbi,' interrupted Mr Dub.

'But it does,' the rabbi insisted gently. 'Think about it. When I give my sermon, you don't listen. You're there but you don't pay attention.' Mr Dub took offence and appeared to rise up in anger but the rabbi insisted. 'Mr Dub, be honest with yourself. You don't listen. You think I don't look down at your faces from the bimah and see the way your eyes are glazing over. It happens to almost every rabbi, every Catholic priest, every protestant minister. It's because we're unable to go beyond the bounds of our duty. We're not free as we'd like to be to tell moral tales or good stories. We have to stick rigidly to what we're paid to tell you.'

Mr Dub and Mr Dayan found his words somewhat insulting and felt themselves bridling.

'Okay,' said the rabbi, sensing that he had caused them discomfort, 'maybe I'm going too far but surely there's an element of truth in what I'm saying. I've decided to hand over my pulpit for a short time to people who are capable of telling good stories. To include intelligent members of the congregation in spreading the moral and ethical messages that are inherent in the behaviour of good people. Now if you don't listen to me, but you do listen to them . . .' The rabbi shrugged his shoulders.

Mr Dub and Mr Dayan stood, and Mr Dub said, 'Goodnight, Rabbi. Shabbat shalom. We still disagree with you but this time we'll let it go. But please. No more stories about crucifixes and Christian bishops.'

'That I promise you, Mr Dub. That I promise you.'

The rabbi walked the short distance to his home, kissed his family and blessed them before he sat down for his evening meal. As he entered the house, he smelled the rich heavy aroma of cholent, a meat and bean stew which had been cooking since early that morning.

Funny how smells were so much an aid to memory. The rabbi had experienced it many times. He would walk into a cinema and smell the odour of old leather seats and his mind would immediately flash back to Sunday-afternoon matinees when his father would give him a few coins and he would lose himself in a world of make-believe. Or when he entered the home of one of his old congregants and there would be the slightly acrid smell of herring. Instantly he was transported to his days as a student at the yeshiva where the traditional Friday-night meal had begun with slices of pickled herring, salty pickled onions and great slabs of challah.

He enjoyed his meal of cholent with great gusto and afterwards relaxed with a good book in order to clear his mind for the following morning's sermon. As he sat in his favourite armchair he read and reread the same paragraph three times before realising that his mind was fixed on the issue Mr Dub and Mr Dayan had raised. He would solve it, he determined, by agreeing to allow Mrs Pomeranz to tell a story.

Now, there was a woman! Not the sort of woman with whom you liked to cross or quarrel, though everybody in the shul had had a quarrel at some stage or another with Mrs Pomeranz.

Although he'd indicated to Mr Glick that perhaps he might be given the nod this coming Shabbat; he now knew that it wasn't the right time for Mr Glick's story about Judaism and rabbis. The rabbi reckoned that he needed something in-between, something non-controversial after Mr Gruzmann's story about Caleb and the crucifix.

It had all happened very fortuitously. Mrs Pomeranz was a member of the Synagogue's Ladies Auxiliary Committee. She was the woman who determined exactly how much wine was required in each glass for the little Kiddush — nibbles and drinks — after the service. She was the woman who organised the purchase of kosher wines for the adults, soft drinks for the kids, chips and nuts and sweets for everybody ... and she was the woman who appointed herself to look at every synagogue function with an eye to making a profit for the Ladies Auxiliary.

Mrs Pomeranz was the archetype of the church/cathedral/synagogue-going lady who could equally well have been a formidable Catholic Church organiser or the backbone of any Anglican community. And not only churches. She was the type of central figure around which every Scout troop, Parents and Citizens organisation, art gallery society, museum friendship society and charitable organisation revolved. Mrs Pomeranz was a doer, an organiser, a facilitator, somebody who put herself forward whenever things needed to be done. And God help anybody who didn't do things Mrs Pomeranz's way, because no matter how carefully they poured the wine in the way Mrs Pomeranz did, their measures were never quite the same as hers. And so it was as clear as daylight that only Mrs Pomeranz could pour the wine and do things properly (as she told the mild and agreeable Mr Pomeranz every evening, filling his retirement years with her scintillating and provocative activities).

In fact, one of Mrs Pomeranz's favourite expressions was 'God help everybody when I'm no longer here, because ...'

Of course many people lived with the theory that Mrs Pomeranz would never die because if she did, God would have too much competition for running the universe, and if anybody really knew how to pour wine, it was God!

The rabbi smiled at the thought, even though it was uncharitable. Mrs Pomeranz had accosted him the previous week.

After listening for several weeks to the speakers, she had decided that she couldn't allow Mrs Finburg to be the only woman speaker, but that she too would grace the synagogue with her story — something which she had hardly told to anybody. And so in the few days before the Friday-night service, Mrs Pomeranz had cornered Rabbi Teichmann and said to him, 'Rabbi, this coming Shabbos. I've a story which I would like to tell. Something which not many people here know and which I think will be very well liked.'

The rabbi had nodded gratefully. 'It's very kind of you, Mrs Pomeranz, but for this Shabbat, we've already got a speaker. It's more or less ...'

'Rabbi,' she said holding up her hand with the finality of the Archangel Gabriel, 'I intend to come specially. I'm a very busy woman. If I make time, I expect you to make a place ...'

But the rabbi had held his ground. 'Mrs Pomeranz, I know it's very kind of you but ...'

'Rabbi,' she said, 'trust me. What I have to say will please everybody. Anyway, whoever you are asking can do it next week. Thank God, one of the things left to Jews is Friday night. I'm sure his story will improve with time. So, it's agreed. Come the time for your sermon, you will stand up and say "Ladies and gentlemen. It's now my pleasure to ask Mrs Pomeranz to tell a story." And then I'll get up and you can leave the rest to me. Thank you, Rabbi.' Then she had turned and walked away.

Now, Rabbi Teichmann was glad that he hadn't argued too strenuously because if he had one failing, it was an inability to deal with pushy Jewish women. He knew he should stand up to Mrs Pomeranz. It would have been easy. Just call her back, and say no. But he was worried about the repercussions of Mr Gruzmann's story, and anyway, he reasoned that on the one hand rejecting her would cause unnecessary problems. Problems! Always problems. The smaller the shul, the more the politics mattered. Mr Dub and Mr Dayan would have problems with another woman speaker. And there would be problems with Mrs Pomeranz if he didn't allow her to speak.

On the other hand, he would get her out of the way quickly. But on the one hand, he would upset the person he had already nominated; but on the other hand, he was sure he could talk Mr Glick into doing it on another occasion. So, with all the hands, he decided that on Sunday he would phone Mr Glick who had spent the week preparing his story, and say to him, 'Mr Glick, I have some wonderful news for you ...'

THE STORY OF
MRS POMERANZ AND
THE CHINESE GIRL
WHO BECAME JEWISH

On the following Friday night, the rabbi felt positively light-hearted, for he knew that when Mrs Pomeranz stood — even if she spoke about crucifixes, devils and martyred saints, even if she spoke about Mohammed and the triumph of Islam — nobody, not one person in the shul, would dare either raise the issue against Mrs Pomeranz or blame the rabbi for what had been said. Everybody knew that Mrs Pomeranz was a voice on her own, a woman who couldn't be denied. Not even by the rabbi. Indeed, if self-righteousness was a currency, Mrs Pomeranz would be the wealthiest person in the shul.

When the time came for his sermon, Rabbi Teichmann stood on the bimah and said to his congregation, 'Shabbat shalom, ladies and gentlemen. Tonight I have great news. Mrs Pomeranz has agreed to tell us a story so, if you will all turn in your seats, Mrs Pomeranz . . .'

People looked at each other. Okay, Mrs Finburg had told a story some weeks earlier. That was the community bowing down to political correctness, but two women storytellers? It was beginning to sound like a Liberal synagogue. Mr Dub, Mr Dayan, Dr Josephs and a couple of others frowned in consternation. Again, they would have to have a word to the rabbi. Or maybe not. After all, it *was* Mrs Pomeranz.

The stentorian Germanic voice of Mrs Pomeranz boomed out and filled the synagogue like a discordant choir as she began her story. 'My story begins,' she told everybody, 'when I was a little girl in Hamburg. In 1937, my parents did everything in their power to emigrate into the United States. We were part of the German quota when we registered but our names were right on the bottom and there were tens of thousands of Jews whose names were above ours. Naturally my father spent a fortune in bribing the Nazi officials to elevate our name to the top of the list. My mother sold her wedding ring; my father his collection of antique guns; one of my sisters even sold her phonogram records, and eventually we had enough to bribe the official.

'I remember my father leaving the house and kissing us all, and saying, "Tomorrow we will leave and start a new life." And when he came home he opened a bottle of Cognac and even poured some for the children. We celebrated with excitement, drinking Cognac and eating poppyseed cake; we felt as if we were the cleverest people in the world. But when my parents went the next morning to collect the visas, they returned an hour later empty-handed. I will never forget their faces. It was as if they were doomed. My father explained to us that the official told him he would have them arrested if they dared to make accusations that a Nazi had taken a bribe. The man had taken all of our money, leaving us penniless and our names were still at the bottom of the list.

'And so we waited, my father being forced to do odd jobs because he had sold everything from his factory, my mother cleaning and laundering. We were taken out of school and forced to do work with my father. But then came Kristallnacht. My father decided that it was the end and we would no longer wait for visas to get to America.

'Now there was much talk about Jews leaving Germany and going to China. Most of you will have heard of the large Jewish community in Harbin but there was another Jewish community before the war at Shanghai. It was the only place in the world where we could go from Germany without a visa because it was under the control of the International Settlement Commission. The British, the French and the Americans had fixed territorial rights in Shanghai and even though we knew that another sector was occupied by the Japanese as a result of the 1937 Sino-Japanese War, we weren't terribly concerned. The Japanese weren't Germans or Nazis. For us the enemy were the fascists of Germany and Italy.

'Our plan was to arrive in Shanghai, and once we were secure, to make application to the Americans for a visa. Okay, it was the long way round. We were destitute with no chance of a visa and the borders of Germany were clanking closed with a horrible finality every minute of the day.

'There were three kinds of shipping lines to Shanghai — the German line went from Hamburg, a Japanese line from somewhere else, and an Italian line from Trieste in the Adriatic. Naturally we wouldn't go on the German line, and so my father borrowed the money for tickets from a friend who told us we were fools, Hitler was just making noises and everything would soon be all right. With the borrowed money, we travelled south, hiding in cattle cars as the train went over the border, and eventually we arrived in Trieste. We waited in line for four days in order to acquire tickets because the Italian fascists under

Mussolini had no great love for Jews. But by a miracle, we were given our boarding passes and got on board, with no money at all in our pockets. Of course, the other passengers were all Jews and we were all in the same boat . . .'

A few people in the synagogue burst out laughing but Mrs Pomeranz hadn't intended to make a pun. She looked malevolently at them. They shut up immediately and she continued.

'And so we worked hard to share the rations which the captain allowed us. I'll never forget the boat ride. These days you go on a ship, you have cabins and two sittings for lunch and dinner, and if you're lucky you sit at the captain's table. In those days, even though it was a passenger liner, the rich Italians, merchants and German industrialists had the cabins on the airy upper decks while we were treated like animals, sleeping in the bowels of the ship in long, noisy, smelly rooms, anywhere where they could put a bunk or a hammock. I'll never forget the smell. Every morning when I woke up the stench of diesel fuel and mustiness was in my nose. But I won't go into that because this is a story and you don't want to hear me complain.'

Rebbetzin Teichmann bit her lip, holding back the words. If anybody could be called a complainer, it was Mrs Pomeranz. But she held the floor, and Rebbetzin Teichmann continued to listen, paying her full attention.

'The ship sailed from Trieste down the Adriatic and then across the Mediterranean into the Suez Canal. When we stopped at Port Said, we suddenly realised that we were no longer in Europe; that suddenly we were free of the oppression of death which had been hanging over us ever since Hitler began his climb to the top of the dung heap. The whole mood of the passengers changed and we rejoiced.

'But the change was even more extraordinary than mere happiness on our part; there was also a change in our confidence. At the beginning of our journey, on the way from Trieste, we had cowered whenever a German industrialist, his wife or children looked down on us from the upper decks. They would spit at us and jeer and the children would throw things to try to hit us as if we were targets. We Jews just tried to ignore them because we were still in their territory. But when we got to Port Said, as I said, something dramatic happened. It was as if we had been released from prison. Suddenly we felt as if we were equals.

'It all began when one of the young men, he must have been eighteen, was walking along the lower decks and a German or an Italian on an upper deck made some horrible remark. The young man picked up a wooden railing which was lying on the deck and brandished it, threatening the man. The boy shouted up that we were halfway around the world and he was no longer scared of him. He said that he and a hundred others would come to the upper deck and toss him into the sea. Well, the cowardly Nazi backed away in fear. No Jew had ever threatened him. God Almighty, what was the world coming to? The man regained his courage and shouted down at the young boy that he would tell the captain and have him flogged, but the boy stood his ground and screamed up at the man, "You're not in Germany now, you old swine. Go away or I'll come up and teach you a lesson."

'Well, even before the young man taught him a lesson, the interchange had spread like wildfire to the upper decks. From the moment the ship sailed from Port Said towards Aden, it was a different ship. Somebody told somebody else, who told another person and suddenly the Germans, Italians, Japanese and Chinese who were in the upper decks no longer peered over to stare at us as if we were animals. Even the crew who brought us food treated us differently. It was the first sign that we were human beings, and no longer the vermin of Europe. I'll never forget the rest of that trip from Aden to India, then Colombo, Singapore, Bombay, Hong Kong and finally Shanghai. As the ship increased its distance from Europe, we Jews increased in stature. We even formed a passengers' committee and sent a deputation to the captain to demand better food. The captain immediately apologised, telling us that he was only following orders; from that moment onwards, our food rations doubled. I honestly think he was scared of a mutiny at sea — even though many more of us would have been killed than they, indeed mutiny was the last thing on our minds — the captain obviously didn't want trouble.

'Every night we sang songs and talked of the adventures we were going to have, and the new life we would be leading. We arrived in Shanghai and were met by members of the American Jewish Joint Distribution Committee, which was there to take care of arriving refugees. We felt as if we had arrived in the Holy Land, and were taken on trucks with our luggage to the Japanese area of that huge and sprawling city. Why the Japanese area? I don't know. All I know is that we had no idea that Japan was about to enter the war. Nor did we have any knowledge of rivalry between the various communities. We thought we had arrived in a very strange Garden of Eden, a paradise after the cold and fear and destitution of Hamburg.

'Of course, it wasn't all luxury and comfort. Quite the contrary. Because we had no money, my father and my brothers were forced to live in huge barracks with one hundred other men and my mother, my sisters and I also moved in with huge numbers of women. It was here that we stayed for the first three weeks until the committee could organise work for us so that we could make our own living and eventually earn enough to move into one of the housing compounds. My father was given work in a fireworks factory. He had owned a glass and enamelling factory in Hamburg and had been very successful. So, being a manufacturer, it didn't take him long to get the hang of making fireworks. What did surprise him was the lack of machinery. It was extraordinary. Everything was done by hand — paper was rolled, the cardboard was glued and gunpowder mixture was manufactured by hand. In the large shed where they made the fireworks there were literally hundreds of people all doing some horribly monotonous job. One man rolled cardboard over a cylinder and glued it. He then slipped it off and handed it to another man who glued on a base. Then it went to another man who did something else. Of course, children today don't know what boredom is, with television and video games and computers but if they had to work in these factories ...' Mrs Pomeranz shook her head.

The rabbi glanced over at some of the younger boys whose attention was already dulled and who were waiting for Mrs Pomeranz to get on with the story.

'Anyway,' she said, 'I was fifteen and already I could see opportunities. What did I do? Well, I'm ashamed to tell you what I did. In fact, when I think today on what I did, I can't believe that I did it.'

Mrs Pomeranz gazed down at the floor. The rabbi looked up and stared at her in astonishment, as did Mr Dub with Dr Josephs, Mr Dayan and all the other people in the congregation. God Almighty, thought the rabbi. What is she going to admit to? That she did something ... immoral? Something where she sold her ... No, it couldn't be! Not Mrs Pomeranz! Anybody but Mrs Pomeranz. The congregation held its collective breath. You could hear a pin drop.

In a whisper, Mrs Pomeranz said, 'I sold cigarettes.' The rabbi could swear he heard a collective moan. 'That's right. In those days, they weren't regarded as they are today. And because the whole world was at war, the only things of any value were things that you could trade immediately, things that would go up in value when the war got out of hand. Things like watches, stockings, soap and tobacco; things that everybody would need and that would be in scarce supply. So that's what I did. I bought cartons of cigarettes from an importer on the Shanghai docks. Not many, just a few cartons. And then I would open the cartons and sell the packets individually, marking them up in price. I would buy the cartons for the equivalent today of $10 and by the time I had sold the packets I would have doubled my money. It might not sound much to you but it was a fortune.

'I did this every day instead of going to school and with what my father and my brothers earnt, we were beginning to do well. When I came to my father and I gave him all the money I had been secretly earning in those few months, he looked at it as if it was manna from heaven. I could see a suspicious look in his eyes but when I explained I had been trading in tobacco, he nodded, kissed me and blessed me. That kiss, I have felt these last fifty years.

'We managed to put enough together to buy a cheap apartment, one street behind the docks in Shanghai, but before I go on with the story, let me tell you a little bit about the life of Shanghai. Now, I've told you that there were a lot of Jews who had moved there out of Europe. We established synagogues, a school for younger children and a youth club. We organised dances, outings, discussions, Torah readings. We had a wonderful life full of gaiety and promise. Those who could play instruments formed a small orchestra which, while it wasn't the New York

Philharmonic, was enough to remind us of the joys of Beethoven and Mozart. And the dances! Oh, they were wonderful. Of course, because our parents were there, the boys almost never danced with girls ...'

Mrs Pomeranz suddenly looked at the rabbi and frowned. 'Oh, I'm not going to tell fibs in shul. Of course we danced together. We left Orthodox Judaism behind in Europe. We all went to shul of course but the old prewar prohibitions of dancing with handkerchiefs and that sort of thing, well, those were the old days. We were in a new part of the world and even though some parents disapproved, we were happy dancing together.'

Most of the people who knew Mrs Pomeranz, the heavy-set, buxom slow-moving and matronly lady, couldn't begin to imagine her as a lithe young woman dancing in Shanghai under the Asian stars to the tune of an orchestra, but they closed their eyes and did their best.

'Life continued very happily for us until the Japanese decided to enter the war. Naturally we had all kept a keen eye on what was happening in Europe. We knew nothing about the concentration camps or about the murder of thousands of Jews. All we knew was what we read in the newspapers and listened to on the radio. We heard about the German attacks on Belgium, France and Greece and how Germany was poised to march across the Channel to take over England. And though we all said how frightened we were, we had the feeling we were so far away we were untouchable.

'Then the Japanese bombed Pearl Harbor. It was the start and it reached us quickly. In Shanghai, I got out of bed because I thought I could hear thunder. But the skies were clear blue. It was the ships in the harbour being bombed and scuttled by the Japanese. The Imperial Army had been preparing in secret. They rolled their tanks into the International Settlement and rounded everybody up. I don't know how many people were killed but for some reason the Japanese seemed to take out their hatred on the Chinese. It was the beginning of the terror. The war had come to us. We lost our complacency and realised that the charmed existence we had been living was no more. From that moment onwards, every Japanese face was the face of an enemy. We knew that life would become tough for us and we thought we had it hard. We had no idea what was happening in Germany.

'In Shanghai we continued to live a fairly normal life except that now instead of being frightened of the Germans, we were terrified of the Japanese. In 1943, they moved us all into a ghetto and even though there was no barbed wire, there were guard posts everywhere and we needed a pass to get in and out. It was said that the Germans told the Japanese that they had to make a ghetto but we were never able to confirm that.

'Of course we all know what ghettos were like in Europe, and we soon got to know what the concentration camps were like in Germany and Poland. Well, the ghetto in Shanghai was nothing like that. We weren't the natural enemy of the Japanese. We just happened to be there. The natural enemy I'm afraid were the Chinese and one of my very best and closest friends was a wonderful fifteen-year-old Chinese girl called Chin Lee. Chin's father was the importer from whom I had been buying my cigarettes. She was, like her father, a Buddhist and having no experience of Buddhism I was very interested in what she believed. I had had very little schooling and so I found everything she told me to be new and exciting.

'Chin Lee was a girl of extraordinary grace and beauty. And I realised that I loved her like I loved my sisters. She was open with me, generous, kind and loving. She taught me so much about the Buddhist views of life and truth and she gave me the knowledge of self which has helped me so much throughout the rest of my life.'

Rabbi Teichmann dug a fingernail into the palm of his hands to stop himself from howling in laughter. Mrs Pomeranz ... influenced by Buddhism? Come on now. We all like a good story, but nothing as absurd as this.

Mrs Pomeranz continued. 'Chin Lee told me that Buddhists believe everything is impermanent, a flowing reality. And that there are four noble truths — the truth of misery, the truth that misery originates from the craving for pleasure, the truth that this craving can be eliminated and the truth that the elimination is the result of a methodical path that must be followed. She taught me of the paths towards enlightenment and about the ultimate goal of the eightfold path to Nirvana.

'Chin Lee and I spent hours every day comparing the joys of Judaism and the joys of Buddhism. In the balance, and Rabbi I say this with no disrespect to you, I think Judaism could learn much from Buddhism in tolerance, understanding and compassion.'

The rebbetzin was about to stand up and protest. For the past few years, Mrs Pomeranz had made the life of every woman at the Ladies Auxiliary a living hell. She was didactic, possessive, authoritarian and self-possessed. The very opposite of what she was now claiming she had learnt from Buddhism. A sixth sense, some form of metaphysical force, must have flowed from Rabbi Teichmann to Mrs Teichmann for she looked at him and he stared at her. The stare said, 'Keep quiet. Sit there. Don't move!' and the whole community, now highly sceptical, allowed Mrs Pomeranz to continue her story.

'Chin Lee and I lived our lives together and planned what we would do together after the war. I agreed with Chin Lee that

I would convert to become a Buddhist and that she and I would go to the north of China and live in a Buddhist community where we would learn true spiritual enlightenment. But what we didn't count on was the Japanese.

'What we also didn't know was that Chin Lee's father, Ah Chuk, was a tobacco merchant by day but a saboteur at night. He was one of the many Chinese guerillas fighting to overthrow the Japanese army. But the Japanese were ruthless and one day caught Ah Chuk leading a band of saboteurs on a daring raid. They tortured him and immediately went to his home where they arrested his wife and Chin Lee's brothers and sisters. If Chin Lee hadn't been with me during that day, she would have been killed immediately. Instead we spent that horrible day in the city and afterwards we went to our homes. An hour later, Chin Lee arrived at my apartment, white-faced and horrified. She begged me to let her stay and I immediately agreed.

'My father knew Chin Lee a little and was quite happy to support what I was doing while the money kept coming in. When I told him the story about Chin Lee's family, he was terribly moved and upset for the girl, saying how hideous the Japanese were and how much like the Nazis they were turning out to be. But when I told him that Chin Lee would naturally have to stay with us, he became aggressive. He told me I was mad. He told me it was an insane plan. That it would lead to the death of all of us. He said Chin Lee must leave our house immediately and not return. The penalty for helping saboteurs was death and he would never take that risk.

'This was in 1943 and by then we all knew more or less what was really happening to Jews in Germany. We had been living our existence away from the true brutality of the war but now it was on our doorstep. So I shouted at my father, the first time I had ever raised my voice to him. I asked him, how could he treat Chin Lee in the way that the Germans, the Poles and the Ukrainians were treating the Jews? That if he sent her away to her death in order to save us and his family, we would be guilty of what Christians were doing to people like us in Europe. Well, my father was faced with the biggest decision of his life. He agreed with what I was saying but knew the risks better than I did. We argued and shouted for hours until he could see I wasn't going to give in.

'Eventually we came to a compromise. Yes, Chin Lee could stay with us but she must become one of us. Fortunately, Chin Lee was a slight young girl from the south of the country and didn't have a round Mongolian face. My sisters cut their long black hair and made a wig for her which we interwove into her own black hair. We dressed her in the same clothes as we wore and we put a scarf over her head. We made her up so that her eyes looked much rounder than they really were, and while she hid in the house for a week we gave her an intensive course in our language and Hebrew. Poor Chin Lee. She tried so hard to get the vowel sounds right but she found it incredibly hard. Several times she wanted to flee the city, but even she knew that that would be certain death and so she stayed with us for two more weeks, never once daring to leave the house, each day getting used to making herself up with her hair, her scarf, the clothes and cosmetics, so that in the end we only saw a European girl when we looked at her.

'And then four weeks after her home and family had been destroyed, Chin Lee and I took our first tentative steps onto the street. We walked down the road to a bakery where we bought some bread and cakes. Chin Lee said nothing but we were watching the reaction of the sales lady who smiled at us both.

This gave Chin Lee a lot more confidence. We returned home and Chin Lee excitedly told everyone in the family what had happened. Everyone was thrilled but my father introduced a note of caution. He said, "All you did was buy bread. Wait until you are stopped by the guards," and he shook his head in fear and went back to his newspaper.

'And so the following morning Chin Lee and I went out and wandered far from my house. We talked animatedly in Chinese until somebody came near to us and then we switched to German and English. Chin Lee spoke little because her accent would have given her away and as people passed by us I did most of the talking. The point is that we walked around the streets of Shanghai passing thousands of people and all they saw were two teenage European girls in animated conversation.

'And for two years this is how Chin Lee lived with us as a sister. We taught her about Judaism and about European culture. She taught us about Buddha and Chinese culture. And all the while our common enemy was the Japanese. When we heard of the end of the war in Europe, we were so excited we lit bonfires, but the Japanese were merciless and came into the compounds shouting and screaming. We had forgotten that the Japanese were still fighting the Americans and that every day the American ships got closer and closer to Tokyo. And then one day we heard the radio talking about a bomb that had landed and how Japanese ministers were going to sign a declaration of surrender on the USS *Missouri*.

'Well, I won't go into the details of how we left Shanghai and came to this country but no doubt everybody here tonight is wondering what happened to my new Chinese sister who looked like a German girl. After the war, Chin Lee became a senior official in the Chinese Ministry of Culture. We corresponded four or five times a year, long and loving letters. She would tell me how her life was under the regime of Mao Zedong and I would beg her to come and live here where I would help her resettle.'

Mrs Pomeranz's voice dropped. The shul community looked at her in hushed surprise. Never one to show any form of emotion, a woman whom everyone saw as bossy and pedantic, suddenly found it hard to speak. She was on the verge of tears when in a quietly subdued voice, Mrs Pomeranz ended her story.

'I never heard from her again after the start of the Red Guard's Revolution. Her letters stopped coming. I still pray every day of my life that my dearest friend will write to me.'

Mrs Pomeranz sat down. Nobody moved until the rabbi stood and walked over to the mehitzah and said a small silent prayer in Hebrew and then walked all the way back up onto the bimah and continued the service.

At the end of the service, people seemed reluctant to leave. Indeed when the rabbi was folding up his tallis, he looked at the congregation and saw that there was a knot of people gathered around Mrs Pomeranz. He stopped what he was doing and looked. And when he saw the reaction, he couldn't help but smile broadly. Now, this more than anything was the answer to his prayers.

At the end of shul service, people would generally pay a courteous regard to Mrs Pomeranz. They would shake her hand, wish her good Shabbos and walk away. Sure, she was often attended by the latest acolyte but she had so many enemies that more people avoided her than came towards her. But look what was happening now!

A miracle? The rabbi felt himself shrugging. Who knows what a miracle is? The parting of the Red Sea, was that a miracle?

It could be explained by science but the Jews knew it was a miracle. Moses' rod turning into a snake; water and manna appearing in the desert; the very creation of the land of Israel from the remnants of Nazi-torn Germany; these were all miracles. Jews had such an intimate relationship with God that miracles were almost a part of their being. And it was miraculous that so many people were now crowding around the often lonely and usually bitter Mrs Pomeranz and warmly congratulating her on her story, asking her questions, needing to know more.

The rabbi looked and saw the beaming smile on Mrs Pomeranz's face. Even Mr Dub and Mr Dayan were smiling. Yes, thought the rabbi, a little miracle is taking place in our shul. And he felt good for the whole of the Sabbath.

MR GLICK'S STORY
ABOUT HOW THE RABBIS
TOOK OVER THE FARM

There was a lighter step in the rabbi's walk as he approached Friday once again. Even his wife, the rebbetzin noticed it. She spoke to him about it on Thursday when the children had gone to bed.

'Things are definitely beginning to happen in the shul,' he told her. 'Not just the increased attendance, although God knows, that's wonderful enough. But I think people are beginning to realise that a synagogue is made up of many different kinds of people, and each has something to contribute. Take someone like Mrs Finburg, or Mr Dayan, or really any one of the storytellers so far. Who would have thought two months ago that any of them had the talent for being so entertaining, or for riveting us with such tales? And the moral behind each of their stories, whether they know about it or not, is wonderful.'

His wife looked at him quizzically but decided to remain silent and allow her husband to glorify in his simple and naïve dreams about the synagogue. He thought that people could change. He didn't have to listen to the sniping, backbiting bitchiness that went on all the time. He was removed from the absurdities with which she had to deal. One day she would tell him what really went on in his shul. One day ... Meanwhile, let him enjoy his dreams about how the people were all coming together through these stories.

But the rabbi was certain that the stories were having a beneficial impact on the place. Now that the event was beginning to take on the aspect of a tradition, however, he had to be very careful about the nature of the stories he was allowing, because he could still feel the underlying tensions amongst the regulars in the front rows of the synagogue.

Tomorrow night, it would be Mr Glick's turn, but before he allowed him to tell his story, the rabbi called him in and asked him to run over the details again.

Mr Glick was a television producer who worked for one of the local television channels. He had come across this story told by a friend and thought it was just wonderful. When Rabbi Teichmann heard it the first time, he was somewhat concerned about its dubious moral value, but accepted it willingly because of what it said about Jews and Judaism. This one, he was sure, would find no offence in the front row. Now he'd heard it a second time, he was even more confident that his censors in the shul would find nothing objectionable.

When Friday night came the rabbi welcomed in the regulars plus the rest of the congregation, men who now brought their wives and children in order to listen to the joys of the storyteller. Fortunately the fall off in population on a Saturday morning seemed to have abated and it now looked as if people were establishing a habit of attending synagogue both on Friday night and on the following Saturday morning. So, above the background hubbub which the rabbi normally experienced on one of the high holy days, he began the service. People prayed, raised their voices in thanks, stood up and sat down at the proper times and everybody waited for the storyteller.

And when Mr Glick stood at the invitation of the rabbi, the feeling of anticipation was profound. 'Many of you here,' began Mr Glick, 'know that I produce television shows, and while I was attending one of the many international conferences which seem to plague our industry, I came across a man from Australia, another television producer, who had just finished a documentary which I thought I would like to share with you.

'The story begins in a hospital in Sydney. A farmer from a place called Wollombi had developed a very nasty abscess on his leg which he hadn't treated. The man lived alone, had no family and tended not to look after himself. But one day the local agricultural inspector came to find out why he hadn't put in certain documents and found the man in his somewhat squalid hut lying in bed, close to death. The man was rushed to a Sydney hospital where he was pumped full of antibiotics and even though his life hung in the balance for many days, he eventually recovered. He was in hospital for four weeks until he was able to leave. During that time he befriended a Jewish doctor, a young woman who knew that he was all alone and never had visitors and so she spent a lot more time with him than she gave to some of her other recovering patients.'

Mr Dub and Mr Dayan smiled as Mr Glick began to talk about the Jewish doctor. Thank God, they thought, at least there's one Jew in this story. The rabbi glanced over and felt a frisson of satisfaction.

Mr Glick continued, 'Now an attachment grew between the young doctor and the old farmer. Nothing romantic of course, he was old enough to be her grandfather. But she liked the old man. She liked his casualness, his open enquiry and his deep love of the land. He told her he had never been married and that all his family were now dead. And yes, she promised to come out and visit him on the farm when she had some spare time.

'The old man eventually returned home and true to her word, the young doctor had a three-day break and, rather than spend it at home reading, thought that she would benefit by driving up to his property two hours north of Sydney to see for herself the wonders he had described.

'And what wonders! As she drove in beside a creekbed, lofty hills rose on either side, studded with multi-coloured bushes, wattle trees heavy with yellow blooms and beautiful pink and white peach trees. The road was rutted and difficult for her urban vehicle but it didn't matter. She drove slowly because every few minutes she would stop the car as the road turned to afford yet another vista and she would get out and smell the champagne air and feel the warm winds which blew up from the creekbed. In the air she could hear the buzzing of flies and mosquitoes, and shafts of light shone through the clouds illuminating patches of forest as though they were brushed by the wings of an angel. Eventually she reached the rise on which the old farmer had built his log cabin. There was no telephone, no gas and no electricity and no running water. Everything he needed came from the sky or from the land.

'She got out of her car and tentatively knocked on the door. When the farmer saw her, his surprise was almost beyond comprehension. Except for neighbours who occasionally dropped in to check on the old man, she was his first visitor in the best part of the three months since he had returned from the hospital.

'"Do you remember me?" she asked ingenuously.

'"How could I forget the woman who saved my life! Welcome to the countryside, doctor." He opened his arms and she kissed him on both cheeks as a granddaughter kisses a grandfather.

"'I'd prefer it if you didn't call me doctor. Especially not here; not in this beautiful place. It sets up a barrier between us. My first name's Ruth. I thought I'd just drive out for the day and have a look at the property you described to me with such love while you were in the hospital."

'Well, the old man fussed around as if she was a member of the royal family. He couldn't do enough for her. He had only just that morning baked some fresh bread in the camp oven over still-glowing coals, and he'd just milked the cow so she had fresh warm creamy milk for her coffee. He began to cut her a slice of ham but she held up her hand and explained that Jews didn't eat ham. Instead, she took a wedge of cheese and satisfied her hunger. Ruth stayed the whole day. They walked over the hills and down into the valleys, and then they returned for more to eat. By the time they had finished talking, it was already dark and too late for her to return home, so the old man insisted she sleep in his bed while he curled up on blankets by the fire.

'What did they find to talk about for that whole afternoon and into the evening, and then the following day and even the day after until she was forced to return to her job? They spoke about Judaism, about the origin of the religion, the Patriarchs, the time of the Kings, the Prophets and the Judges. They spoke about the Diaspora and about persecution, about the urbanisation of the Jews and their life in ghettos. And they spoke about modern-day Israel and how the Jew for the first time since the Diaspora had returned to his own land and was able to farm and feel the soil and nurture the crops. And the old man took it all in and nodded as she spoke, frequently asking questions about why this happened or what was meant by that. And at the end of the third afternoon, a few hours before it became dark, Ruth threw her arms around the old man, kissed him and thanked him profusely for the time he had given her and for showing her around his beautiful 300-acre farm.

'As they walked to her car, her arm through his, he helped her in and said to her, "Ruth, I'm a lonely old man with nobody ever to talk to. All I have is my farm and the wonders of nature. If ever you want to come up here again, I would consider it an honour."

'She promised him she would and as she started the car, he bent down and said through the open driver's window, "And thank you for telling me all those things about what it's like to be Jewish. It has meant a great deal to me. I have never been a religious man and you've shown me what Jews have suffered by being cut off from their land. I realise now how lucky I am to have been blessed by being able to live amongst nature all my life."

'He kissed her again on the cheek and she drove off. Three months went by while Ruth was studying for a professional examination, and then another three months before she was able to take her next period of time off from the hospital. Having no way of phoning the old man or letting him know she was coming, she drove north of Sydney with a feeling of trepidation. Even if he wasn't in, it was only another three-hour drive back home, but she had been so looking forward to the break that she knew she would feel bitterly disappointed if the old man wasn't there. The minute Ruth drove through the gates, she knew there was a problem. There were no blossoms on the trees, the sky was overcast, the insects were no longer flitting through the air. It was as if a heavy hand had been laid upon the farm.

'When she eventually arrived at the cabin, it was firmly locked and bolted and from the look of the spider webs over the door frame, Ruth knew it had been like this for some little time ... not long enough for the place to look abandoned, but certainly unoccupied for at least a week or more. She travelled the twenty kilometres to the nearest town and there she went into the police station to ask if they knew what happened to the old farmer who lived alone. The young constable asked if she was a relative and she told him that she was the old man's doctor from Sydney, which in part was true. She explained that she was a hospital doctor who had looked after him and was coming to check on his wellbeing. The policeman called his sergeant who explained that the old man had died ten days previously and expressed his sympathies. He said that the local solicitor was handling the matter and perhaps she might like to go and talk to him.

'John Conroy was the only solicitor in that part of the country and rarely got out to meet his clients, but he remembered the old man very well for his gentleness and his love of nature. He also remembered him because four months previous he had visited Conroy's office and made a change to his will which, when granted probate, would come as a shock to a small but intensely religious group of Jews who lived in Bondi at a place called a yeshiva.

'Ruth felt her jaw drop in amazement. "I know I'm not supposed to read you the contents of the will until probate has been granted but as you were his doctor it appears that you in part were responsible for the change. Apparently you told him about this yeshiva where ultra-Orthodox Jews are cut off from the land. Your description went straight to his heart. He was thinking of leaving the farm to you, but didn't want you to be burdened with the responsibilities. Having nobody else, he's left the whole damn place to this group of religious fundamentalists."

'Conroy shook his head in amazement. "I did everything in my power to talk him out of it but he wouldn't be dissuaded.

I have to tell you that when those gentlemen come to this area, all hell's going to break loose. There's a very strong Christian fundamentalist group here, a big Baptist community, and they're not going to like these Hasidim or whatever you call them, in their midst. Not one little bit."

'Too shocked to argue and somewhat offended by his remarks, Ruth felt no obligation to explain the reality of the situation. Instead she returned to her home and here, I'm afraid, Ruth completely drops out of the story because, ladies and gentlemen, boys and girls, I have no idea what happened to her after that.'

Rabbi Teichmann looked up in sorrow. All along he had harboured a secret hope that Ruth would inherit the property, but he knew that it wasn't to be. The rabbi had a particularly soft spot for the young doctor's namesake, the Ruth of the Bible, who had supported her mother-in-law, Naomi, when the old woman was distressed and needed help. Ruth, a Moabitess, willingly accepted the dictates of the older woman, and told her 'Do not force me to leave you, for where you go, I will go; and where you lodge, I will lodge: your people will be my people and your God, my God.' Ruth had then gone into the fields to glean barley where she met Boaz and eventually lived happily ever after. It was a delightful story, one in which the writer subtly criticised the dictates of Nehemiah and Ezra concerning their law against mixed marriages ... o tempora, o mores!

Mr Glick continued. 'And so probate was granted and a letter arrived on the desk of Rabbi Goodmann, the Hasidic leader of the yeshiva which told him that a Christian gentleman of whom he had never heard and with whom he had never had correspondence had left him a valuable 300-acre farm of some of the best land in New South Wales, two hundred kilometres north of Bondi. The gift was absolute, and was worth many hundreds of thousands of dollars, but there was one codicil attached to the gift, a rider which at first made the old rabbi laugh but then concerned him. The rider was that the property couldn't be sold for ten years after the death of the old man or it would revert to the state. Now, as is the case with most yeshivot, this particular one was invariably short of funds and was always making appeals to the community to support its students and its rabbis. The work of the yeshiva was to teach, to enquire, to study, to try to understand, and to fulfil the obligations that God places upon Jews, which was to know the Torah. Hasidic Jews had no place on a farm, nor did they understand anything about agriculture. What were they going to do with 300-acres of farm land? Especially three hundred acres which they couldn't sell.

'So the rabbi consulted the yeshiva solicitor who wrote a letter and then made a phone call to Mr Conroy. Now the yeshiva's solicitor, apart from being an ultra-Orthodox Jew, was one of the most senior lawyers in the state and well-known, both in the legal profession and also in the wider community, for chairing a number of high-profile commissions. For this simple country lawyer to receive a phone call from a man of his stature was something which he would remember to the end of his days. But no matter how much the two men spoke, debated, discussed, and argued back and forth, neither could see a way out of it.

'Mr Conroy said, "You, I know, will be the first to understand that I'm bound by the terms of the will. Please don't think that your clients will be happy in this community. We here are composed of a large number of strictly fundamentalist Christians and I can see nothing but tension."

'"And please don't think, Mr Conroy," said the yeshiva's solicitor, "that my clients want to accept this gift. The last thing these Orthodox rabbis want to do is to milk a cow or push a plough. Please send me a photocopy of the will so I can examine it and see if I can find a way around it." But by the end of the week the yeshiva's solicitor told the rabbi that there was nothing he could do, that they must either accept the gift and take possession, or forfeit land which could be worth almost a million dollars, and give it to the state.

'The rabbi spent that day and the following in consultation with his colleagues and they made a decision. The first thing they did was to get into their car and drive to see the property they suddenly owned. They followed the route that Ruth had taken six or so months earlier but unlike Ruth who was an Orthodox but much more secular Jew, these rabbis had rarely been out of the Jewish areas of Sydney's eastern suburbs ... except to fly to their spiritual homelands of Israel and New York. Even when they had to go to visit a large Jewish community on the north shore of Sydney, they felt as if they were entering strange and uncomfortable circumstances, for the north shore was much leafier and greener than the concreted and oppressively treeless eastern suburbs.

'So imagine their amazement when they went beyond the city limits and found themselves amongst the forested hillsides and plunging gorges which are a feature of the national parks surrounding Sydney. Try to imagine their feelings, surrounded each and every day by car fumes, bitumen and rectangular concrete houses, as they looked through their car's windows and saw blue ribbons of water intersected by precipitous cliffs, vast acres of impenetrable wilderness ... Nature as far as their eyes could see.

'In fact, even trying to imagine a car full of Hasidic rabbis with their strange black coats, their hats, their bushy beards driving along a country road amidst Ford pick-ups, flat-bed trucks, tractors and the ubiquitous four-wheel drives leads to a question of perspective — what was stranger: the scene inside the car, or what they saw outside the car?'

The shul community laughed as they imagined the picture which Mr Glick was painting. Even Rabbi Teichmann, who was the one closest to the description which had been used for the rabbis, found the scene amusing. He had always harboured the view that a Jew belonged in two places: a synagogue and a coffee shop, and couldn't quite cope with a car full of Hasidic rabbis kicking up the dust on country roads.

Mr Glick continued. 'But there they found themselves. Driving down the rutted track, getting out and opening gates, batting away the flies from their faces, wrinkling their noses as they smelt the cow manure, looking in amazement at kangaroos hopping through the bush and disdainfully avoiding the thousands of cowpats all over the area from the stock of local farmers who now agisted their cattle on the dead man's property.

'The rabbis arrived at the farmhouse and Mr Conroy, the solicitor, was already there. He had arranged to meet them in order to prevent what he was now certain would become another problem in the area. But what he saw shocked him more than he thought possible, for he had taken a book on Judaism out of the library and had seen pictures of rabbis from England, America and the Arabic countries, all dressed differently; but these people standing in the middle of the Australian bush ... Well, these people were similar to pictures he'd seen in the encyclopaedia of Jews in seventeenth-century Russia. With their ringlets, beards and long frock coats, they looked like the Amish Mennonite farmers of Pennsylvania he had observed from the windows of a tourist bus on his last trip to America and he wondered whether these were indeed the same Jews that he was instructed to contact.

'The rabbi shook hands and introduced his colleagues, and the party opened the old man's house and walked inside. With no light they were forced to ignite a hurricane lamp which illuminated the dirty and somewhat squalid condition in which the cabin had been left. One of the rabbis, seeing some aged meat covered in mould and flies on the table, was forced to walk out before he was sick. The smell of rancid milk and fungus-ridden decaying cheese was all through the hut. After a few moments of looking at their new domain all of the men agreed to discuss matters further outside.

'"I would strongly suggest," said Mr Conroy, "that the first thing you do is bulldoze this place. It has no value for men of your religion, I would think you would want to start off afresh."

'"But what do we do with it?" said the rabbi. "We're not farmers. We have no idea how to farm this place. What crop does it grow? What animals are there?"

'Mr Conroy shook his head in surprise. "There are no crops, Rabbi. And no animals. It was just a place where the old man lived. It was once cleared to run cattle but when he took over sixty years ago, he put up fences to stop the cattle coming in and the trees have now all grown back. All you have got here, I'm afraid, is a huge area of wooded hills and valleys and a creek. It has no current income-earning potential."

'"But what should we do with it?" asked the rabbi again.

'Mr Conroy, the solicitor, shrugged. "I don't know. I'm afraid that's up to you."

'"How did the old man live?" the rabbi asked.

'"Apparently he sold firewood. He spent his life cutting it up, putting it into trailers and then the local merchant would buy it from him. It was enough to pay for the food that he couldn't grow or produce. He did have one cow which gave him milk but when he died that had to be shot because it got mastitis."

'Conroy looked again at the rabbis. The whole scene was incongruous. They stood there in the baking sun of an Australian summer, clad in their black coats with locks hanging behind their ears, the strings of tsitsith hanging from beneath their garments, like sheep lost in some strange paddock.

'The head rabbi rounded on the solicitor and said to him, "There's no way we can take this place. You must realise this." Each man began talking in Yiddish to the others. They spoke at a different level of intensity motivated by whatever level of fear they felt during their brief sojourn on the property.

'But the solicitor stood his ground against the rabbinic onslaught. "I'm sorry gentlemen, your distinguished lawyer and I both agree that you have no option or you forego the property."

'The rabbis slunk into a huddle and began to speak to each other. Because they conversed in Yiddish, Mr Conroy felt like an outsider. Then the senior rabbi said, "What about a tenant? Could we put somebody who will pay us rent, then at least we can get some income from the place and we don't have to be here?"

'The solicitor looked at them as though they were crazy. "This is three hundred acres of wooded property in the middle of a couple of thousand acres of prime cattle and sheep land. Who on earth is going to lease this from you? Farmers are walking off their properties because they can't make a profit. You've got trees all over your hillsides so it makes it useless as a cattle property. If you wanted to farm it and grow crops it would cost you hundreds of thousands to clear the trees and to sow the crops and then you would have to wait a couple of years before you got anything like a return. The only thing I can suggest is that you use the land close to the creek for an orchard and that you do what the old man did and sell wood."

'The old rabbi nodded and conversed again with his colleagues. "We'll go back to our yeshiva and pray for guidance from the Almighty. He will tell us what to do," and with that they departed, the keys to a filthy and totally unkosher shed in their pockets — the possessors of three hundred acres of virgin countryside and the most unwilling urban farmers in the 12 000-year history of agriculture.'

Mr Glick looked up and studied his audience for a few moments. Everyone had a wry smile on their face, not the least Rabbi Teichmann who thought the story was delightful but was wondering where it was going. And he missed poor Ruth. He wished she had stayed in the story. He really liked her, and would have welcomed a metaphor between the modern-day Ruth and her biblical namesake. But there were to be no morals or metaphors in this talk ... not if he was to pacify the front row.

'The rabbis returned to their yeshiva and called a meeting of the Board of Governors, their senior Talmud students, associates and friends. There were sixty people in the room by the time the rabbi led the group in prayers, and then explained the situation carefully and logically to everyone. The suggestions came thick and fast from the floor.

"'Give it away. Who needs it?"

"'Challenge the will in court. Maybe you can sell."

"'Put cows on the land and a milkmaid to milk them."

"'Clear some land and use it to grow crops for the yeshiva."

"'Form a trust company and put the assets into a trust, then liquidate the assets and ... "

'At this point, the last speaker was howled down.

'Eventually the rabbi called for order. Well, to tell the truth, the rabbi called for peace instead of order, because the room was in a commotion. "Friends, something is becoming obvious to me. We're very much like the Jews who left Mount Sinai and got stuck with being the chosen people whether they liked it or not. I'm afraid that we're stuck with this block of land. Now it seems to me that a good number of us here are strong and healthy. It also seems the property contains plenty of axes and spades and something which the solicitor up there called a chainsaw. Now with these we can cut down trees and then we can grow things. And who knows? It could be a holiday place when we need to go somewhere. Maybe we could even put up a little building and some of our young man could have a ... well the Christians call it a retreat."'

At this point Mr Dub looked up in anger. The word 'Christians' had arisen again. He hoped this delightful story wasn't going to take a wrong turn.

Mr Glick resumed, '"What I'm saying to you," continued the old rabbi, "is that we should give it a go. Try it. Who knows? Maybe God will smile on us and something good will come of it."'

'If you think that the rabbi's decision was welcomed by everyone, then you're wrong. But he was the rabbi, it was his decision and everybody went along with it. A week went by, and a further week and after a month, nobody had left the comfort and security of their yeshiva, or even the eastern suburbs, to take the risk of going into the country. In fact, truth to tell, many of the prayers which the congregation intoned silently were asking the Almighty to make the rabbi forget his decision.

'But rabbis don't forget decisions, and he managed to keep interest in the farm among the younger men. So it came as no surprise to him, though considerable surprise to the rest of the community, when a couple of the younger men decided that maybe, just maybe, it would be nice to go up there and pitch a tent and spend Tuesday, Wednesday and Thursday in the country. After all, before they became Hasidic, they had been boy scouts. So, they got the keys, promised to make the hut kosher by clearing it out and burying all the rubbish as well as the pots and pans, the knives and forks, the glassware, and taking some clean crockery, cutlery and food up there. When they returned on Friday morning they reported that it was the most wonderful few days that they had enjoyed in a long while. The peace, they enthused, the quiet, the relaxation, the air. Oh friends, they said, you have no idea what wonders we saw.

'Now this, believe it or not, encouraged some other people to go up on the next Tuesday because they couldn't go up on Friday or Saturday and Sunday was the big day for cheder where they taught Hebrew and Bible studies to the local children who weren't part of the yeshiva. So on Tuesday morning another group of rabbis and their students set out, but unlike the first group of pioneers, these arrived to find a clean kosher hut with kosher cutlery. With the provisions they brought, including a tent and sleeping bags they'd borrowed from a congregant, they were able to make themselves very comfortable.

'When they returned on the Friday morning, they reported exactly the same story as the group which came to be known as the pioneers. Long peaceful walks in the country, communing with God, struggling up mountainsides and sitting on rocks overlooking the majesty of the environment, bathing in crystal-clear brooks and seeing the glories of Australian wildlife — the multi-coloured parrots, wallabies and kangaroos, the possums and even a platypus in the river. They spoke of the miracles which they saw during their time in the bush; of how the clarity of the air and the vast night sky with its intense black and the impossible multitude of stars made them realise what infinity really meant when they spoke of God. They explained that they hadn't fully understood before the relationship between God, the creator of Israel, and God, the creator of all things. That when they saw themselves in the enormity of the landscape, or at night as a paltry addendum to the universe, they comprehended as never before the beginning lines of the Book of Genesis.

'The effect of this ecstasy encouraged more and more people to go. This continued for three more months until by then almost all of the yeshiva community had visited and stayed for a couple of days on their farm. And the universal comment was of how their days away from the enclosed walls of the yeshiva somehow gave them a deeper appreciation of the power of God; that their bookish experience, while fulfilling, was made more complete with the demonstration of God's presence in the land.

'And the rabbi had an idea . . . '

Mr Glick took out a handkerchief and wiped his lips which were dry. Normally when he made speeches he liked to have a glass of water but unfortunately people didn't think of this in a synagogue. Undaunted he continued, 'The rabbi phoned one of the leaders of the Hasidic movement in New York, discussed the situation and put the proposition to him.

'The rabbi in America thought about it for a few moments and then told the local rabbi that it was a great idea and that he should proceed immediately, which is what happened. A special fund for building and maintenance in the yeshiva was raided and the money used by the rabbi to build ten wooden shacks on the farm. More money was then put into connecting electricity from the grid, running water into the farm to make the cabins more inhabitable, and ultimately, in a miracle of modernity, a telephone line was run to the central cabin. It took a fair amount of money but a mere three months for the farm to be turned from a camping ground for adventurous rabbis into a retreat where the entire yeshiva community — men and women, boys and girls — could go during the week in order to commune with God under the infinity of His creation. Here the teachers held lessons, talks, debates, arguments, discussions and prayers.

'And in the little town which serviced the area their presence became more and more of a feature. Of course the rabbis would rarely shop in the town and instead brought everything with them — kosher meat, kosher milk, their own bread and supplies which they used when they needed to cook. But sometimes they had to go into town for supplies of equipment such as nails, screws, planks of wood, batteries and personal items such as toilet paper and tissues. On these rare occasions they were a curiosity for the local community. People would come out of their shops or pubs to look at the couple of men who had drifted into town, dressed in black and resembling (so they were assured by Mr Conroy) the Amish of Pennsylvania. And in time the Hasidim became accepted as they walked around the town.

'Mr Conroy, the solicitor, of course knew what was going on. Although he tried to be a voice of moderation, he would sit in his office dreading the appearance of these aliens. Not that he was an anti-Semite. Not at all, but he was concerned that not everybody was as liberal as he, and there would be resentment about the appearance of ultra-Orthodox Jews. But no! He couldn't have been more wrong. At first suspicious, but then welcoming, the townspeople tried to strike up a relationship with the Jews ... and the Jews found the locals not only laconic and easy to talk to, but inordinately friendly. In some people, there was a little bit of suspicion; in most, there was curiosity. One of the locals was particularly friendly, telling the rabbis that it was important to stack the cowpats one on top of the other beside the main gate, so that the Cowpat Collection Service would come and pick them up on the first Tuesday of every month. The rabbis thanked the local for his help. When their car disappeared over the horizon, he fell on the floor, howling with laughter, and spent the next week telling all of his friends what he'd done.

'And for their part, the rabbis drove away, wondering how anybody could possibly believe that they'd fall for that kind of practical joke.

'And so a year went by since the first group of rabbis came out to inspect their sudden inheritance. On the Monday morning, in order to mark the anniversary, half of the yeshiva population took themselves out in cars and travelled north through Sydney, through the national forest and into the bush. The senior rabbi looked at the way in which the workmen had cleared the wooded section of the land and had built the wooden cabins with blissful views of the nearby hills and gentle walks down to the stream. He blessed the cabins and the trees and the animals and sat down to say prayers with his whole community, and to eat lunch.

'And as the fifteen rabbis and many students sat around outside in the glorious fresh air, arguing and debating moot points about the nature of a Jew in relation to the environment, the cacophony of their voices was interrupted by the sound of a truck coming along the track.

'Now you have to understand that their property was so large and so far from the nearest road that the only sounds apart from their voices which could be heard were the calls of the bellbirds, kookaburras and whipbirds and the buzzing of insects. Oh, and I forgot to tell you about the whispering sound of the wind in the trees. They heard the noise of the approaching truck from far off and immediately stood at the crest of the hill to survey the road and see who was approaching. The man who got out was tall, rugged and muscular. He walked up the hill to where the group of rabbis and their emaciated-looking students were standing, looking back at him suspiciously and in some consternation. But his cheery face and open manner disarmed all of them.

"'Good day," he shouted up in a broad Australian accent. He felt like a conductor before a choir. "I'm Bill Foster. I own the next-door farm." He pointed in the direction of the hill opposite. Then he walked up the hill to meet them.

'One by one, the rabbis shook hands and told him their names. One was Reb Dovid, another Reb Yosef, a third Reb Yoel and one Reb Yechezkel. But by the time he had met all the rabbis and their students, the Australian farmer's eyes glazed over in incomprehension. For a man who had grown up with Franks, Syds, Phils and Arthurs, these exotic Eastern European and Yiddish names were just too much for him to cope with.

"'I heard youse blokes were moving in here. I've seen youse from time to time. I've dropped over a couple of Saturdays and Sundays to introduce meself, but there was nobody here," he said.

'The head rabbi invited him in for a glass of water. "No," said the rabbi, they couldn't give him a glass of wine, because they weren't permitted to drink anything unless it had been prepared in the presence of a person specially appointed. And the rabbi went on to explain why the community was only ever there during weekdays. "Would you guys care to come across to my place for a cup of tea. I've told the wife I might be bringing some people home. She's just baked a batch of scones." Again the rabbi reiterated the nature of kashruth, and why they couldn't even countenance eating any food in his home, however delicious he was sure it would be. The rabbi begged his neighbour to understand the restrictions.

'But what he said he would happily do was to bring a small group along to drop by later in the day to be neighbourly. Which they did. Five of the party spent a most pleasant afternoon in the house of their neighbour who lived six kilometres over the hill.

'And not only did they enjoy it, but Bill Foster found the experience rewarding, and he recounted how interesting these old Jews were when he was drinking in a pub later that night. The following week Bill's experience encouraged a couple of other neighbours to drop by and invite the curios to their home. But these men began their invitations differently. They made it very clear to the rabbis that they fully understood why they wouldn't be able to eat or drink in their homes and should feel no need to apologise for failing to be hospitable.

'Over the weeks the Hasidim were able to visit half-a-dozen more homes in the district and became something of a cause célèbre. At Country Women's Association meetings or in the pub or at the National Farmers Federation get-togethers, the talk of the town was no longer the immorality of the Federal government and its attitude to farmers, nor of the drought, nor of the bushfire dangers but was of the way in which the Hasidim had brought real interest into their otherwise humdrum lives.

'But that wasn't the only thing that was happening to the rabbis. Word began to spread in the Jewish community that the farm was something of a garden of paradise and members of the Board of the Synagogue and their families began to ask if perhaps they could stay at the farm for short breaks. And so more money began to come in, which enabled improvements to be made until more cabins were added and an entire little settlement began to grow on the banks of the stream. Where the old man who had owned the land three years previously had lived a solitary life in a single run-down shack, now there was a small tourist settlement growing.

'So the year and the following year went by and the farm became an extension of the Hasidic community and the yeshiva. And a strange and wonderful thing began to happen. Jewish boys who used to know only the ghetto existence of a tightknit Jewish community, who once knew only concrete streets and petrol fumes, got back in touch with the land. The first to appreciate the real ramifications was the head of the yeshiva, Rabbi Goodmann. The young men who came back from the farm had ruddier cheeks, stronger bodies and sunburned faces. They thrilled to the experience of chopping down trees or digging the soil or tending the small menagerie of animals which the farm not only boasted but also needed in order to provide milk and eggs.

'One night after prayers, Rabbi Goodmann was sitting in his study talking to two or three of his colleagues and ruminating on the way in which the children of Israel were meeting the modern world. "It's interesting, isn't it?" he mused. "We were always farmers or goatherders or growers of crops when we had our own land, Eretz Yisrael. And then 2000 years ago the Romans came and kicked us off our land and we became outcasts throughout the world. And in almost every place where we found ourselves, we incurred the hatred of Christians who forbade us from entering professions and who forced us into occupations for which we were not suited, like usury and moneylending. But what hasn't occurred to me until we became owners of this farm was how central the land is to our very being. How much the Jewish nation is a nation of farmers and goatherders and how, like our father, Abraham, we count our wealth in the Torah which was given to us by God ... and in sheep."

'The other rabbis began to object but Rabbi Goodmann held up his hand. "Oh I know we always talk about being in our land of Israel. I know that every year at the Seder service we say 'L'Shana Haba'ah Birushalayim ... to Next Year in Jerusalem. And that's what Israel has always meant to me — the cities of Jerusalem, Safed and Jericho ... and perhaps even the River Jordan. I've never thought of our attachment to Israel as being as a result of its agriculture. Yet now, we, through the intervention of God Almighty, have been forced to expand our yeshiva into the countryside, and we have become farmers. It has enabled me to understand how central the land is to us because God is everywhere in the land ... in the trees, in the valleys and in the mountains. You see, in my arrogance, I thought that our study in this yeshiva was the central core of Jewish existence. But I now realise it is only one pillar of our strength."'

Mr Glick's talk created an interesting mixture of confusion in the congregation. The Friday-night congregation was now up to seventy. It was composed of the nine regulars, plus another sixty or so who had come anticipating a ripping good yarn — the sort of story which they could repeat at a dinner party or from which they could learn an interesting moral lesson. And these people were, well, frankly ... disappointed.

Yet in the front two rows the nine regulars, who of course included Dr Josephs, Mr Dub, Mr Dayan and a few others, were beaming and nodding and calling out 'Shekoyach' and 'Amen.' The small group of regulars had thoroughly enjoyed Mr Glick's story. It was full of Yiddishkiet and sound Jewish principles. It was an exemplary tale, the type told at Jewish functions and on Friday nights when the family got together. It was a heroic tale, a Jewish struggle against adversity, only this time, thank God, the Jews won.

Let's face it, until the creation of the state of Israel, the Jews could hardly have been called the world's greatest warriors, or farmers, or agricultural luminaries. Yes, the regulars enjoyed Mr Glick's story enormously ... but for the others? Well, that was another story. They were far from impressed.

So what, they asked? So a bunch of Hasidic rabbis had taken over a farm and turned it into something nice. So Jews had regained a foothold on some land. Okay, big deal. But where was the moral? Where was the message that they would take away and think about for days following? Where was the story with the strong moral standpoint which they could retell to their children and grandchildren when they committed the minor sins which children and grandchildren tend to commit?

As he stood, being super-sensitive to the feelings of his congregation, Rabbi Teichmann sensed a growing dichotomy between the front and the back, the old and the new, the traditional and the modern. Having heard Mr Glick recount a synopsis of his story earlier in the week, he felt sure that the large majority would find it unsatisfactory. And by the audible lack of appreciation as Mr Glick, full of youth and vigour, self-importance and self-confidence, sat down to be patted on the back by the traditionalists, the rabbi knew that he had to regain the agenda from the front row, or else the following week and the week after, the numbers would gradually erode. And this is how he did it.

'Before we begin with the rest of the service, I would like to thank Mr Glick and the other storytellers whose tales we have all enjoyed so very much during the past weeks. They have all delighted us with their superb storytelling techniques and with the wonderful stories which they've told. You know, my dear friends, not even I as your rabbi had any idea that there was such a depth of talent in this little shul of ours. It's often said that the times produce the leaders. Normally it refers to adversity and in our case, there were circumstances which could indeed have been termed adverse, circumstances which I think will not be unfamiliar to our regulars. We had a falling attendance on a Friday night and so I decided to forego my sermon and lesson in favour of letting the congregation tell its stories as a way of attracting more people. It has patently worked, as may be witnessed by so many of you being here.

'Now that we have more people coming however, I intend to return to the sermons and to give everybody a break from the demands of storytelling,' and so to the shocked and disappointed community, the rabbi simply turned his back, and continued the service.

The following Friday night, attendance was dramatically down to just above twenty and the Friday night after, only one person more than the regulars turned up. That was Mr Finburg, who had substituted Friday night for Saturday morning. It was then that the rabbi called Mr Dayan, Mr Dub and Dr Josephs into his study on Monday night. 'What am I to do?' he asked. 'You've seen the results. We're back where we started; it's a disaster.'

Mr Dayan nodded. 'You have to go back to storytelling.'

'Only if there's a compromise, Mr Dayan,' said the rabbi. 'Only if you agree that some of the stories are going to please you, some of the stories are going to annoy you but that you and Mr Dub and Dr Josephs and all the other regulars will sit there and listen with patience and open-mindedness.'

'Of course.' They all agreed immediately. 'We wouldn't have it any other way.'

The rabbi and rebbetzin spent the next three days sending out letters to all the congregation which read:

MAZALTOV!! GREAT NEWS!!

By popular demand our storytellers have been asked to come back.

Every Friday night, instead of the rabbinic sermon, the storytellers of our congregation will tantalise your minds and inflame your intellect with wondrous fables and tales of times past, present and future.

Plus there's a Kiddush at the end of the service.

Bring your family. Bring your friends. Join us for a Friday night Festival of Stories.

Signed,

Rabbi and Rebbetzin Teichmann

And on the following Friday night, not ten, not twenty, not even the previous record of seventy, but one hundred and thirty people crowded into the synagogue. The rabbi and rebbetzin couldn't believe their eyes. Even old Abe Flaxman the beggar, freshly washed and laundered courtesy of the rabbi was there, (would he never leave the rabbi's home? He'd been there for six weeks).

Now in order not to embarrass anybody, the rabbi had made it a policy not to stand up and make a particular mention of the newcomers. It would identify and discomfort them, but even he was so amazed to have such a large congregation in the small shul that he felt impelled before the service started to turn around and to say 'Shabbat shalom, dear friends. This is a miracle. I welcome you all for whatever reason you have come,' and he turned around and continued with the service.

MR AARONS THE WRITER TELLS HIS STORY ABOUT THE THREE RINGS

When he came to that time of the service when he otherwise would have given a sermon, Rabbi Teichmann called upon David Aarons to stand and delight everybody with his story. It was something of a coup to get Mr Aarons. Of all the people in the synagogue, he was the most publicly recognised in the wider community. Mr Aarons was a novelist, a playwright, a poet and a regular contributor to the Op-Ed sections of the intelligent newspapers. He frequently appeared on television when there was a programme to do with the arts, and was often sought out for his opinion when there was a literary controversy somewhere in the world.

Mr Aarons rarely came to shul, except of course twice on Rosh Hashanah and once on Yom Kippur. He was always away at international meetings or in some writer's retreat, writing his novels, or at his mountain home composing poetry for months on end. So when, the previous day, Mr Aarons phoned the rabbi and told him that word had got to him about storytelling in the synagogue, the rabbi was most flattered. But his delight turned to shock when the great writer offered himself as a storyteller.

Although he had somebody else lined up, Rabbi Teichmann had no hesitation in thanking Mr Aarons and accepting his offer most gratefully. He'd have to cope with Mr Udovitch's sensitivities at some later date.

Now Mr Aarons wasn't the type of author who looked like some aging philosopher, one whose picture appeared on the back cover of his books smoking a pipe, sitting at his trusty old typewriter and stroking the head of his golden retriever. Mr Aarons was in his early seventies, short, balding, with ears which stuck out almost at right angles. The rebbetzin was fond of saying that he looked like a Volkswagen with its doors open. Mr Aarons also suffered from a head which resembled that of a gnome. His beard clung to the outskirts of his otherwise clean-shaven face. He had probably been a beatnik in the 1950s and had not progressed sartorially since. But all this was of no concern, because to the rabbi's delight, he appeared in the shul, right on time on Friday night and looked completely at ease as he mounted the bimah, shook hands with the rabbi and turned to address the congregation.

'Ladies and gentlemen,' he began. 'Rabbi Teichmann, Mrs Teichmann . . .'

Mr Dayan and Mr Dub looked at each other in surprise. What was this? The beginning of an after-dinner speech? This was a story. You don't begin a story with 'My Lords, ladies and gentlemen'.

'There wouldn't be many people here who are not intimately familiar with one of William Shakespeare's greatest achievements, *The Merchant of Venice*. If you will remember, in the *Merchant*, which was written by Shakespeare around 1596, Shylock the Jew is portrayed as a villainous buffoon. When it was played to the Elizabethan theatre it was received as a comedy but more recently, especially over the last hundred years, we have come to judge the masterpiece as a serious drama with only a few overtones of humour. The figure of Shylock has changed from being an evil and villainous usurer to a dignified and very much wronged figure of tragedy. In the time of Shakespeare, a Jew was considered a natural and inevitable buffoon, and a rightful victim of Christian trickery, and the Elizabethans considered it absolutely proper that he should be dealt with harshly by Portia. But since the time of the Enlightenment and the emergence of the Jew from the ghetto, the wider literary world has been somewhat kinder to the image of the Hebrew people.

'Although he was Elizabethan to his bootstraps, William Shakespeare took great pains to examine the figure of Shylock very carefully from a number of different angles and, rather than presenting him as a one-level cardboard cutout of a character, the Bard gave us luminous insights into his motivation, rationale and justification.

'So why am I giving you a lesson in literary deconstruction? Simply to introduce you to one of the minor, but still important elements of the play — the incident of the three caskets. You may remember that Bassanio tries to woo the wealthy and noble Portia; but in her father's will it has been specified that whosoever wants to marry her must chose one of three caskets: a casket of gold, a casket of silver or a casket of lead, and each one of these bears a legend which defines much about humankind.'

Mr Aarons looked at the congregation who were listening to his every word. Most people were still amazed that the rabbi had attracted so prominent and important a visitor to the shul. Only Mr Udovitch sat there, feeling unhappy and disregarded.

'It's an interesting device which Shakespeare used, the three caskets. Indeed, it has a certain resonance in another religion which, for the sake of propriety, I won't name.

'But out of the ancient mists of history and retold more recently as a famous play called *Nathan the Wise* comes a story which has a certain similarity with the caskets seen in Shakespeare's *Merchant*. This story doesn't involve caskets, but three objects which have a more profound significance, as will soon become clear. So with your permission, I would like to tell this story of the three rings, which I've adapted from the play, *Nathan the Wise*.'

The entire shul was hanging onto his every word. Despite the fact that he looked so odd, his ability to hold the congregation in the palm of his hand, like the great storytellers of a past era, was extraordinary. Even the rabbi examined his technique, intending to use it the following Saturday morning when he rose to give his sermon.

Mr Aarons continued, 'My story begins in Jerusalem at the time of the Crusades. It was a time when the fearsome Saladin was positioned against the approaching King Richard I, known throughout Christendom as Richard the Lion-Hearted.

'The year was 1190 and the First Crusader kingdom of Jerusalem had fallen three years earlier. It had lasted from 1099 until its final, miserable dissolution in 1187 when it was put out of its misery and overthrown by the greatest warlord that the Arabian nation has ever produced.

'Now most people think of Saladin as a man of intense viciousness, bitter brutality and inhumanity. Few things could be further from the truth. Oh, certainly he committed numerous barbaric acts, but in those days they weren't considered to be barbarism and Saladin rarely acted brutally unless people had acted brutally towards him. Saladin, in fact wasn't an Arab at all, but a Kurd born in Mesopotamia. At a very early age, he came under the influence of the Turks in northern Syria and when he was thirty-one, he was appointed commander of the Syrian troops and vizier of Egypt. He would have just been another ordinary Middle Ages ruler had it not been for the insanity of the popes who used the Crusades as a way of bolstering up their petty powers, entertaining their political machinations and implementing their fight for land.

'After the Second Crusade and the hideous defeat of the Knights Templar and the other Christian armies at the Battle of Hattín, Saladin took Jerusalem and thought that he would bring peace to the land. What he didn't count on was the reaction many Western rulers like King Richard of England, the German Holy Roman Emperor, as well as the jealous and suspicious King of France would have to the loss of Jerusalem. But I don't want to turn this tale into a history lesson . . .'

Mr Dub said a silent prayer of thanks. All this talk of Crusades and Saladin was beginning to worry him.

'. . . but there was one event that happened in 1187 which is noteworthy. It has nothing to do with my story, which I'll come on to shortly, but it's always been a source of wonder and amazement to me. On October 21, Pope Gregory VIII succeeded Pope Urban III. Now Gregory was a particularly pious and learned cleric who came to the throne intent on reconciliation. But he was dogged by the problems in the Holy Land. Three weeks before his enthronement, Saladin had taken Jerusalem, and it's believed that when the new Pope received the news, he became terribly distressed. Gregory proclaimed a new Crusade . . . the third — because in his opinion, the catastrophes of the Christians in the Holy Land were a punishment from God for the sins of the Catholic Church and the Christian community in general. Yet just a few short weeks after declaring the Crusade, Pope Gregory VIII died of a broken heart. What amazes me is that if the Crusades were divinely inspired, as the Church told its followers, then why did the Almighty cause the most devout Pope in centuries to die so suddenly before he could see Jerusalem recaptured and back in Christian hands? But that's something which must be answered by one much wiser than me . . .'

Mr Aarons looked at the congregation for a rebuttal of his deprecation, but nobody made a movement. So he continued.

'But back to the Holy Land. It is generally regarded that whilst he was in control of Jerusalem, Saladin brought an amazing degree of tolerance to the government. Jews were allowed to pray at the remains of the Herodian Temple and in their synagogues, and they happily worshipped alongside Moslems and whatever Christians remained in the city. From this point of view Saladin can only be regarded as a leader of civilisation and courtesy.

'And now to my story proper, which begins in the years between Saladin's takeover of Jerusalem in 1187 and his need to defend the city from the Third Crusade led by King Richard the Lion-Hearted. Armed with a huge following and motivated by extraordinary zeal, Richard arrived in Palestine in 1191 with the intention of recapturing Jerusalem.

'As many of you will know, the tragedy for Richard was that he came to within sight of the walls of Jerusalem but was forced to return home in order to settle affairs with his mischievous brother John and to protect his French and English kingdoms.

'So what did happen inside Jerusalem during those few years of peace and tranquillity, of civilisation and tolerance between 1187 and 1191 when the Kings of Europe again brought war to the Holy Land?

'Well, as I've told you, Jews, Moslems and Christians prayed side by side, walked in the streets chatting amiably to each other and lived a full and peaceful life. Now those four years might not sound like much but when you consider the brutality of the Christian kings of Jerusalem from the beginning of the twelfth century until close to its end, it was as if Jerusalem had become the Garden of Eden. And so it must have seemed to the residents after the way in which Jews and the Moslems had been persecuted by the various orders of Knights Chivalrous. Yes, my friends, this brief moment of sunshine was a period of intense joy and growth for the local community.

'And it's here that my story proper begins ...'

The rabbi breathed a sigh of relief. It was the third time that Mr Aarons had said that his story was beginning. All this history was quite interesting as background, but people had come for a story, not a lecture.

'In this local community was a man called Solomon the Merchant. Although for many years the Jewish community had been oppressed by the Crusader Christians, through his intelligence and gift for flexibility and adapting to the needs of the times, Solomon the Merchant had amassed a great fortune. Of course in those days there were no banks and so his money was cleverly deposited in secret compartments around his house. Since the advent of Saladin, however, the vast bulk of his fortune was securely locked in the treasury of the new ruler's palace where Saladin protected it in return for a not-inconsiderable fee.

'Solomon's business was in equipping caravans to trade between the great centres of population of the day. Some of his caravans travelled from the Fatamid caliphate of Egypt, where its capital Cairo was a bustling metropolis, then north through Ashcalon, Caesarea, Sidon and Tripoli; then further north through the Seljuk empires into Byzantium where, after many weeks of exhausting travel, they eventually unloaded their exotic produce in Constantinople. But that wasn't their only route, Solomon's caravans travelled far and wide around the Levant, and extended their trading to many towns en route around the fertile crescent — into Greece and southeast into the bustling cities of Mecca and Medina. But his primary trade route was along the ancient kings' highway where the fabulously wealthy caliphates of Egypt were eager to buy his silks, golden jewellery, precious perfumes and ointments, and the traders of other empires were eager for the produce of other exotic and faraway lands.

'Solomon used to supply all the food, drink, camels and money that the camel owners needed when they joined one of his caravans. Because in those ancient times, it could be many days journey between one caravanserai and another. Often the journeys were long and arduous but these days Solomon was very rarely robbed by brigands on the way or by the caravan drivers who carried his stock. And the reason? Because everybody knew of the love and respect in which he was held by Saladin. You see, Solomon had known Saladin for many years. While the young man was ruler of Egypt, Solomon had recognised his brilliant gifts of leadership, and had helped to make his Court one of the most glittering of the ancient world. Solomon promoted Saladin wherever his caravans travelled and artists, poets, and craftsmen were attracted to Cairo, which quickly became the centre of creativity and excitement. And Saladin didn't forget his old friend when he came to rule over Jerusalem.

'Saladin made it very clear to everybody throughout the lands over which he was now the ruler that anybody who attacked a trader's caravan attacked him, and he would be merciless in his pursuit of the evildoers. So only rarely were thieves and brigands stupid enough to attack caravans and nobody for many years had dared to attack a caravan belonging to Solomon.

'It might surprise you that Saladin, a Moslem and a fervently religious follower of the Prophet, held an old Jew in Jerusalem in such high regard and respect. These days, thanks to propaganda and the media, we have been conditioned to think that Jews and Moslems have been at each other's throats for centuries. Not so. It's only in the last hundred years that real enmity has been present between our brother nations, and this is over the thorny issue of Zionism. Contrary to what many people think, history doesn't show the same thing happening through the ages; for most of their existence, Jews and Arabs have coexisted side by side, often cooperatively and amicably.'

Rabbi Teichmann nodded his head in agreement.

'The Moslems had great respect for Jews as the originators of their own religion and Saladin especially was as close to Abraham, Isaac and Jacob as he was to Mohammed, the founder of his own religion 570 years earlier. The two religions shared the same God, though known by different names, Elohim and Allah.

'As is so often the way with these kinds of stories, Solomon the Merchant was a widower, but he had a beautiful daughter. And they lived together in rich and luxurious surroundings in a large mansion on the top of one of the city's most prestigious hills in sight of the palace in which Saladin lived when he was in Jerusalem.

'Of course, I might have given the impression that for those few years between the fall of the Christian kingdom, and the arrival of the Third Crusade to retake Jerusalem from the followers of Islam, everything was rosy in the city, but it wasn't. You see, there was a thorn in the side of the peacefully co-existing Moslems and the Jews, and these were the few remaining Knights Templar that had not been killed at the Battle of Hattín. Does it surprise you that Saladin allowed his enemy, the knights dedicated to protecting Christian pilgrims to the Holy Land, and dedicated to the overthrow of Islam and the restoration of Jerusalem as a Christian kingdom ... does it amaze you that Saladin would allow these men to remain at liberty? That he would allow them the freedom to worship? Remember, these were the selfsame men whose brotherhood had mercilessly slaughtered tens of thousands of Jews and Moslems in the past 70 years; the men who had vowed to destroy Saladin and all like him.

'But allow them freedom of existence is precisely what Saladin did. Just think about that for a moment. A few years earlier at the Battle of Hattín, Saladin had watched the incompetent Christian army led by King Guy of Jerusalem and the equally incompetent contingent of Templars, throw itself unprepared into one of the most calamitous battles of the Middle Ages. Saladin beheaded hundreds of Templars in his anger at the injustices of the past, yet, when he had won, he was also merciful and forgave many of those that remained, allowing them to live a peaceful life in Jerusalem under his protection. I can't see any modern ruler doing that, can you?'

Rabbi Teichmann shook his head as did many of the people in the congregation. 'And that was how a young Templar, a vigorous and virile knight called Ranulf came to be living in peaceful Jerusalem alongside Moslems and Jews.

'Ranulf was the second son of one of the nobles of the Champagne area of north France near Rouen. He had taken up the cross ten years earlier and enlisted as one of the Knights Templar because, as a second son, he knew he would not come into any property on the death of his father. So, being a pious young man, he devoted his life to assisting pilgrims, and swore to protect the lives of those who were travelling to the holy shrines of Jerusalem. With thirty of his fellow knights he had travelled to the south of France where he boarded a boat to Acre and then walked, bareheaded in the blistering heat, up the hills of the Holy Land until he entered the city of Jerusalem. That was five years before our story begins, and there he stayed.

'Had Ranulf not fallen victim to a fever, he would undoubtedly have been one of the victims of the massacre at the Horns of Hattín, but as fortune would have it, Ranulf survived and, under his bitter enemy's protection, lived a peaceful and quiet life in the stables of the Temple of Solomon along with a dozen other older Templars who had somehow survived the battle.

'One day Ranulf was walking the streets of the ancient city when through a window he spied a sight which literally took his breath away. It was the house of the rich merchant Solomon, and the sight he saw was Solomon's daughter Rebecca. She was combing her hair and playing with a pet monkey that had been brought back as a present from Egypt. Being a young man, Ranulf found the vow of chastity that he had taken as a Knight Templar particularly difficult to maintain when he saw Rebecca through the window. At that very moment, he experienced an epiphany and realised he would have to break his vow.

'She was extraordinarily beautiful. Her face was fair. Her eyes black as jet and her hair fell in cascades below her shoulders. Sensing she was being looked at, Rebecca turned and glanced down into the street where she saw the tall dark-haired young man staring up at her, his mouth agape, his eyes fixed on her lips.

'Now Rebecca had been instilled with the humility of a young Jewish woman and her upbringing told her that she must look away immediately and close the shutters. But there was a momentary delay — was it a second, a minute, even an hour? — before she closed the shutters, and that told the young Ranulf everything that he wanted to know.

'Eventually, pretending that it was the monkey on her shoulder which caused her to tarry, she closed the windows and went into the depths of her boudoir where she sat on the bed, her face flushed, her head spinning. Her maid looked at her with concern and thought she was ill but Rebecca assured the servant that she was perfectly well and had a temporary moment of faintness. The girl took some smelling salts out of her bedside cabinet, a present from a rich Greek merchant, and placed the pungent aromatic oil under her nose. For the whole day, and for the following day, Rebecca kept her bedroom window closed. In part because of the stifling heat of summer but mainly because she was terrified of setting eyes on the young man again.

'It was on the third morning that she reopened her shutters on the brilliant blue and white sky of Jerusalem. In the distance were the gold and silver domes of the mosques of Al Aksa and Omar, and the minarets which pointed up to the heavens. And side by side were Christian churches with their crosses, and synagogues with their Shields of David, but Rebecca wasn't looking at the skyline. Instead, as she threw open the shutters, she cast her eyes down in the hope that the young man, who had been the centre of her dreams, would still be there. Her heart pounded and again she nearly fainted when she saw him, standing there as if in three days he had never moved. He looked up as she looked down and in her fright she began to pull the blinds closed but he called up, "Wait! Wait! Beautiful maiden. I beg you. I have stood here for two days in the broiling sun, hoping to catch sight of you. What is your name?"

'But in fear, she closed the shutters and ran downstairs to one of the salons where she sat in a fluster breathing deeply. There she tried to read a book. It was a beautifully illustrated manuscript written in Latin by an Egyptian scribe retelling the legend of Harun al-Rashid . . . '

Mr Aarons looked at the congregation, knowing from Shakespeare the power of a soliloquy, and said, 'You may be interested to know that this great man, whose name means Aaron the Upright, lived in Arabia in the eighth century and was later idealised as the caliph of Scheherazade.' He coughed to indicate the end of his aside, and continued with his story.

'But the words swam before her eyes and she realised after a while that she had read nothing. And so she put the book down and walked into her father's library where he was busy writing orders for a caravan. She went into the kitchens to instruct the cooks on the provision of the day's food and then found her way back upstairs to her boudoir where an intense and irrepressible magnetism drew her again to the window. Silently, she opened the shutter until a crack of light found its way into the room, and she saw the handsome young Templar standing in exactly the same spot in the burning sun looking up at her window, waiting for her appearance. She closed the shutter instantly and determined to go down and tell her father. It could not be allowed. He was wearing the hideous white tunic and red cross of her most hated enemy. It was intolerable that he should be staring at her home. The man spying upon her was the natural enemy of her people.

'Her father would know what to do. He would go out and deal with the young man, or tell Saladin, who would have the man punished severely for this intrusion. She stood outside her father's library but some indefinable force prevented her from entering. Her heart was pounding. Her face was flushed. She felt as if she was coming down with some fever. She poured herself water from a glass carafe and told her maid to prepare her outdoor clothes for she would walk down to the Western Wall in order to say prayers.

'As the door was opened, Rebecca, accompanied by her maid and bodyguard, walked out of the house and prepared to amble down the winding hills towards the last remaining vestiges of the Temple of King Herod. But as they turned into the street, the young man crossed the road and said, "Lady, please talk to me."

'Her bodyguard, a tall muscular and fearsome Abyssinian, drew a huge scimitar from its scabbard and turned to face the young man. Uncowed, Ranulf put his hand on his scabbard preparing to draw his sword out in order to fight, but Rebecca ran between the two, calling out "Stop!". She turned to the Abyssinian and said, "Put away your sword. This man presents no danger", then turned to Ranulf and said, "Who are you and why do you wait below my window?"

'"I am Ranulf. I am a Knight of the Temple of Solomon. I saw you days ago and have hardly slept or eaten since. I must know who you are. Your name, and whether you are married."

'"You're impertinent and impetuous," she said. "Be off or I'll tell the Grand Vizier," and then she turned and continued to walk down the hill towards the wall of the temple.

'But Ranulf wouldn't be put off. He ran down the hill, dodging between donkeys, carts and old beggar women bent double in their suffocating black robes holding their hands out for money.

'"Not until you have told me your name and whether you are married. One will suffice but both will make my life complete."

'Rebecca refused to answer, walking beyond her maid and in front of her bodyguard down the hill. As he walked parallel to them, the young man called out, "I've already told you my name. It's Ranulf. I'm the second son of the Count of Champagne. I should have died at the Battle of Hattín but God saved me to meet you. Tell me your name, I beg you, or you will do to me what the Saracens have failed to do."

'But Rebecca ignored him and when she and her small party continued to walk on, Ranulf quickly realised that his efforts were in vain. When they turned a corner into another street to approach the Western Wall, Rebecca surreptitiously glanced back and felt a tinge of annoyance that the young man was no longer pursuing her but was standing fecklessly in the street just looking at her. Well, she thought, if that's all he cares.'

Rabbi Teichmann was beginning to become concerned. This story was sounding as if it was heading for a mixed marriage, something which he couldn't possibly countenance. He hadn't checked the details of the tale with Mr Aarons, it had all happened too late and the rabbi didn't know him well enough to be absolutely certain that Mr Aarons wouldn't embarrass the congregation.

'The following day,' Mr Aarons continued, 'Rebecca threw open her shutters and saw that Ranulf was standing in the same place. But this time she didn't close them. This time she felt a tinge of annoyance. If he was any sort of a man he should have pursued her the previous day, and not be put off by her harsh words. "I told you to go away," she shouted.

"'Not until you tell me your name," he called out. He pulled his sword out of the scabbard. "And even if your Abyssinian guard comes to kill me, I shan't move. I'll stay and fight him to the death. Just tell me your name."

'She sighed and thought for a moment. It was the only way to get rid of him. "My name is Rebecca. Now go!"

"'Wait," he shouted as she began to close the shutters. "You promised me another answer."

"'I promised you nothing," she shouted down angrily.

"'Then tell me, Rebecca. Are you married?"

'She looked at him. He had such beautiful, dolorous eyes, such a clean complexion, such jet-black hair. He was slighter than her bodyguard who was a giant but he was still taller, broader and obviously stronger than almost everybody else in her circle of friends. She began to close the shutters but imperceptibly she shook her head. Watching her every movement, Ranulf realised that this was a signal and threw his cap up into the air, shouting in joy.

'No, she wasn't married. Yes, there was a chance. His heart exploded with elation and he shouted out "Yes! Yes! She's unwed" to the surprise of passers-by.

'Later that morning, Rebecca interrupted her father's business affairs by asking, "What is the greatest sin a Jewess can commit?"

'Her father Solomon sat back in his chair and put down his sharpened writing reed. He was surprised by her question. "Have you committed a sin that you need to discuss with me?" he asked. He and his daughter had grown close since the death of Solomon's wife ten years earlier but when she became a woman he had found it more and more difficult to talk to her about matters of intimacy. He prayed that his strength and resolve would not fail him.

"'No father, I haven't committed a sin."

"'Then why need you ask this question?" Solomon asked.

"'I'm just interested in what you consider to be the greatest virtue of a Jewess and the greatest sin she can commit."

"'The virtue is easy. To walk upon the path ordained by God, to follow the laws of Moses, to be modest, to obey each and every one of the ten commandments, to study the law, to be educated."

'Rebecca nodded. "And the greatest sin?"

'Solomon frowned and stared up at the ceiling, choosing his words very carefully. "I can't answer that question. For to each person, sins mean different things. For a person who has murdered once, a second murder isn't such a great sin. For a person who is a thief, stealing another's purse is no great sin. Yet if you, my child, were to steal even the smallest coin from your father's purse, for you it would be the greatest of sins. For you are an honest young woman who knows the difference between right and wrong. So for you, my daughter, the greatest sin could be deceit or immodesty or uncharitable thoughts. As you can see, the question cannot be answered."

'Rebecca nodded and thanked her father but before she could leave the library he said, "Rebecca, do you need to talk to me about something?"

'The girl hesitated in the doorway and as if she was suddenly carrying a heavy burden, she returned and stood over her father. She kissed his head and said, "There's a Christian man who stands outside our door. He has been there for the last four or five days," and she told her father everything that had happened.

'Now, you might expect that her father would have been incensed, that he would have called the guard and had the young man soundly thrashed. That's undoubtedly what would have happened if a Jewish man had stood underneath the bedroom window of a Christian girl. But this isn't what happened. In fact, quite the opposite. To her amazement, Solomon said, "We mustn't be inhospitable. We must invite him in. We must explain to him why his interest in you will always be unfulfilled."

'And that was how Ranulf, second son of the Count of Champagne found himself drinking rose-water and eating delights at the table of Solomon the Merchant. The young man unabashedly told Rebecca's father of his love for her. Not once did he prevaricate or lie or evade the truth when confronted by Rebecca's stern-looking father. He impressed Solomon by explaining simply and eloquently how he planned to marry her. He said that he wasn't able to get her out of his mind, and told Solomon how he had taken vows of chastity but was now prepared to forego those vows in order to marry the Jewess. He was even prepared to leave the order of the Knights Templar just so he could marry Rebecca and devote himself to her for the rest of his life. And old Solomon nodded and listened carefully not once interrupting, but according the tempestuous young man the rights of an equal.

'But when he had finished his declamation, Solomon asked the young man, "These vows you took. Were they sworn on the Bible?"

'"Of course," replied Ranulf.

'"And when you marry my daughter, will you swear your fidelity to honour and respect her on the Bible?"

'"Naturally," said the young man.

'"But if you break the vows you took when you became a Templar in order to marry Rebecca, why will you not break vows of a similar gravity which you will take when you marry my daughter?"

'"But that's different," protested the young man. "I love your daughter."

'"And don't you love the order to which you belong?"

'Ranulf pushed back his chair, stood, and said angrily, "You're saying then that I can't marry your daughter?"

'"What I'm saying," said the old man slowly and cautiously, "is that before you can look to involve others in your duplicity, you must examine your own heart. How can you be true to another,

Ranulf, when you cannot be true to yourself and to your own beliefs? Vows cannot be picked up and put down again like some child's plaything."

"'Imagine you are a passenger on a ship when another, more attractive ship sails close. It might look simple to transfer from one to the other, but life teaches us that to change in the middle of a heaving and uncertain sea invites disaster. Of course, it can be done, but the dangers are great, for your immortal soul and for your life."

"'Can I become a Jew?" asked Ranulf.

'Old Solomon shrugged. "Do you really want to? Do you want to become one against whom the Popes have excoriated? Christians see us as the murderers of Christ, as the harbingers of evil. I have no doubt, young man, that when you came here, you were burning with the desire to cleanse Jerusalem of Jews and Arabs. Yet now, because of a romantic burning passion in your heart, you want to become one of us. Do so, and you will become just like us, wanderers upon the face of the earth, hated by Christians everywhere. Reviled because we refuse to believe in your Christ. Is your love for my daughter really that strong?"

'Ranulf gripped the chair that he was leaning against and closed his eyes. Reason began to seep back into his befuddled mind. He no longer saw Rebecca as the perfect embodiment of beauty. Instead he saw her through the eyes of his father ... as a Jewess, the daughter of an old Jew, a usurer, a merchant, one of the hated band who refused to convert to the true faith of Christianity.

'The young man nodded and apologised for his intemperance. He begged to leave but Solomon wouldn't let him go. "I see the light of reason shine in your eyes, Ranulf. But you are a good young man with many virtues. Don't just leave us. Learn from us. My daughter has to marry a Jew. That you must realise. But she is a wise and educated woman who can teach you much. Spend time with her. I know she'll enjoy it and, provided you behave modestly, I know that you will learn a great deal. Rather than waste your time in those stables, get to know more about us."

'And that's precisely what Ranulf did. Although in his heart he still harboured feelings of great passion and would run up the hill every morning to be by her side, Rebecca maintained her decorum and modesty and over the next year introduced Ranulf to the depths of Judaism, to the genius of the great Greek and Latin writers, to Arabic poetry, to the arts of astronomy, algebra and geometry, to medicine and alchemy ... and during the year, Ranulf quickly learnt the difference between the mind and the body, between the spiritual and the corporeal.

'So much a part of the daily life of Solomon and his household did Ranulf become that one day, when Saladin was in Jerusalem, he invited Solomon and Rebecca to join him at dinner that night, and Solomon wrote a note begging that Ranulf, a Knight Templar, be permitted to join them. Saladin unhesitatingly agreed, though privately he said he was surprised that such a friendship existed.

'That night, over dinner, they talked for hours about the coming Crusade of Richard the Lion-Hearted who was by now wintering on the island of Sicily and the advance of the fleet of ships commandeered by King Phillip II of France. Of course, Saladin, realising that a Knight Templar was present, gave no further details but assured the company that he knew about Richard and that he felt sure he could avert a new war.

'During the evening, Saladin became quiet and pensive. For some reason, he kept looking at the old Jew and his daughter sitting beside the young Christian, staring at them as though some strange thought was passing through his mind. He was thinking how odd were the circumstances which led to these followers of two different religions to sit at a table in the company of a Moslem prince. And a thought occurred to Saladin, something which he had pondered upon many times in the past and now seemed a good time to ask.

"'Dear friend,' he said to Solomon, "which one of ours is the true religion? I ask this in the presence of a Christian and a Jew. I ask from the standpoint of a man who follows Mohammed and believes with all his heart that He is the true Prophet."

'Solomon thought for a moment. He took a sip of rose-water and looked at his daughter. Her friendship with Ranulf for the last year had taught the young man much about their religion. He hoped that the parable he would tell would help the young man understand even more. "Let me tell you, Mighty Ruler, the story of the ring. Once, many hundreds of years ago, a jeweller was commissioned to make a beautiful ring. And the jeweller invested this ring with much love and craft, so that when it was complete, it was the finest ring ever made with the very finest gold and most precious stones. The jeweller loved the ring so much that he could not bear to part with it. In fact, he became convinced that it had magical powers, that it could protect the wearer against harm, that it would give its master great insight and wisdom, and that it would enable its owner to answer every impossible question in life. The great craftsman loved the ring so much that he decided to keep it for himself and make another for the client, though he could not invest this second ring with the same love and care and devotion as he had invested in the first ring.

"'And so the jeweller wore the wondrous ring unto his death. And with his last dying breath he called his only son over to his bedside and whispered into his ear the secrets of the ring, saying to him, 'You may have the ring but you must use it wisely.'

"'The son took the ring from his father's dead finger, put it on and he too was endowed with the same ability to see further and clearer and understand more than any other man. And for generation upon generation, father gave the ring to son until one day one of the sons married and his wife gave birth to triplets who grew into three healthy and virile young men. The father couldn't separate or divide his love between any of the three, each of whom was perfect in his eyes. And as he grew older, he grew more and more desperate because he knew that only one of the sons would gain benefit from the ring.

"'So what did this man do? After many months of painful thought he had a jeweller make two more identical rings. Now only the father knew that these new rings were not blessed with magic like the real ring, but as he grew weaker and weaker, he called the three young men together and he said to them, 'These are three rings, each of which has great and magical power. Powers of insight, powers of knowledge, powers to let you see further and know more than any other man.'

"'And he picked up the three rings and put them onto the fingers of his three sons. Now, the father had no idea which of the rings was the original because each ring was a perfect replica of the other. And so when the three young men put the rings on, each believed in his heart that he was wearing the original, and each, through his faith, was able to see further and to know more than any other man."

'Solomon looked at Ranulf who was smiling. Then he looked at Saladin who nodded in understanding. And so the dinner party ended and Ranulf walked home with Solomon and Rebecca. He was unusually quiet, and the reason became clear when they arrived at the front door. For Ranulf said, "Although I love you both dearly, and will never forget you, I fear that I will never see you again. Tonight, I have made a decision that will take me away from you, and may perhaps mean my death. For tonight, listening to your story about the three rings, I have decided that I will ride north from here to Acre where I will demand to see King Richard the Lion-Hearted. I know he will see me, because I am a Knight Templar, and he will think that I bring news of Jerusalem. But when I am shown into his presence, I will throw myself at his feet and I will beg him to be merciful when he comes to the Holy City. For I will explain the nature, the true nature of the three religions we profess. And I will beg him to be like Saladin and allow men and women of true faith to worship side by side in peace and love and harmony."

'When she heard the news, Rebecca, who secretly loved Ranulf, objected strongly because she knew that the young man was riding to his certain death. But her father stayed her objections, and Solomon kissed the young man on his forehead, telling him that he loved him as a son, and that what he planned was the best thing that a young man could do. He wished him Godspeed and said he would pray for him everyday for the rest of his life.

'Rebecca never saw Ranulf again. I have no idea what happened to him, but one thing I do know, which is recorded in the pages of history, is this: that when Richard left Acre something miraculous happened to him. It was always known that he was the bravest and most valiant warrior in Christendom. But when he came into contact with the forces of Islam, he developed a great and enormous respect for the religion and for its most valiant leader, Saladin. And privately, although I have few grounds for saying this, I also suspect that he had great respect for the Jews. It is even recorded that Saladin offered

Richard the hand of his daughter in marriage in order to make a permanent peace between the brother kings, something he would only have done if he held Richard in high regard. Richard couldn't accept because he had to rush back to Europe, but who knows what would have happened if, eight hundred years ago, a Christian king had married into the family of an Islamic ruler, both of whom had been captivated by the stories and wisdom of an old Jew.

'Who knows ... maybe Ranulf did get through to King Richard. Maybe he did tell the story of the rings, and maybe something did change in the warrior king. Who knows? Amen.'

Mr Aaron's story seemed to have found precisely the right balance. It was short, shorter than most others, and the men and women in the shul managed to get home a few minutes earlier than in previous weeks. Also, according to Mr Dub as he walked home arm-in-arm with Mr Dayan, it had a very good moral to it. Yes, he really liked the story of the three rings, although strictly between the two of them, he knew in his heart which was the true religion.

'Let's face it,' said Mr Dub. 'If I had a look at those three rings I would have known which was which. You get my point?'

Mr Dayan stroked his beard with his free hand, getting his point straightaway.

The rabbi was happy as the story seemed to have pleased everybody — it had an elegant moral, a nice twist at the end, had kept everybody guessing and didn't compromise either the art of the storyteller or the nature of the Friday-night service. And so the following week another carefully chosen story was told. And the week after, and the week after that until Rabbi Teichmann realised that there was standing-room only in his shul. The congregation had now reached a regular group of two hundred and more. Never, ever had they enjoyed such numbers. It became a bit of a problem in itself because the crowding was so great that every Friday night was just like Erev Yom Kippur, the great and awful Kol Nidre service where Jews throughout the world congregated to be present as God begins the process of closing the heavenly books in which are determined who will live and who will die, who will prosper and who will fail during the forthcoming year.

Six months after Rabbi Teichmann's storytelling part of the Friday-night services had begun, having already been written up twice in the Jewish newspapers and even occasionally in the national press, he received a letter from the chief rabbi asking him to drop in for yet another visit. This time he approached the meeting with no real feeling of trepidation. What could possibly be wrong, he reasoned as he walked into the chief rabbi's office in town? His services were overflowing with people he had never seen before at shul. There was nothing untoward being said by the storytellers. His profile had even risen beyond its previous obscurity.

The chief rabbi was courteous indeed, shaking the rabbi's hand warmly, offering him a sherry, inviting him to sit in an armchair instead of at the desk. The conversation between the two men began effortlessly. The chief rabbi asked about things at the synagogue, how were things in the rabbi and the rebbetzin's life and things in general.

Until just as effortlessly, with the consummate skill of the politician, without even the rabbi knowing that the subject was changing course, the chief rabbi asked, 'So tell me, Rabbi Teichmann. These Friday-night stories of yours. How do you feel they're going?'

Rabbi Teichmann told him with a great deal of pride. He told him the numbers. He told him the effect. He told him the way in which Jews he had never seen before were flocking to his synagogue.

'You see, Rabbi, that's the trouble,' said the chief rabbi, sipping his sherry. 'What you're doing is wonderful for your little shul, but the effect it's having . . .' the chief rabbi sucked in his breath, shouldering the burdens of the world '. . . it's attracting the Friday-night Jews from other synagogues. It's causing a lot of problems for your brother ministers. They're having difficulty filling their services. Some have even told me that they can no longer guarantee a minyan.'

He took a couple of letters out of a portfolio and handed them to Rabbi Teichmann who read them briefly. They were from the rabbis of neighbouring synagogues asking the chief rabbi to intervene and put pressure on Rabbi Teichmann to stop the storytelling or they would soon have to take drastic action . . . though in none of the cases was the action specified. The rabbis said that they were most put out, because depleting the congregations of such otherwise large and prosperous synagogues was a serious matter, and one which should not be taken lightly by the chief rabbi.

'You can see my problem, Rabbi Teichmann. Your success is based upon the defeat of others. I'm afraid you're being just too successful.'

'What should I do?' asked Rabbi Teichmann.

'I'm afraid you'll have to cut out the stories. I can see no alternative.'

But Rabbi Teichmann refused simply to accept this as a solution and argued vehemently, explaining that if he did this, then his congregation would shrink to the previous level of nine men and himself. The chief rabbi said that he knew this would happen, and had been searching his mind for a solution.

And so the two men sat in the armchairs, sipped their sherrys and pondered how to solve the knotty problem.

Until the chief rabbi's face suddenly brightened. In his mind he had been searching the Talmud, that vast treasury of wisdom written over centuries by great rabbis and he remembered something told by one of the most learned of the rabbis. He looked up at Rabbi Teichmann, and said to him, 'Let me tell you a story ...'

OH, AND ONE
SMALL THING I FORGOT
TO TELL YOU . . .

Oh, and by the way . . . remember I said that I'd tell you ten of the stories which were told in the shul? Ten, the number of men you need to hold a minyan. Go back to the beginning, and you'll see I'm right. Well, in this book, there are eleven stories. But I'm a storyteller, not a mathematician. What do I know about mathematics? I remember there was one occasion when my son asked me to help him with an algebra question that he had to do for his homework. Well, do you think I could do it! How on earth the Arabs worked out algebra, I'll never know.

But even before the Arabs, there's a record on papyrus in the British Museum of a problem dating back to 1650BC:

Divide 100 loaves among 10 men including a boatman, a foreman and a doorkeeper who receive double portions. What is the share of each?

Sure, the Arabs might have taken algebra into Europe . . . it comes from the Arabic word *al-jabr* meaning the reunion of broken parts . . . but it was originally brought by them from ancient Babylon, Egypt and India to Europe.

What? You didn't know that algebra had anything to do with Arabs? They used it as a way of working out how to divide up property between children as inheritance. Let me tell you the story of what happened when algebra was first. . .

GLOSSARY

Many of the words found in the stories of this book will be unfamiliar to people who are not of the Jewish faith. Some of course have become a normal part of the English language. Words and expressions like 'oy vey' and 'schlep' and 'nu' are part of the currency of everyday conversation. Over the centuries, however, words from German, Russian, Spanish, French, American and of course Hebrew have been added to Jewish literature to enrich it and to act as an itinerary of where Jewish people have been sent in their exiles. Here are some simple explanations of words used in this book.

Aron Hakkodesh The Holy Ark situated within the wall of a synagogue which faces towards Jerusalem. It contains the scrolls of the five books of Moses, or Torah, which are taken out on Mondays, Thursdays, on the Sabbaths and on Holy Days to be read by the rabbi to the congregation

Alav ha shalom
or
Aleha hashalom A phrase used or said when mentioning the name of a departed relative or friend. 'May he or she rest in peace'.

Alef-bet

The alphabet. The Hebrew alphabet, which was possibly appropriated from earlier languages such as Phoenician, is itself one of the earliest written codes. From the Hebrew alphabet developed the Greek and the Roman and of course European writing scripts. It begins like a,b,c,d 'aleph, bet, gimel, daled ...' The letters can even be traced through to modern letters in the English alphabet today.

B'rachah

A blessing. Jews say blessings over everything. There are hundreds of blessings. Only the most Orthodox say all the blessings; everybody else has to get on with their life.

Bar mitzvah

Literally 'a son of the commandment'. The coming of age of a Jewish male, usually at the age of thirteen, but can be said at any age after this. A boy is called from the congregation, and reads blessings and prayers as well as a segment of the Torah (five books of Moses) and a lesson by the Prophets ... all in Hebrew. He ascends the bimah as a boy, and descends as a man ... quite a performance.

Beth Din

An ancient judicial court, first associated with the Temple, and now a rabbinic court which decides all manner of Judaic matters. There is usually one in every large city.

Bimah   A rostrum in a synagogue where the rabbi stands in order to read from the holy books and to conduct prayers. Men are called up to the reading of the law in order to recite prayers before and after the rabbi reads the portion from the five books of Moses.

Black Hundreds   One of dozens of different Cossak, Ukrainian or Eastern European Christian groups often impelled by priests to rise up and strike fear in the hearts of Jewish communities. They would ride their horses into Jewish villages, setting fire to houses and slashing people to death with their swords; often drunk; invariably terrifying; this was just another form of racial cleansing.

Challah   The twisted loaf used at the beginning of a Sabbath. Often it is made with egg and poppy seed. On Rosh Hashanah, it is traditional to include raisins in the loaf to ensure a sweet year.

Cheder   Literally a room; actually a room where children come to learn Hebrew and scripture.

Cheder ochel   A dining room.

Chevra   'Brotherhood' or 'community'.

Cholent A bean stew from the east of Europe and Russia. Often served with huge lumps of delicious meat.

Cohanim Priests. In the days of the First and Second Temples, the Cohanim, the descendants of Moses' brother Aaron were given the task of being priests in the newly built Temple. They were attended by Levites and the congregation was made up of Israelites. Today's most common Jewish surnames are Cohen and Levy, which indicates a descent from these ancient 3000-year-old roles.

Kavod Glory or honour. If children do well at school, they cover their parents with kavod.

Diaspora The dispersion ... any place outside of Israel. The Jews were dispersed into an enforced Diaspora by the Emperor Vespasian in 70AD, and remained so until the re-creation of the land of Israel in 1948. All Jews who continue to live outside of Israel still live in the Diaspora.

D'rashah A sermon; a lesson; a speech by a wise man or woman to any congregation or audience.

Eretz Yisrael The land of Israel.

Erev Shabbat	The evening before the Sabbath i.e, Friday night. The Jewish Sabbath begins about one hour before three stars separated by distance can be seen in the evening sky on Friday night and ends when three stars are visible on the following Saturday night.
Eshkol	A grape or bunch of grapes with the same name as the Israeli Prime Minister Levi Eshkol.
Goldeneh medinah	Literally the golden land, often used to refer to America more than anywhere else.
Goyim	Literally 'nations'. Often now a term of disparagement by Jews about Christians and Moslems.
Habdalah	The ceremony to end the Sabbath.
Kaddish	Memorial prayers said for a close relation. This is a solemn prayer, and is usually recited on the anniversary of the relation's death.
Kashruth	Literally, 'proper'. Kashruth is the term denoting everything which it is correct and proper for a Jew to eat. It is, in effect, the science of keeping food ritually clean.
Kiddush	Hebrew for sanctification. Before particular meals we recite prayers and blessings over a

cup of wine at the commencement of the Sabbath and festivals, as well as after the end of the morning service and before lunch. When a father returns home on Friday night from synagogue, he recites the Kiddush for his family and this is followed by the evening meal. Often this is done communally in a synagogue

Kein ayin hara   The fear of the evil eye. Because of thousands of years of persecution, Jews have always looked deeply into the holy books for hidden signs as to God's purpose to explain their misery. This has led to much superstition and kein ayin hara — no evil eye — is one such expression of personal protection.

Maggid   A wise man or preacher. When a maggid speaks, everybody listens.

Mehitzah   A curtain or structure dividing men and women in an Orthodox synagogue. It is a barrier placed to prevent men being distracted by women in their prayers and vice versa. Liberal synagogues throughout the world have dispensed with the mehitzah and there men, women and children in a family sit together in prayer.

Melamed   A teacher; often an old man, dearly beloved by his students.

Mezuzah	A sign, object or small elongated box placed on the right-hand lintel of every door of the house. It contains passages from Deuteronomy.
Minyan	An assembly of ten men who come together in order to pray. A man is defined as any person who is over the age of thirteen. Most prayers can be said with fewer than ten, but certain crucial prayers such as memorial prayers for the dead can only be said with a minyan.
Pale of Settlement	An area of restricted settlement for Jews in Tsarist Russia stretching from the Baltic to the Black Sea. In 1791 when Russia absorbed parts of Poland it also captured a large Jewish population who were segregated in the Pale of Settlement. At the end of the nineteenth century, there were five million Jews living in this area. The Pale of Settlement came to an end with the Russian Revolution in 1917.
Rosh Hashanah	Literally, the Head of the Year, or the New Year. Traditionally the date on which God created Adam, the first man. It is a day of celebration and prayers and repentance for past sins. For ten days Jews think about the errors of their past and repent them prior to Yom Kippur when God then seals the Holy

Books and the fate of all men and women in the forthcoming year.

Seder
Literally, 'Order'. Today the Hebrew expression, 'Hakkol B'seder', means, 'everything okay', or 'everything in order'. Ritually, Seder refers to the first two nights of the Passover (one night only in Israel), when the father of the household follows a strict order of service.

Shekoyach
'May you have strength' or 'congratulations'

Shabbat/Shabbos
Friday night and Saturday, when Jews traditionally go to synagogue to say prayers and welcome in the Sabbath. A day of rest commanded by God when no work is to be done and one must be penitent and think only of the writings of the scriptures. The difference in pronunciation between 'shabbat' and 'shabbos' is the difference between Jews who hail from the east of Europe (Ashkenazim, who say Shabbos) and those who hail from Israel, Spain, the North of Africa and Arabia (Sephardim, who say Shabbat).

Shaharit
Morning prayers. The Jewish day is divided up into three distinct phases of prayer: Shaharit for the morning, minhah for the afternoon and arvit for the evening prayers.

Shalom	Literally 'Peace'. A greeting said when meeting somebody, when saying goodbye, or when wishing them peace.
Shiur	A lesson given by someone learned.
Shema'	Literally 'Hear'. The beginning of the glorious words from Deuteronomy 'Hear O Israel, the Lord our God, the Lord is one' is called the shema'. It has even been thought to be the central tenet of Judaism, and is often the last prayer on the lips of a dying man or woman.
Shul	A synagogue; a meeting place for Jews to come together and pray. Any building (from a simple home to a palace) can be used as a shul. In Orthodox shuls, men are divided from women by a curtain called a mehitzah.
Shtetl	A collection of Jewish houses huddled together, usually on the outskirts of a Christian village. These invariably were found in the East of Europe and in Russia.
Streimels	The fur hat or cap used by some Hasidic Jews on Sabbath, festivals and other festive occasions. Different branches of Hasidim wear different kinds of streimels. The Lubowitcher Hasidim have for many years

given up the practice of wearing streimels and instead wear stylish black hats.

Tallis/Tallit A prayer shawl used by men when in synagogue.

Tallis beitel A colourful bag, often embroidered, used for carrying the tallis.

Talmud, Mishna and Gemara The great teachings and commentaries on the five books of Moses by the rabbis written over many centuries.

Tsitsith A garment worn by Jewish men underneath a shirt. It is put on over the head and the front and back have eight strings attached to the corners, tied in a particular way which then protrude beneath the shirt and over the trousers. Usually now only worn by the most Orthodox men.

Ulpan Where people (often adults) go to learn to speak Hebrew. Many kibbutzim in Israel have special ulpans attached to teach migrants how to speak Ivrit (modern Hebrew).

Yeshiva A rabbinic school or academy where students learn all aspects of talmud and talmudic study. The method of learning is that of argument and discourse.

Yiddishkiet	Anything to do with being Jewish. It's a more homely and user-friendly way of expressing what it means to be Jewish, rather than 'Jewishness'.
Yom Kippur	Literally the Day of Atonement. The holiest day of the Hebrew calendar. In ancient times it was the one and only occasion when the High Priest entered the Holy of Holies in the Temple. It begins the previous evening with a solemn Kol Nidre service and the entire following day is spent in fasting and prayer, asking for forgiveness and listening to writings from the Torah as well as the writings of the Prophets. The day ends when God traditionally determines who will live and who will die and who will prosper in the forthcoming year.
Zeida/Bubba	Grandfather and grandmother in Yiddish.